Seeking the Dark

Paula R. C. Readman

www.darkstroke.com

Discover us online:
www.darkstroke.com

Find us on instagram:
www.instagram.com/darkstrokebooks

Include **#darkstroke** in a photo of yourself
holding this book on Instagram and
something nice will happen.

For all the angels that have touched upon my writing career, especially lovely Rita, Nicky Slade, Ivy Lord, Jill Dalladay, Dot Walker, Mum & Dad. You all left us too soon.

About the Author

Paula R C Readman lives in a village in Essex with her husband and two cats. After leaving school at 16 with no qualifications, she spent her life working mainly in low paying jobs. In 1998, with no understanding of English grammar, she decided to beat her dyslexia, by setting herself a challenge to become a published author. She taught herself 'How to Write' from books which her husband purchased from eBay. After 250 purchases, he finally told her 'just to get on with the writing'. In 2010, she had her first taste of success with fiction when English Heritage published her short story in their anthology, Whitby Abbey-Pure Inspiration. In 2011, Paula took the opportunity redundancy offered her to take up writing full-time and started concentrating on writing short stories for publication in anthologies and for competitions while mastering the skills needed to write novels. Paula has had many short stories published, and a collection of short stories, Days Pass Like a Shadow, published by Bridge House, a crime novella. The Funeral Birds, published by Demain Publishing and a gothic crime novel, Stone Angels published by Darkstroke.

Acknowledgements

A big *thank you* to darkstroke for all their encouraging words and for the opportunity to finally see my first novel published after its completion in 2005. Thank you to Laurence and Steph for your suggestions with editing to help make *Seeking the Dark* shine.

Thank you to my husband, Russell, for all his continuing support and belief in my dream to write. For my darling son, Stewart and daughter-in-law Kathryn *thank you* for your words of encouragement.

To my two dearest friends, Joan and Ana, *thank you* for sharing this writing journey with me, plots and all. To Mum

& Dad, thank you for giving me life. May your stars shine for ever bright.

A big *thank you* goes to Lisa Moulds who read my first short story, the inspiration behind *Seeking the Dark,* and for wanting to know more about Amanita. A big *thank you* to lovely Rita, though we only worked together briefly your interest in my dream to become a published author made a big impact on me, along with your passing comment about how your name Rita seemed only to be given to prostitutes in novels, and could I use the name Rita for a more interesting character. I'm just so sad that you were taken too soon, and never got to read *Seeking the Dark* for yourself.

A big *thank you* goes to Bex Green-Fortey and Anne Shaw for their encouragement in the early days of the development of *Seeking the Dark.*

And, for everyone else who has briefly touched upon my life. Good or bad, you've created the writer I've become.

the barman. "Does he really think we're stupid enough to believe...*I can put you in the movies, doll*?"

"Must think we were born yesterday."

"Compared to him, we are," she giggled, and flicked the card over the bar where it fell into the slops. As the girls moved away, Jake looked at the man and was surprised to see him raise his glass as though acknowledging someone. Jake looked in the direction the man was looking but all he saw was a group of youngsters seated at the tables near to the dance floor. No one seemed to respond to him. Then Jake saw his angel. Her crown of thick white hair cascaded around her shoulders as she perched on a high, chrome stool, her short pale-yellow skirt revealing more of her thighs while lengthening her long, bare legs. She pulled a mirror from her bag, pushed her hair away from her face, and checked her make-up.

The lothario crossed to her. Jake wondered if they were already acquainted as the man placed his hand on her knee, leant forward, and whispered something in her ear. His angel responded by tossing her head back, making her long hair shimmer. Jake turned away, overcome by a sense of voyeurism. He took a large gulp of his drink. Maybe he was in the wrong business to get women interested. He glanced back to see the man slide his arm around the young woman's neck and kiss the top of her head, making her laugh again.

The black dog slipped its leash, in his head, at the thought of heading home to piles of outstanding bills, so Jake did what came naturally and held his glass out to the barman for another one. Like most journalists, he was chasing an exclusive story, one that would change his life forever.

Jake glanced over at the lothario but made eye contact with his angel instead. She smiled at him as the man chewed at her neck. Stunned, Jake nodded back. *Did she really smile at him?* Had the whiskey finally hit the spot? He looked at his glass and inhaled, catching his breath. A stirring in his loins added to his discomfort. He looked back at the couple. She looked as though she was enjoying the man's attention. *No accounting for taste,* Jake decided, downing the last of his drink. *Time to head home.* The walk would soon clear his head, hopefully enough to finish the articles he was working on. He signalled to the barman, wanting to leave a message for Mariana. But before the barman had time to respond, Jake felt a hand on his shoulder, the familiar sweet smell of *Obsession,* and the warmth of lips brushing his cheek.

"Darling Jacob, you're not leaving me so soon, are you?"

"Mariana…" He returned her kiss. "As formal as ever, you must be the only person other than my Aunt Kate to call me Jacob."

"That's me. Daring to be different."

"I thought you had stood me up."

"Never! Have you eaten yet?"

"You read me like a book."

"Jacob Eldritch—" She feigned anger. "You'd better come on upstairs now."

He followed Mariana to her personal lift and glanced around for the white-haired beauty, but she and her companion had gone.

"Were you looking for someone, Jacob?" Mariana said, glancing back over her shoulder.

"I thought I saw someone I recognised." He slipped his arm around her waist and kissed her hair. As the door to the lift closed, the sound of the music faded. It amazed Jake how quiet her apartment was considering it was over a nightclub. Mariana let go of his arm and walked ahead. Jake inhaled at the sight of the rise and fall of her firm buttocks. The red, silk dress clung to her like water, showing off her voluptuous body. Many a man believed he could win the black widow, Mariana's hand to reign as the new emperor, but none could melt her ice-locked heart. Their friendship had a long history. Over a hot meal, she would talk business, while he ate. Sometimes, on cold, lonely nights, a simple smile would pass between them, and they would share a moment of comfort and warmth. She knew he wouldn't outstay his welcome and that was enough for both of them.

"How's your day been?" she asked, gesturing to a table set for two.

"You know. The same as always."

She opened the oven door, and the smell of her oxtail stew flooded the room. Jake's appetite returned. "Why haven't you gone to London and followed your dream?"

"You know I can't leave here. Not when the story is so close to breaking." Jake saw the old familiar look in her eyes as she set a plate before him. He had seen it in other people's eyes too.

"Come on. How many more years are you going to—" she paused, reaching back for her plate. "Tuck in. There's bread if you want it. I'm sorry, I shouldn't have said that. I hate seeing you wasting your life. Someone special is out there for you, but this obsession with these murders means you'll miss out."

Jake allowed the meat to melt in his mouth. The term 'Dead Men Sleeping' wasn't his, but a coroner's description. All the victims looked as though they had just fallen asleep. Jake stumbled across this fact by chance as it had been kept out of the newspapers. All the victims' blood was missing. At first he wanted the police to explain why this wasn't common knowledge, but he decided to keep it to himself. Once hooked on uncovering the truth, he became a driven man. According to his contacts, the police uncovered no links between the men while alive, but they all had a high level of an unidentifiable substance in their bodies. It's similar to a spider's venom when used to incapacitate their prey. Of course, the police believed the bodies had been moved after death. The only visible marks on any of the bodies were two small insect bites on the neck. The lack of evidence brought their investigation to an end.

Jake had his own theories, but he too needed more information. He pushed the plate to one side. "Wow, that was beautiful."

"I'm glad you enjoyed it." Mariana cleared the table. On returning, she set a strong cup of tea down in front of Jake, a black coffee for herself.

"Have you seen a young woman with white hair in the club before?"

Mariana took a sip of her drink before answering. "White hair? No, the young women all blur into one for me. Too many different hair colours and contact lenses these days to tell one girl from another. One day, dark hair with cat's eyes, the next who knows. Why?"

"Not sure. Probably, nothing I suppose."

"Are you interested?" Mariana gave a slow wink.

"No. Not in that way."

"Good. I'm glad." She reached for his hand and led him to her bedroom. The white-haired beauty strolled across his mind. Something about her told Jake their paths would cross again very soon.

Chapter Three

"Come on, you can do it. Just a quick look and if it's nothing, then it's back to bed. If you find something, then what's the harm?" Bard Walker steadied his breathing ready to face his demons lurking in the alleyway. "Pull yourself together and stay focused on the job." Fear was ready to overwhelm him and send him running in the opposite direction. "Come on, it'll be worth it to wipe the smug smiles off their faces tomorrow. Then they'll know they can't mess with you."

Walker peered down the gloomy alleyway, his words echoed back at him. "I bet those bastards set me up, thinking I'll make a complete arse of myself. Well, we'll see who'll have the last laugh." He pulled out a pen-torch. Its beam bounced off the piles of rotting restaurant garbage and take-away cartons. "Oh God! This is all I fucking need. She'll never forgive me now!" The stench filled his nostrils and clawed at the back of his throat.

Just after midnight, when his wife and he had finally stopped fighting and fallen asleep, peace was shattered when he received a call telling him to investigate a reporting of a body in an alleyway. Walker was sure he heard stifled giggles in the background as he was given the assignment.

The sounds of the heavy traffic faded as he searched between the doorways, dustbins, and rubbish skips. Halfway down the alleyway a flickering streetlamp threw half shadows over everything, causing him to stop and turn slowly.

"You bastards! Is this my initiation into joining you because I'm new to the area? Thought you'd have some fun, by having me running around here all night." Walker strolled on. Google had highlighted the criss-crossing paths that ran

15

through most of the Deep Water Wharf. He shone the torch beam along the path and saw nothing out of the ordinary. His heart rate slowed as the tension in the back of his head eased. He turned to head out of the claustrophobic alleyway and found himself back at the first intersection. He stopped, unsure which direction he had entered by. All the alleyways looked identical in the flickering light with its windblown rubbish. He cast the torch beam around and froze. "Shit!" The word echoed back at him. Caught in a beam, a pair of legs protruded like some semaphore signalling from a doorway. Walker let his breath out. "A fucking shop mannequin…the bloody bastards. What a sick joke!" As the beam travelled up the discarded mannequin, his anger rose. A sleeping man leant against a grimy door.

"Oh, for fuck's sake! Come on, get up, you lazy sod." Walker kicked the man's foot. "There are places for the likes of you."

The body jolted but gave no signs of waking up.

"Shit!" Walker squatted, aware of an icy chill cutting through the night air. "Look for signs of a struggle," he muttered, but everything seemed normal in such an unloved place. Walker pulled out his phone and took some photos, just as his radio burst into life.

"Walker?"

"Yes—here"

"Where's here?"

"I think—"

The man's face had the recognisable trademarks that were in all the police reports on the other unexplained deaths. Soft lines around their eyes and mouths gave them a strange untroubled look as though sleeping, the report had said.

"Absolution!" The word roared out of the darkness. Walker struggled to his feet as his chest tightened, making it hard for him to catch his breath. "What?" Walker spun round but saw nothing.

"Absolution!" The word bounced off the walls and reverberated inside his head. He covered his ears in an effort to silence it. "Darkness!" The word came to him from another time as horrific images crowded in. There were babies, children and women, their faces melting in the burning heat while all around lay heads torn from bodies and pale limbs scattered about. Walker's stomach churned as the bile rose at the sight of these half-remembered things. A voice in his head... No, not in, but somehow closer. Sweat ran down his back as he tried to block the ever-changing images out. Then the screaming started, and he didn't want to go back there.

Four years ago, a car crash left three of his friends dead. Walker hadn't slept well since the accident. The terror of the metal coffin haunted his dreams. Trapped by the seatbelt that had saved his life, he had been left hanging, staring into the bloody faces of his dead friends. Unlike him, they hadn't been wearing their seatbelts.

The day had started with laughter. Under a clear blue sky, and bright sunshine, they had all become Indiana Jones. Halfway up a mountain they found a hole near a ruined settlement in Albania. In a moment of madness, with no safety equipment they went hunting for lost treasure.

Justin shouted something about in the late 90s the site was excavated, so whatever treasure had been there was now long gone. Tim and Andy ignored Justin, following Walker into the small cavity. Once inside they found stone steps led into a chamber. At first, Walker believed the change in temperature was due to being underground, but the solid wall of darkness seemed to eat up the torch light. There were voices too that echoed around him. Behind him, he heard his friends' laughter as they howled like ghosts, but as their laughter echoed back it sounded more like screams.

On the drive back to the hotel, the laughter had dried up as Tim took the corner too fast. A wall of darkness appeared on the road before them. Tim swerved, and the car took flight.

Walker was woken by the sound of a reassuring voice coaxing him back from the dark. A miracle, they said, pulling him from the wreckage, but he hadn't been so sure. Something still lingered in the back of his mind, telling him it wasn't a matter of luck, no miracle of life. If he had learnt one thing from the accident, it was that death had a distinct smell.

The smell in the doorway had him retching. It transported him back to the moment in his friend's car when their laughter ended as the car sailed through the air and crashed into the ravine below. Once again he saw his friends, a tangled mess covered in a mixture of blood and grey matter as he hung over them. After three days, he had given up calling for help. In the pain of dying, the darkness had appeared to him. In a straight swap a life for a life, Walker had taken the chance to breathe again.

"It's payback time..." a singsongy voice said.

Walker tried to back away from the body in the doorway, but his legs were rigid. The smell bubbled up around him. Death seemed to eat its way out of the body. It crossed the space between the man's body and him and grabbed his legs. The torch in his hand overheated, so he tossed it away. Its beam flickered across the dead man's face as the body began to convulse. It seemed to be fighting against an unseen puppet-master.

Walker, overcome by a sensation of falling, felt the ground disappear from under his feet. Flat on his back, he witnessed the dead man haul himself up. His body, bent as though it had no backbone, moved like some bizarre marionette. Its limbs shook as it swung one leg before the other in a peculiar gait. Its black eyes bore into his like pits of despair. The stench of the man's rotting breath seemed to find its way into Walker's mouth and nostrils. The dead man's features shifted into his. A sound of someone screaming filled his ears until unconsciousness bore him away to a place of safety.

"At last, for a moment, I thought I had two dead bodies on my hands." The easy-going voice seemed to come from every direction.

Walker blinked.

A shadowy face peered closely at him, their breath smelled of roast beef or some other pleasant-smelling odour. Walker tried to sit up, but his throbbing head wouldn't allow him.

"Are the rest of them on their way?" The voice said as it

moved away. "Or did you just happen to stumble across this one by yourself, DI Walker?"

'*For Christ's sake, leave me alone,*' Walker wanted to say, but instead he said, "Who *the fuck* are you?"

"Do you need to go to the hospital?" the voice asked.

"No!" He struggled to his knees and reached for his torch. In its beam, he saw the body was back where he had first found it.

"If you're sure you're okay," said the disembodied voice. "Can you tell me what happened? This guy seems to be too dead to do you any harm?"

"I'm not sure. Must've blacked out. Who... are... you?"

"Your worst nightmare."

"What?" Walker rubbed the side of his head. His fingers met the stickiness of an open wound.

The disembodied voice shone its torch on Walkers' hand, highlighting the blood. "Are you sure you don't want to get that checked out? You look as though you've been hit over the head."

"No— I'm fine."

"Suit yourself." The torch turned its attention back to the dead body. "He looks the same as all the others, doesn't he?"

"Are you going to tell me who you are? And, what you're doing here."

"Here you go. Hold this on it." The voice turned into a magician and conjured up a hanky. "It's clean. The bleeding will stop sooner if you put pressure on it."

Walker held the hanky to his head, just as his phone rang.

"Oh, that's been doing that all the time you were out cold. I didn't like to touch it in case it put me in a bad situation."

"Hello. Sorry the signal's not too good around here," Walker said, answering his phone. "Yes, there's another body. It looks to be the same as the others, but I can't be sure until forensics has had a look. Yes, of course I'll be here." He slipped the phone back into his pocket. "So, Mr Nightmare, what's your angle?"

"No angle. Jake Eldritch, a journalist."

"What were you doing here, Mr Journalist?"

"On my way home from the Golden Hart. It's a short cut."

"Golden Hart?"

"A night club. You're new, aren't you?"

The alley suddenly filled with blue flashing lights and the sound of running feet. Bright lights filled the darkness. Walker turned to the journalist. "Where can I get hold of you for further questioning?"

The journalist smiled. "Your best bet is to try the Hart. If I'm not there, just leave a message with the owner. I'll see you around."

Chapter Four

Amanita paused under a streetlight to reapply her makeup, paying special attention to the corners of her mouth. She crossed the road and followed the footpath into the park. The park lay gloomily at ease with itself as Amanita made her way to the bus stop.

On reaching it she pulled out her phone. "Hello. I need a taxi to pick me up from Old Hall Lane bus stop, please. My name's Amanita Virosa. Will it be long? No, that's fine. Thank you."

She slipped the phone into her bag and hugged her thin jacket to her. A rustling behind her made her turn and she scanned the darkness. The amber moon freed itself from behind a cloud. Its light filtered through the shrubs highlighting the rubbish that gathered at the bottom of the bushes. Amanita inhaled, trying to relax. The cold air was tinged with a pungent smell of decomposing leaves and rotting wood. She focused on the bushes, sensing something moving and stepped back into the shadows.

From the undergrowth, the slinky form of a cat appeared. It skulked among the discarded beer cans and litter. Amanita, impatient to get home, sat on the park bench, eased her shoes off and rubbed her aching feet she noticed some specks of blood mixed in with the red wine on her skirt and laughed, recalling the warmth of the man's touch on her thigh.

"Men like Charles Keys are such fools. One less to worry about…" She ran her tongue around her mouth, savouring the memory when his warm blood trickled down her throat. "They never believe me when I tell them the truth. Hmm, I must check on Marco Le Bianco."

Then Amanita brought to mind the watcher. Was it

possible the Dark had found her? She shivered. At the sound of the approaching vehicle, she gathered her belongings, walking barefoot to the taxi. In the half light of the car's interior, she caught a flash of the cabbie's smile.

"I'm sorry, pet, but had a bit o'trouble getting through. The coppers were running about like headless chickens. Dunno what's got into 'em. Strange goings on, if you ask me. Sorry, yer look done in. Best get yer home, pet. Where's it yer want to go to?"

"To St Hilda's Terrace, Whitby, please."

"Yer niver know who's about at this time of the night. Yer ought to be more careful. My old Grandma used t'call it the witching hour."

"Once upon a midnight dreary, while I pondered weak and weary—" Amanita muttered.

"Err, what?"

"Edgar Allen Poe. It's from—"

"Whatever," the cabbie sighed heavily. "A young girl like yer ought to be more careful and not be out on your own."

"Next time I will. Thank you."

Away from the insipid town lights, Amanita relaxed as they crossed the pitch-black moors. Above the stars sparkled brightly as the moon's light shone across the vast, empty landscape. Amanita opened the window and breathed in the night air. They drove in silence. Sleepily, she watched the back of the cabbie's head sensing his unease as he kept furtively glancing up at the rear-view mirror. At last he spoke. "Do yer mind if I put the radio on?"

Amanita saw confusion in his eyes as he glanced in the mirror waiting for her reply. Of course, she knew there was no reflection of her. As he glanced over his shoulder, she cried, "Look Out." Caught within the beams of the headlights a lone sheep stood in the centre of the road.

"Oh God!" The cabbie swerved in time to miss the beast.

"I don't mind, if you do." She yawned.

"Err, what? Sorry?"

"You wanted the radio on."

"Oh yeah. Thank you. I like a bit o' noise, not one for the

quiet life."

She closed her eyes as the cab filled with a gentle melody. *"Who knows where the time goes? I'll still be here. I have no thoughts of leaving ... "* the radio sang out until a newsflash cut the music. "Earlier this evening at Deep Water Wharf in Middlesbrough the police are investigating the grim discovery of a man's body. We hope to update you with more details in our next bulletin."

"So that's what the fuss was about. Knew something was amiss. Good job I picked yer up when I did, pet. The killer could've still been in the area." The cabbie glanced in his mirror again.

The taxi drove through the deserted streets of Whitby until at last, the driver pulled over at the railway station. "Which number on St Hilda Terrace did thee want?"

"This is fine. How much is it?" Amanita asks pulling out her card.

As the taxi taillights disappear from view, Amanita ran barefoot across the road and up a steep alley before passing under an ornate arch. At the front door of a large, Georgian house, she pulled an iron key from under a flowerpot and unlocked it. A wave of security swept over her.

Within its quiet interior, a dull green light shone softly from room to room. Heavy curtains at the windows sealed out the advancing light of the day. Amanita made her way along a small passage and then down two steps into a large kitchen at the back of the house. She dropped her shoes and bag onto the breakfast bar and took a glass from a cupboard and water from the fridge. While sipping her icy drink, she remembered the specks of blood on her skirt. In the utility room, she rubbed some devil stain remover which her housekeeper swore by on the blood, before dropping the skirt into the washing machine and switching it on.

Back in the kitchen, she noticed a flashing light on the answering machine and pressed play. "You have a new message: Hello, Miss Virosa. I am so sorry. I'm having problems with my daughter, so I won't be in at my usual time. I'll be there as soon as possible. Bye for now."

After placing her empty glass in the sink, Amanita climbed the backstairs and headed to her bedroom. She stripped off the rest of her clothes and slipped into bed, barely able to keep her eyes open.

ankle, but he pushed past her. The picture shook as Charlotte placed the camera on the ground. Plants and leaves obscured part of the screen as she crawled on her belly after Robert. A scream shattered the silence and Charlotte froze. Then edging forward, she peered over the edge of the trench. "Please, Robert, come on."

His head reappeared. "Here, take this."

A rucksack appeared next to her.

"Let's go, please." Charlotte put out an arm to help him up.

Another shot rang out. Puzzlement clouded Robert's face for a second as he began to fall backward. Charlotte muffled a sob and pulled the bag away from the edge. She crawled back to where the camera continued filming. Her voice barely audible called, "Robert, where are you?" Charlotte leant over the side of the trench and began to pull Robert up.

From nowhere, a dark-cloaked figure loomed up behind her. Robert's bloodless face stared in horror over her shoulder. Charlotte turned as Robert's lips parted while his arms tightened around her torso. The dark figure raised an arm, and a loud crack rang out.

"Sweet Jesus. No!" Robert cried dragging Charlotte with him.

From within the trench, her sobs faded as the dark figure came into view. As the wind swept the cowl away from Cula's head, a thin-lipped smile played across his pale face as he raised his gun and pulled the trigger. "It is such a pity you did not listen to me—"

"Oh, my dear God! I'm so sorry, Jacob. If I had known, I —" Caroline's hand flew to her mouth.

"So that's what happened to my parents." Jake slumped onto the settee next to her.

Chapter Eight

The Games People Play

Amanita stretched, cat-like, trying to shake off the heavy sleep. She swung her long legs over the side of the bed.

The only room in the house not modernised was her parents' bedroom now hers. Her mother's favourite painting hung over the fireplace. It depicted her in a shimmering gold and silver dress that hung in soft folds about her naked feet. Her hair fanned gently away from her face as though a soft breeze blew and, in the background the artist had added a ruined temple surrounded by trees.

Amanita crossed to an ancient-looking glass which allowed her to compare herself to the painting. In the glass, a tall, slender woman with alabaster skin, white lashes that curtained her large amethyst eyes while translucent hair hung down to a slim waist. She picked up a silk wrap from a chair and slipped it on before crossing to the bathroom. "In two hundred and fifty years, I haven't changed at all."

She disrobed and stepped into the shower. As she rubbed her hair dry, her tongue caught against her protruding top teeth. She checked her looking glass and lifted her lip. Her gums were slightly swollen, but that didn't worry her. Last night in the nightclub, for the first time, she had been visible to a man other than her victim, but *why?* Was she sensing the same fate her mother had felt on the day her parents died?

She dressed and went to the attic. Seated at the antique table her mother had once used to write her correspondence, a computer sat. On her right, another screen displayed images from cameras that surveyed the entire house. She logged in, her long slender fingers dancing across the keys. The birth of the 21st century had made life so much easier. How she had wished her parents had lived to see it. On her homepage an animated, winged, Lara Croft-type figure descended from the top of the screen with its arms folded across its chest and a gun in each hand.

On alighting with its legs astride, the creature folded back her wings, holstered one of the guns before cocking the other one and asked, "*Is your man cheating on you?*" It crossed to the left side of the screen, dropped to one knee, and aimed its gun. From the top right hand corner, a cupid fluttered down, carrying a large red heart. The creature took aim and fired. The heart broke in two and the screen became drenched in dripping blood.

When it cleared, a photo gallery appeared and the winged figure said, "My name's Nyrene. I'm your avenging angel." With a sweep of her hand, she pointed to the photographs. "Here, in my Rogues' Gallery, are the men who've broken their loved one's hearts." Nyrene pointed her gun. "You, too, can add '*your unfaithful lover*' by clicking here." Next, she pointed to the small floating cupid, holding a broken heart.

Amanita clicked on an image. The photograph of the cheater in the rogues' gallery rotated allowing her to read the details of the man. She clicked on the cupid and was taken back to Nyrene.

"Let us at *ManWatch* be your eyes and ears. We can keep an eye on your man and tell you all you need to know to end your heartache. *Click here* for our message board." Nyrene pointed to a cupid holding a pen.

In *The Rogues Gallery* forum, women posted dates, times and any other information onto the site to help others to avoid the heartache of dating a cheater.

<u>Lucy from North Yorkshire:</u>
"Hi Girls. I've just seen **Malcolm Edwards** in June's wine bar in Middlesbrough with a blonde bimbo. Sorry, hope it wasn't his wife. Don't think so. He was enjoying himself too much and kept winking at me while I was serving behind the bar. After the bimbo had gone for a pee, he asked me for my

number... The Bastard!'" see photo.

Sue from Middlesbrough:

"Hi *ManWatch*. I love your web site. Its Gr...eat! Saw **Charles Keys** from your 'Rogues Gallery' at the Golden Hart on Saturday night. Tell his wife he's the best fuck ever and pays well too."

Celia from Suffolk:

"Hello *ManWatch*. I love your web site and downloaded your Rogues' Gallery app. After sixteen wonderful years, my husband left me. Men like that need stringing up by their balls!"

The list went on.

Amanita clicked back to the gallery and began hunting for the next rat that needed terminating. She looked for the golden rodent logo which indicated the newly-added men and worked her way through the photographs.

Some were professional-looking pictures while others were just family snapshots, with or without children. Some were wedding photos, all smiling, happy faces, but most were just head and shoulders shots, with the occasional shots of a man laid naked on a bed or sunbathing on a beach.

Elizabeth believed these men were using the site like some sort of dating agency, unbeknown to their wives. Amanita often found even overly-jealous wives used the site too, posting photos of their husbands. Lucky for them, she was able to detect innocence on meeting them.

On one such occasion, while she was sitting at the bar in the Golden Hart sipping a glass of red wine, she caught sight of the intended target. He was making his way through the bedlam, apologising to everyone, while trying to reach the bar. He sidestepped to allow a space for a young woman, who turned clutching two glasses of wine. On seeing a barstool in her way, the man moved it. Another man standing next to him yelled, "Hey Mate! That's my seat. Fuck off!"

The nervous man tried to explain he wasn't taking it, only moving it to help the woman. He turned for her support, but she was gone, leaving him to face the aggressive man. Mr

Apologetic continued along the bar to where Amanita sat.

"Excuse me," he called, on failing to attract the attention of the bar staff. He turned and collided with Amanita, knocking her drink into her lap. Panicking, he tried to wipe the spilt red wine from her pale skirt with his handkerchief. "I'm sorry, so sorry."

Their hands touched briefly.

He pulled his hand away. On his face, confusion. "Please allow me to buy you another one." Without waiting for an answer, he leaned over the bar and shouted, "A glass of house red here, please!"

Immediately one of the bar staff turned, nodded and returned with one. He passed the glass to her. "It was very clumsy of me."

"Is that all, sir?" The barman asked.

"Err, can I have a glass of mineral water, please?"

The man handed a banknote to the barman before addressing Amanita. "Hope the wine washes out all right."

"Don't worry. The stain remover I use will shift it." She dabbed at her skirt with a napkin.

"Andrew Hull." The man held out his hand.

"Pleased to meet you, Andrew." She went to take his hand and saw a look of discomfort cross his face. Instead, Andrew reached for his glass. They sat in silence, drinking. Amanita sensed him watching her from the corner of his eye but waited for him to speak.

"Do you come here often?" He set his glass down.

"Not really."

"Sorry. That sounded like an awful chat-up-line. Do you work round here?"

"Sort of."

"Sort of—" He met her eyes and long forgotten memories flooded in. She saw him recall his teenage years. The painful memories of feeling a fool the day he tried to speak to a girl in his class and dropped his books. The girl tossed her dark brown hair over her shoulders, closed her green eyes slightly as she tilted her head, and looked past him towards her waiting friends.

45

"You remind me of a girl from my schooldays. Strange, I should've thought of her—" He sipped his drink and then looked down, studying the melting ice.

"Do you have children, Andrew?"

"Yes, two girls." His face relaxed as he chatted. "My job pays well, but the downside is I'm away from home too much. My wife doesn't seem to understand that I'm doing this for them, for us."

"Maybe you need to talk to your boss. If you lose your family the money will be for nothing."

"Do you have children?"

She shook her head.

"First your drink and now I'm boring you to death—" He stared into his empty glass.

"Go home, Andrew. You've but a short life to live." Amanita turned away from him and looked into the crowd for her next target.

Puzzled, Andrew turned and looked to see who the woman was looking for, when his attention was drawn to her skirt. The stain was gone.

Amanita ignored his confusion, knowing her transformation was instant once her attention had shifted. No longer was she the woman Andrew Hull had spilled wine over.

Andrew placed his empty glass on the bar and took out his phone. After speaking to his wife, he touched her shoulder. She looked up and flashed her baby-blue eyes at him.

"Thank you for helping me." Andrew turned and pushed his way through the crowds.

***

Amanita hugged herself as her tongue teased the edge of her gums. She paged down to the next selection of photographs until a face leapt out. She clicked on the *golden rat* logo and the picture rotated to reveal the details.

Anthony Sharp, 36 years old, 5'9" dyed black hair, with blue eyes, neat fingernails, well dressed and well spoken. Annabelle his wife wrote. *He works for Acorns Financial and Management Services, a company set up fifteen years ago, by my father. In all the years of our marriage, he hasn't stopped womanising. However, my father doesn't believe me, telling me I've an over-active imagination. I would like some sort of proof so I can start a new life on my own. Please, can anyone help me? Thank you.*

"I think I can do better than that." Amanita ran her fingertip over the photo.

Chapter Nine

Seeking The Dark

Jake and Caroline stared at the blank screen in stunned silence. Without a word, Jake rose, went through to the kitchen and switched on the kettle. After a little while, he emerged, carrying two mugs.

"Are you all right, Jacob? Sorry, stupid question."

"I wasn't expecting that, Caro. Guess the film was unfinished after all. Not a good idea to share it with Kate." Jake passed a mug to her.

"I agree. But we really need to talk to her about what happened. Did you know how your parents died?"

Jake took a deep breath and pulled forgotten memories to the surface again. "The day I found out, Kate didn't really tell me anything. She showed me. She just handed me a newspaper. I unfolded it and read the headline. *As in Life, so in Death; always and forever together.* Underneath the headline was a large photo of two bodies lying with their arms around each other. In the picture, clearly seen, was a bullet hole in the back of their heads. To me, it wasn't my parents. We've never really spoken about it since. They were dead, and she brought me up."

"Oh, Jacob, I didn't know. I'm so sorry about the DVD." She put her arms around his neck and hugged him.

He laid his head against hers and felt the warmth against his cheek. Any other time and he would've kissed her, but now numbness overwhelmed him.

"Don't be silly, Caro. After all these years, it's come as a bit of a shock. We've just witnessed a murder and I want to find out why they were killed." Jake took her arms from around his neck and kissed her lightly on the forehead.

"I know that look, Jacob." Caroline gave a nervous laugh. "It's your *doggys got his teeth into a bone* look."

"My— what look?"

"You'll not let it go."

"Talking about getting teeth into something. What about the skulls with eye-teeth like a snake?"

"Your Mum called them, Taba'ta, son of the serpent."

"She wasn't happy about them being in the graves. Why?"

"They were supposed to be angels, not demons."

"Or vampires?"

"Come on, Jacob, vampires? There's a logical answer to why the skull had teeth like that."

"Forever the practical one, Caro. Think outside the box for once."

"All right. Why were they killed then?"

"They uncovered something they weren't supposed to. But what? Who knows?"

Caroline placed her cup back on the table. "In one way, I think you're right, but not because it would prove the existence of vampires."

"Oh dear. Caro. For a moment there I thought you'd escaped your box."

"Dearest Jacob; I'm too practical to be foolish." She nodded in the direction of the map covered in brightly coloured stickers. "What's that all about?"

"That's my dead men sleeping campaign map."

"Dead Men Sleeping?"

"Yes. I've been amassing details about some bizarre deaths in Yorkshire. Each of the stickers represents one. Some are well over fifty years ago.

"Wow, a serial killer at work? Haven't the police any suspects yet?"

"None. That's my point. A puzzle with no logical answers."

"Just one point."

Jake knew if she stopped calling him Jacob and referred to him as Jake, she'd outsmarted him again.

"You can't be serious. One person has caused these deaths

for over fifty years?"

Jake opened his mouth to argue his point, but Caroline cut him off.

"Don't interrupt. I know how your mind works. You think there's a link between your parents' deaths and those." She gestured to the wall.

He raised his arm. "Please, Miss, can I speak now?"

Caroline nodded.

"Okay. There's no link at the moment. And I'm not out to make a name for myself by proving the existence of vampires. After seeing these brutal killings, I'm sure my father would approve of me wanting to hunt out the truth."

Caroline squeezed Jake's hand. He studied hers, the slenderness of her fingers and the lack of rings on any of them. He noted the delicate shade of pearly pink nail varnish. He raised her hand to his lips and kissed the back of it.

Caroline pulled her hand away and smiled softly. "Jake, I hate to burst your bubble, but there's another reason for killings. The gold—oh, I forgot—" She reached for her bag, pulled out an envelope, and passed it to him. Jake emptied it onto the table. Six coloured photographs slid out.

"The details of the gold boxes are exquisite. That's why they were killed. Both Robert and Mike had doubts about Doctor Cula. Didn't they say there was a change of plan at the last minute? He might have been a criminal. It's not uncommon for antiquities to be stolen to order."

The photographs showed the highly decorated box from all sides. In each of the pictures was an angled ruler to give an idea of its dimensions. A patterned boarder ran across the bottom and up the side of each panel. They depicted an assortment of birds, plants, and animals. In the centre of the front panel was a seated man, dressed only in a robe, which was draped across his lap. He held a staff in one hand and a scallop shell in the other.

"They're beautiful, Caroline. Have you seen anything like them before?"

"No. Not in all the years I worked at the university and studied ancient cultures of the bible. However, I do recognise some of the symbols."

"And?"

"It doesn't make sense. They're early Christian symbols. Yet the box and site they came from are Pre-Christian."

"So what are you saying?" Jake tossed the photographs back onto the table.

"I'm not sure. Scallop shells have been a symbol of pilgrimage. The early pilgrims used the shells as a drinking cup. Over time it was linked to St James."

"So more questions than answers. What are the boxes telling us— something to do with a pilgrimage the travellers were on? What do the boxes contain, or did they once contain?"

"The archaeologists thought they were an offering. Would you mind if I showed a copy to a friend?"

"By all means, if it'll give us a lead. Does Kate know anything about what Mum and Dad were working on?"

"Come to dinner and ask her yourself."

"Okay, you win. How much of my parents' stuff is there?"

Caroline laughed. "You wouldn't believe me if I told you. Kate wanted me to clear it out, but it's only right you saw it first."

"The time's getting on now. I can't come today, but I'll try to make it sometime this week. Take that look off your face, Missy. I will, I promise. I've got to see Mariana first and finish off a couple of articles—bills need paying. Some of us can't live for free."

"Hey, what do you mean by that, Mr Eldritch? I do freelance work as well as looking after your aunt." Caroline's face softened. "You get me every time."

"So you have a word with your friend, and then get back to me. If you leave the disc with me, I'll look at it again."

In the hall, Caroline slipped her coat back on and took her car keys. "I've not had this much fun since we were children, Jake. It's like a detective story."

"We'll see what you think when it all becomes mundane. Thank you for coming over. It's what I've needed. I'll speak to you later."

51

Something buzzed in the back of Jake's mind as he tried to focus on the two articles, but after two hours he found he was reaching for the green folder. He needed to check something and pulled out a yellowing newspaper cutting dated 1967.

Young Man's Body Found Yesterday, the headline read.

Yesterday, a dog walker, in Dalby Forest, near the beautiful village of Thornton Dale, North Yorkshire, explained to our reporter, 'I noticed the car parked in amongst the trees with its driver's door open,' the dog walker said. 'It crossed my mind that he might've been sleeping off a late night. I went over to check he was all right. When I touched his arm, he just fell out. It was awful. I shall never forget it as long as I live. To think, he had been dead all that time, and not asleep. He looked so peaceful.'

"The only information the police were willing to give was they weren't treating the death as suspicious as they are unable to say how the 25-year-old Mr Theo Green had died."

Jake flicked through a few more articles until he found the one with the results of the tests.

"Scarborough police were aware of Mr Theo Green due to his criminal record for dealing in drugs. It's believed that his death was caused by substance abuse with hallucinogenic mushrooms, Psilocybe Semilanceata, local name, Liberty cap. High levels of toxins in his body, though no explanation can be found to explain the large amount of missing blood as none was found at the scene, or in his car."

"Interesting that none of the other reports followed up on what caused the blood loss, or even how much was missing." Jake read aloud while typing the information into a new document. Next, he looked at the lists of victims' names. Somewhere he recalled one from Whitby. The name John Blackstone jumped out at him.

Blackstone was found dead on the North Yorkshire moors in 1996, according to his information from a newspaper cutting. His wife reported him missing. On the night in question, the reporter said, the neighbours had phoned the police because of the noise. By the time they arrived, Blackstone had left, and his wife didn't want to press charges. In the newspaper, his death was reported as accidental poisoning while not being of sound mind. Again, high levels of toxins were discovered in his body.

Jake wrote down John Blackstone, ringed it, and then underlined it before phoning Mariana.

"Hi, how's it going? Have the police finished yet?"

"Jacob. It's fine. They do want to speak to you. I gave them your mobile number. I hope you don't mind. Would you like to come for a meal?"

"Of course. Tonight?"

"The place is still buzzing. I'll give you a ring when."

"Did you see one called Walker?"

"Yeah, bit of an odd one. Not quite with it. Nice enough. I'm sorry, but I must go. One of my new bar staff is having problems."

"Okay."

Jake stared at the name on his pad. "I wonder whether it's a local family name."

Chapter Ten

The Next Player

On the edge of Middlesbrough, the Grand Hotel stood surrounded by a large country park with its 18-hole golf course and health club. Over the years the clientele had changed from holiday makers to the owners of big international companies. Now it was an upmarket meeting place, turning the hotel into an exclusive club. Within its five-star restaurants, the rich, beautiful people clinched business deals while consuming exquisite meals and glasses of expensive champagne.

Anthony Sharp always arrived early, to take his favourite seat at the bar. From his view point he was able to watch everyone else's arrival in the mirror that ran the full length of the bar. He signalled to the barman who stood polishing glasses.

"Yes sir. What would you like?"

"Same again, Jim." Anthony smiled confidently into the mirror as he ran his fingers through his jet-black hair. Here he was one of the wealthy, beautiful people. He sipped his drink and watched the women who came to ply their trade, though he never paid for their services. Some were looking for rich husbands, but there were a few who ran their own companies and could afford fancy cars and fine clothes for themselves. After a hard day at the office, they enjoyed letting their hair down.

Anthony looked around, wanting a piece of the action, but not wanting to have to work for it. Away from his family responsibilities, he enjoyed himself, laughing at another little white lie he had told his wife. "I'm so sorry; it's another one of those god-awful business trips…"

He eyed the rich, young men. No matter how well he dressed or drove the right sort of car the one thing he lacked most was plenty of easy money. He gulped down his drink, deciding not to allow a little thing like maxed out credit cards spoil his evening. Tonight was all about having fun. "Hey, another one of these, Jim," he called to the barman.

The grandeur of the Victorian panelled ballroom was still visible in the contemporary setting. Opposite the bar four French windows opened onto a large stone balcony. In the centre of the room was an area for dancing, and at the far end were large, comfortable leather chairs set around tables. Beyond these were snug areas with soft lights for private chats. Above, a musician's gallery allowed the guests to sit at tables and watch the comings and goings below.

Anthony sat acknowledging the same old faces. Like him, some registered at the hotel through their company, some were just passing through, but most came to be part of the scene. The most chilling thing was while everyone enjoyed the atmosphere, millions of pounds changed hands, and countries over the odd glass of wine, a laugh, and a pat on the back. Breathe in deeply enough and Anthony was sure he could smell the sweet scent of a successful deal going down.

"Another drink, sir?"

"Thanks, Jim. Just add it to my bill." Anthony took a sip and nearly choked. Over the rim of his glass, he saw her. "How long have you been sitting there?"

"Sorry?" The woman lowered her glass and offered him her hand. "I'm Grace, with Electronic International. Pleased to meet you."

"Sorry."

"Which company are you with, Mr, err?"

"Company?"

"Yes. Who do you work for?"

He swallowed his drink in one go. "Acorns Financial & Management Services, if you must know. The name's Anthony Sharp, not Tony. If you'll excuse me, I've just seen a friend. Nice talking to you."

Taken aback by his rudeness, Grace's smile disappeared. She watched his retreating back.

"Forget him. The guy's a complete arsehole. Would you like me to get you a drink?" The barman said.

"Please. A glass of dry white wine, thank you."

He placed the glass in front of her and then offered his hand. "My name's Michael, but you can call me Mick." They both laughed.

"I take it you know him well."

Mick nodded. "I'm afraid so. He's a regular, stays here about every three weeks. Always calls me Jim. For the life of me, I've no idea why."

Grace watched Anthony make his way across to the snug area. She liked the look of his strong back and small butt, and wondered what he would've been like in the sack. She turned back to Mick. "It's a shame. I quite liked the look of him, but why's he an arsehole?"

"He's married… and has no money, though he likes to think he has."

"I'm intrigued. How can you tell?"

"Well, a dead giveaway is the white band round his finger. I see it all the time. It makes me laugh. These men think you women are stupid."

"His financial state. Do tell?"

"Well…" Mick leaned forward. She moved closer.

"When you've been in this business as long as I have, you get to know the signs. First they flash the cash, then everything goes on the bill, which tells you he's either broke, or his company's paying for it."

Grace ran a long fingernail up the stem of her glass. "Or he could own the company."

"Yeah, right." Mick picked up a freshly washed glass and started to polish it. "If that's the case, lady, I own this hotel. Believe me, that man doesn't have a penny to his name."

***

56

Anthony moved among the dancers, their sweaty bodies pushing against his as he crossed the dance floor. He half-greeted a scantily dressed girl, he had danced with last night. She wrapped herself around him. "Hello, Anthony, darling," She purred, brushing her hand against his crotch. "Let's make sweet love again."

Anthony pushed her away and carried on without looking back. He caught tantalizing glimpses of a young woman seated alone, cradling a glass of wine in her hands, through the crowd. A cold trickle of sweat raced down Anthony's back as she met his gaze. The gap closed again, and a spell released Anthony. He forced his way through the throng, "Please, sweet God, let her still be there."

Standing before her, he cringed on hearing himself muttering. "I say, is this seat taken?"

"No, not yet." The young woman said and then preoccupied herself with her glass of wine.

Anthony plonked down in the chair opposite her and turned his attention on the dancers.

Amanita crossed her legs and leaned forward, sipping her drink. It tasted bitter to her and she forced herself to swallow it. On the dance floor a young couple caught her attention. The man slipped his arm gently around the woman's waist. With slow steps, he brought their bodies close together. They seemed only aware of each other. Amanita wished it could be her he had his arms around. She closed her eyes and swayed gently in time with the beat and imagined the man's hands touching her body.

"Could I buy you another drink?"

Amanita opened her eyes to find the man seated opposite was asking her the question. "Let me introduce myself." He extended his hand over the table.

"A glass of red. Thank you." She placed her glass in his open hand.

"It looks as though we've been stood up." He rose. "Why don't we keep each other company?"

"Okay. Thank you for the offer, Mr Mmm—" She winked

at him.

He coughed and swallowed. On regaining his composure, he said, "My name's Anthony. And yours?"

"Amanita."

"Mrs?"

"No, just Amanita."

"What an unusual name?"

"Is it? My father named me after a seaport where he was born in Illyria"

"Illyria, where's that? My geography's a little rusty." He laughed.

"In the Adriatic Sea, I think."

"I've never seen you here before. Which company did you say you worked for?"

"I didn't say. I work for my father's shipping company."

"Really. I'll just get us both a refill." He held up the glasses and winked. "Keep it warm for me."

Amanita watched him disappear into the crowd and furrowed her brow, puzzled by his last remark.

Anthony muttered while weaving between the dancers on his way back to the bar. "I can't believe it. Talk about my ship coming home. Oh, baby, this is my lucky day, I can't wait to see the look on my wife's face when I ask for a divorce. Should've done it years ago, being misled by her lies. Her father controls everything. This time it'll be different, I'll make sure."

Back at the bar, Anthony found himself standing next to Grace again.

"Hi. I see you found your friend," Grace said.

He nodded and looked to see if he could see Amanita from where he stood. Satisfied he couldn't, he said, "Hey, Jim."

Once the barman finished serving a customer, he made his way back down the bar to Anthony.

"Hello, sir. What can I get you?"

Grace picked up her glass and drained it.

Anthony gave a wry smile. "A glass of house red and a whiskey, please." He turned his back on them and looked to where Amanita sat. "I guess, for once, I've got lucky," he murmured.

Mick rolled his eyes and picked up the two glasses. Grace laughed at his gesture.

"Would you like another drink too, Grace? Mr Sharp is paying," Mick said with a smirk.

She nodded and turned to Anthony. "Your friend, is she someone you work with?"

"What the hell has it got to do with you?" Anthony snapped back.

"Hey, no need to be rude. Only making conversation," Grace retorted.

Mick returned with the glasses and placed them in front of Anthony who snatched them up and walked away.

"He's a complete arsehole," Grace said.

Mick moved Grace's drink to where she could reach it. "Did you see who he was talking to?"

"Not really. He's headed over to the snug to some unfortunate female, no doubt."

Chapter Eleven

The Perfect Kiss

Amanita watched as Anthony moved through the crowds. To her surprise, she saw someone she hadn't expected to see again. The man from the Golden Hart sat staring at her, only this time, he wasn't alone. He sat with two other people, including a woman with jet-black hair, who was in deep conversation with an elderly gentleman.

The man studied her with a deep interest. *Did he see through her disguise?* She wondered. If he saw her natural self, then it was worrying, but for now, she didn't have the time to find out.

"So what part do you play in your father's company then?" Anthony asked, placing the wine glass in front of her as he sat beside her.

Amanita raised the glass to her lips, laughing sweetly. "What part do I play? None. I work nights."

"You're a working girl, or maybe vampire?" He laughed at his own joke, and she flashed her perfectly formed teeth while sipping the wine.

"How did you guess?" She cradled her glass in her hands.

"You're a bit of a joker. I like a woman with a sense of humour."

"Are you married?"

"Err, I was. My wife left me. The bitch took everything, even my kids." He looked away as he wiped his cheeks. "It's so hard for me. The ring was a constant reminder of what I've lost, so I removed it."

"That's understandable." Amanita leaned forward and placed her glass on the table.

"I knew you'd be the sort of girl I could talk to." He slipped his arm around her shoulders. "It's been hard for me not seeing them." He rested his head on her shoulder and breathed in a sweet fragrance before kissing her neck. Amanita arched her back at his touch. It sent his pulse racing as he inhaled deeply. "Let's go to my room for some privacy," he whispered, placing his hand on the top of her leg.

Amanita didn't answer.

"God, you're so beautiful," he said, his children quickly forgotten.

He took her hand and led her over to the lifts. "If only you had some idea what you are doing to me." The doors opened, and he pulled her into the empty lift, and then hit the button for the third floor.

Amanita could feel his hardness as he pulled her to him and whispered, "Feel what you're doing to me?" He moaned softly and gathered her hair at the back of her slender neck, pulling her head back as he kissed her. "Just wait until I get you to my room, honey."

There were changes happening to her body too, but unlike his, these weren't just the sexual kind. She ran her tongue around her mouth feeling the slight tingling in her gums. Her body quivered, and her breathing deepened. Her heart echoed his beat. The sound of life to her was like the sweet summer rain after a long drought. She pulled away, wanting to get out of the lift. "No, not here please! Not here." She moaned at him.

"Okay. Nice to know you're just as hungry as I am," Anthony whispered.

The lift stopped with a jolt. As the doors slid open, he reached for her hand, and led her along the empty corridor. At his door, he fumbled for his key card, almost dropping it. Amanita hesitated at the door until he invited her in.

The spacious cream-coloured sitting room had two large leather settees that faced each other. Between them was a large glass-topped, dark-brown coffee table.

He guided her through to the bedroom. "You wait here. I'll

just make us some drinks. We'll need one afterwards," he added with a wink.

The bedroom, decorated in the same unfussy cream-colour had, at its centre was a large round bed. Amanita heard him in the bathroom, and then the sound of him filling two glasses before the familiar clink-clink of ice.

She closed her eyes, ran her tongue around her front teeth, and tasted her own blood. She inhaled deeply as her whole body started to quiver so much that she had to sit down. A licentious smile lit up Anthony's face as he brought the drinks through. He set the glasses down on the bedside cabinet, then knelt before her. First he removed her shoes. After no resistance, he slowly unbuttoned her jacket.

Amanita reached out and stroked his cheek. He responded by kissing the back of her hand. Anthony stood and removed her jacket before starting to unbutton her blouse. He pulled her up off the bed and slipped the blouse from her shoulders. At the sight of her firm breasts, he ran his tongue around his lips and reached out to caress them. He bent and took a nipple into his mouth. Amanita ran her fingers lovingly through his thick hair, and then closed her fingers tightly around a clump and jerked his head up.

Shocked, he stared deep into her amethyst eyes and saw flames of passion burning within. She let out a groan of agony, but Anthony only heard ecstasy. She closed her eyes, threw her head back as her mouth filled with her own blood, and moaned softly as the burning liquid slipped down her throat.

Anthony pulled her close, searched for her mouth with his, wanting to taste the sweetness of her kisses, but she pulled back. He pushed her onto the bed and tore off her skirt. Hastily, he removed his clothes and leant over her, his body betraying his excitement. He kissed her flat stomach and the insides of her long legs, inhaling the delicious perfume of her body.

His body drove his mind now. She trembled at his touch. His suntanned body contrasted against the whiteness of hers as he brushed the hair from her face.

"Don't be shy. This isn't your first time, is it? You're driving me crazy, your body, so white, so pure, and so sexy. I want to make it special for you." He caressed the inside of her thighs as he prised her legs apart.

Amanita allowed Anthony to make his choice. He caressed her face, his words like soft rain dancing around her mind, inflaming her soul with the urgency of his wants and needs.

"I'll show you such pleasures. Sharing a perfect kiss to taste your honey lips," he whispered in her ear.

Amanita slipped her leg over Anthony's hips, and pushed him on to his back. Stunned, he found himself looking up at her. Fear slipped through his mind and disappeared as she smiled warmly down at him. He winked and placed his hands around her slim waist in one controlled movement. He pulled her on to him, slipping his hardness between her legs. She arched her back seeming to come alive under his control.

"Oh, sweet God, yes! Oh, I knew there was a whore in you." With deep thrusts, he entered the warmth of her body.

She responded in perfect timing to his movements. She opened her mouth a little and ran her tongue around her lips, watching the pleasure of their lovemaking build on his face. His eyes began to close as he reached his climax. Arching his back, he uttered, "Sweet Jesus," with the full thrust of his orgasm.

In perfect timing, she sunk her teeth into his neck. Anthony's eyes flew open, but he saw only the whiteness of her shoulder as a searing pain coursed through his body, followed by a sweeping numbness.

Aware her weight had lifted off him, he tried to find out what damage he had suffered. Surprised, he found his neck no longer hurt. There was nothing more than a dull ache. When he went to reach up to touch it he realised he couldn't move his arms.

What's wrong with me?

He tried to move his head but couldn't. Panic washed over him. Aware now, he saw only what was in his peripheral vision. He tried rolling over on to his side, but he remained on his back. Get help! Anthony heard a shower running, and tried to shout for help, but his body remained uncooperative. Paralysed. What had she done to him?

She reappeared. Naked. Her wet body and hair glistened, and her skin had more colour to it. Dear God, she's so fucking beautiful.

"Hello, Anthony," she whispered.

The bed gave a little as she sat next to him. As she caressed him, she whispered, "You've a fine body. I adore men who look after themselves." She ran her tongue over his thigh and across his flat stomach. "How perfect was my kiss?" She smiled down at him. "You were right. I'm not a working girl." She kissed him. "Please, Anthony, relax and enjoy your last moments. Soon you'll be free from sin. After all, you've had your fun, so now it's payback time for betraying your wife."

She brushed his hair back from his forehead. The smell of fear mingled with soap and aftershave. In his eyes the familiar look of not understanding why this was happening to him. She had seen it many times before when men realised they had no control over their own destiny. Some wanted to talk, mostly about themselves and the injustice of their lives. She smiled and gave little sighs of sympathy and understanding until the moment they showed their true colours. Sometimes she indulged in a little small talk allowing her body time to change back. Leaning forward, she whispered in Anthony's ear, "No one lied to you."

He let out a whimper.

"But how often have you lied to others?"

She saw he understood that his betrayal of his wife and his family had brought him to this moment. She gently caressed his face and neck. Then she licked her lips and leaned into him. Her long needle-like teeth slid painlessly in and drew away the last of his blood to allow him salvation.

She stretched and arched her back. The buzz of the new blood rushed through her, energizing her body. She quickly dressed. Once satisfied with her appearance, she opened the door, checking the corridor was empty and made her way to the lift.

In the lift, she pushed the button for the ground floor and leant back. Tiredness made her vulnerable. Then the lift stopped on the second floor. When the doors opened, the man from the nightclub stepped in with a woman. He smiled at her.

"Hello. Didn't I see you at the Golden Hart nightclub the other night?"

Amanita hit the emergency button on the control panel. As the doors burst open, she slipped out, ran down the last flight of stairs, and out to the car park to find her car.

Chapter Twelve

Reflection

Slowly backing out of Room 54, an ashen faced chambermaid on the third floor of the Grand Hotel gave an ear-piercing scream. She cast aside the fresh towels she had been carrying and shouted, "Oh God, he's dead!"

The hotel manager charged up the stairs, hissing, "In heaven's name, please think of our guests, you silly girl!" He leant against the carved banister to catch his breath as Ginnie flung herself into his arms.

"Oh, Mr Andrews, he's dead!"

"Please lower your voice. Who's dead, Ginnie?" The manager asked.

"Mr Sharp! He said I would kill him?"

"Dear God, I'm going to lose my job!" He shook Ginnie by the shoulders. "Are you saying you murdered him?"

"Mr Sharp said I would." She covered her face with her hands.

Andrews took hold of her arm. "Show me, and a little less noise. Please!"

Mr Sharp's door stood open. Down the corridor, one or two of the other doors were ajar. Woken before their personal alarm call, bleary-eyed guests stood with questioning looks. Andrews puffed his chest, and with as much confidence as he could muster, said, "I'm sorry you've been disturbed. There's no need to be alarmed. Everything is under control." He pulled Ginnie into the room, and closed the door behind them.

For a moment, Mr Andrews faced the closed door, fearing what he was about to see; a blood-spattered room with a disembowelled corpse, maybe. He inhaled deeply and turned slowly to find Ginnie standing by the bedroom door.

"He's in...there..." She pointed.

Mr Andrews entered a softly lit room. A stale odour hung in the air. On the bed was the sleeping Mr Sharp. "Ginnie, are you sure he's dead?" he whispered.

She nodded.

"Don't touch anything, I'll phone the police."

Within an hour, the hotel buzzed with life. Not its usual state, with guests coming and going, but the hum of police activity. Detective Inspector Walker stood patiently outside the door, talking to a uniformed police officer when the senior investigating officer Skinner arrived along with Detective Inspector Brookbanks and Detective Chief Inspector Martin.

Brookbanks, a local man, was the first to speak to the new officer.

"Good morning, sir," Walker said.

"Another body! On a Sunday morning too. Bloody typical, DI err!"

"Walker... DI Bard Walker."

"No peace for the wicked then, Walker. Well, what have we got?"

"Well, sir, we've a Caucasian male. The police surgeon has been. No sign of a weapon, but something familiar— about the death."

"We better take a look then." Brookbanks followed Walker to the open door. "Oh, one thing."

"Yes, sir."

"Let me give you two pieces of advice as you're new here. If I want your opinion, I'd ask. Second, let my team of experts do their job."

Walker narrowed his eyes as Brookbanks passed him.

"Where's the victim?" Brookbanks yelled on entering the hotel suite.

"Through here," Skinner called. On entering the bedroom, Brookbanks and Walker found Skinner and Martin standing either side of the bed.

"Good God, you'd think he was asleep," Brookbanks said.

"I'm sure I've seen this before..."

"Leave it to the experts," Brookbanks interrupted Walker. "Well, it's nice to see someone got a peaceful lay in this morning. Right, Walker, who found him?"

"The maid, Ginnie Maxwell. Mr Sharp ordered a personal alarm call for 7.30."

"What's known about Sharp?" Skinner asked.

Walker thumbed through his notes. "Anthony Sharp, thirty-six, a regular. He worked for his father-in-law's company, Acorns Financial & Management Services. They book this suite regularly. The family has been informed, sir."

"Excellent," said Brookbanks. "And the maid, we need to talk to her."

"She's next door, sir."

"Can you photograph this too?" Skinner said as a crime photographer made his way around the room.

"It's odd the covers have been lifted from the bottom of the bed," Martin said.

"The maid, Ginnie, err, gave Mr Sharp, a personal... hmm...wake up call, sir."

"She's a call girl?" Martin asked.

"No sir, they'd an understanding." Walker coughed, clearing his throat. "She'd give him a blow job to wake him up, sir. Only this morning he was..."

"A little stiffer than usual," Skinner sniggered.

Walker eyed the laughing senior officers condescendingly. "The maid seems to think she's responsible for the man's death. He'd told her on numerous occasions, she'd be the death of him."

The officers stopped guffawing and looked at him as though they'd just missed the punchline.

"What did you just say?" Brookbanks asked.

"I said that the maid said she..."

"Confessed to the killing?" Brookbanks said.

"No real evidence to show that she did, sir. I've spoken to the bar-staff that were on last night..." Walker checked his notes. "Michael Tucker, the barman, said the victim spoke of meeting someone. One of the guests, a Grace Middleton had the impression he had met a woman."

Brookbanks turned to Skinner. "How long before your team can let us know what's what?"

Skinner's phone rang before he could answer. "Okay," he said into his phone before answering Brookbanks. "The pathologist's team are on their way up, so we'll soon have a better idea of what's happened here."

By the time the pathologist's team had arrived, the crime photographer had finished his job, allowing the forensic team in to collect samples. The forensic pathologist, Heather Easton, peeled back the sheets, and leaned over the body. To her assistant, she said, "Please take notes." Easton then addressed her digital recorder. "At a guess, I would say he's been dead between six to eight hours. His skin is cold and clammy to the touch. Hmm, that's interesting. See here." She turned to her assistant. "Could I have a photo of the two small puncture wounds to the right-hand side of the neck? Possibly an insect bite, maybe not... but something has definitely punctured the skin."

"Is that what killed him?" Brookbanks interrupted the pathologist's train of thought as he had the hotel manager, on his back, complaining on behalf of the guests who wanted to leave.

"I'll need to have a proper look back at my lab." Easton glared over the rim of her glasses at him. "Once all the results from the samples come in from testing, I'll have a clearer picture. Until then, I won't be able to tell you anything."

Skinner sighed. "How soon do you think you'll be ready to move the body?"

Easton frowned and chose to ignore his question. She turned to her assistant. "I'm ready to remove the bedding now—" The assistant carefully scooped the bedding up and placed it in a sealed bag. "That's interesting. I would've expected..." Easton said, taking a closer look.

Walker looked up from his notebook. "Wouldn't there be signs of fixed lividity as the blood would've settled by now?"

"Yes, that's what I would've expected."

"DI Walker, ma'am."

"Well, Walker, there's no discoloration to the face." Easton looked into Sharp's eyes. "The cornea is cloudy. That puts the death within my estimate. Can you help me turn the body?" The assistant stepped forward as Walker stepped back. "No, I meant you." Easton nodded to Walker.

The pathologist took a closer look at the marks on the neck. "Look here." She gestured to Walker. "See, there's slight bruising around each of these marks." Her assistant passed her a magnifying glass. Easton jerked her head back. Walker leaned forward and studied the marks on the man's neck. Easton spoke with her assistant before turning to Martin. "I'm ready to turn the body now." Between them, Easton and Walker turned the body as the photographer took shots. "It's just as I thought, this man has lost a lot of blood, to the point where he's been drained."

"Are you saying he was killed elsewhere?" Brookbanks asked.

Easton removed her gloves. "That's your job. Once the body is back at my lab, I'll be able to give you a clearer picture." She left with her assistant in tow.

"Get that bloody body out of here," Brookbanks shouted.

"Sir, I've come across this sort of murder before."

Brookbanks narrowed his eyes with a look of disdain. "Right, lad, what is it?"

Walker flicked through the pages of his notebook just as Skinner called from the other room. "Hey, Brookbanks, we're ready to take the body now."

The stout police officer dismissed Bard Walker with a flick of his wrist and went back into the bedroom.

Walker's eyes raged at Brookbanks' attitude towards him. On pocketing his notebook, Walker caught a glimpse of his reflection in a mirror. A disagreeable thought flicked across his mind and, for a moment, he didn't quite recognise his face in the mirror. The stubble on his chin felt uncomfortable as he ran his hand over it. Though, overall, he was pleased with the keenness of his new mind, and he was good looking.

In the mirror's reflection, he observed the scene in the other room as Skinner and Brookbanks moved in and out of view.

"It's a pity about the bumbling assholes I have to work with," Walker heard himself saying. Surprised by the bluntness of the voice, he turned from the mirror, unsure whether it had been him, or someone else. On seeing no one, he turned back and rubbed his forehead. Since the encounter in the alleyway, he had found the voice inside his head was getting stronger and even egged him on.

"No," he said sharply. "These are my thoughts?" His hand touched his forehead again. "Am I going crazy?" he asked his reflection.

"What do you think, sucker?" the voice said, and he grinned back at himself. "Typical sort of place I would've expected to find her handy work." An anger rose in Walker's gut. "Who the bloody hell was her!" Walker rubbed at his head again. There hadn't been any mention of a woman in any of the police reports, but the voice in his head had other ideas. Anthony Sharp lay in a peaceful pose, just like the other unexplained deaths. A beautiful death, some might say.

Walker's thoughts struggled with the voice. The doppelganger in the mirror carried on studying his face. His eyes were unchanged; the same piercing dark green stared back at him. No matter how many rebirths he went through, he could still recognise them. He turned sideways and eyed himself up and down, nodding proudly, satisfied with his body. Tall, lean, and physically fit, his reincarnation had done well yet again. A pain shot through him as his host's mind fought back. Unwanted thoughts crowded in, of children, a woman other than the one he was looking for. Most of his earlier human hosts felt and remembered nothing. This one seemed to be putting up a fight.

The voice fought back. All he had to remember was the angel, his angel of death. Humans believed they were winged messengers from God, all halos and beautiful smiles, creatures of pure beauty, innocent, and incorporeal. How disappointed they would be on knowing the truth. The only angels he knew sucked the life out of you and left you where you fell. The white corpse lying on the bed knew the truth about angels.

The entity went back to studying his host and opened his mouth and studied Walker's teeth. No eyeteeth for him, no sweet taste of sin. He smiled at his reflection, opened Walker's jacket pocket and took out the small painting, enclosed in its own carrying case. It always surprised him how he had managed to know where he had placed it for its own safety along with his knife. The knife, he had been given so long ago by one of the first betrayers.

"Walker! What are you playing at, lad?" Brookbanks' voice echoed around the room. "There's no time for standing around daydreaming, there's work to be done!"

Walker winked at his reflection. "True, so true."

Chapter Thirteen

A Missed Opportunity

Jake's mobile woke him and swept away the fragments of a dream. A white-haired beauty was dancing around the bodies of dead men leaving a trail of blood. Jake reached for his phone, his fingertips probing the surface of the bedside cabinet. He snatched it up and grunted, "Hello."

"Sorry. Did I wake you, Mr Eldritch? It's Miles Hammond. I'm so sorry I couldn't be of any help to you. I'm not sure what happened last night. Please let me know."

"Don't worry about it. Of course, if we find out anything more, we'll let you know. Bye."

The haunting vision of the white-haired woman slipped into Jake's mind, unleashing dark thoughts again. Had Caroline really failed to see her last night? Jake replayed the scene. They had entered the lift, making their way down to the car park. Maybe she was concerned about Miles' odd behaviour, though he couldn't believe she had missed seeing the woman pressing herself into the corner of the lift. Caroline had only turned in her direction when the doors burst open. In that split second, the woman slipped through the gap and was gone.

The whole evening had been rather bizarre.

Jake placed a small wager with himself after Caroline had described Miles to him as an upper-class English gentleman with cut-glass accent. Jake guessed that he would be wearing tweed trousers and a jacket, with a cotton open-necked chequered shirt. Jake's only disappointment was the lack of a bow tie, but his passion for ancient civilizations made up for the lack of it. Miles stood as they approached the table.

"Please do allow me to buy you both a drink before we get started, my dear chaps." Miles pulled out a chair for Caroline before Jake even had chance to think about being a gentleman. Once he had gone to fetch the drinks, Caroline whispered, "When I phoned and told him I had a problem he might like to help me with, I didn't mention where the pictures came from, or how we came by them."

"He's bound to ask."

"You're the journalist. Make something up," she said just as Miles appeared with a tray of drinks.

"My dearest Caroline, you sounded perfectly intriguing on the phone. Do tell." Miles handed out the drinks.

Caroline handed over copies of the photographs. Miles flicked through them, stopping occasionally before returning them to their envelope. Jake glanced at Caroline who gave a slight nod.

Miles placed small, narrow spectacles on the end of his thin nose and opened the envelope. He selected one of the photos before tucking the envelope back between his knees. Jake finished his drink, and asked Caroline if she was ready for another one. She gave a nod and handed Jake her glass without taking her eyes off Miles' face. By the time Jake returned, Miles had finished looking at all the photos. He held the envelope in both hands as though evaluating something of great value. Finally, he focused his grey eyes on them. "Can I ask you how you came by these?"

Jake and Caroline looked at each other.

"It's all right. If you don't want to tell me, I'll understand."

"We—" Caroline started, but Miles cut her off.

"I take it you do not know what you have here."

Jake suddenly felt as though his lungs forgot what they were supposed to do as he gasped for air. Had his parents died because of what they had found?

Caroline touched his arm. "Jacob, are you all right?"

Air rushed into his lungs as he caught sight of a familiar figure moving through the crowd. He coughed the words out. "It's—her—again!" Caroline looked in the direction Jake was pointing. She saw a man making his way towards the lift. *"Her*? Who do you mean, Jacob?"

"Sorry—my mistake. Miles you were telling us," Jake said.

"Horebbah," Miles said, closing his eyes.

"Horebbah. Do you mean the ruins?" Caroline asked.

"I'm not sure. But it could've come from there." Miles pulled out a clean handkerchief and wiped the sweat pouring from his forehead.

"Obviously you both know, but enlighten me," Jake said.

"You've heard of the Dead Sea Scrolls?" Caroline asked.

"Who hasn't? Since their discovery Christianity became more exciting with the mention of angels and demons."

"There's more to them than just the angels, Jacob. Among the collection of scrolls was one made of copper. Hence its name, *Copper Scroll*. Inscribed on it is the location of buried treasure."

"Wow, that's a bit Indiana Joneish, isn't it?"

"In a way, but to some, the treasure was as fictitious as Indiana Jones. However, others argued that the list does contain some real locations in and around Jerusalem. According to the scroll, hidden somewhere at Horebbah, in the Vale of Avhor are several dozen tons of gold, silver, aromatic spices and manuscripts. Some believed that the deposit of the treasure was the results of the first Jewish Revolt about AD 66-74."

"Why hasn't anyone found it before now?"

"They haven't pinpointed the location."

"You're... not a believer... Mr Eldritch." Miles' voice slurred slightly.

"I never said I wasn't."

"Please, Miles," Caroline interrupted. "It isn't important whether Jacob believes in God or not. What can you tell us?"

"If this box is what I think it is, then it's time we all question our beliefs. I would've thought that you, Caroline of all people, would know what we have before us."

"You believe it is part of the copper scroll treasure?"

He leaned forward, his voice taut. "Speak freely,

expressing my various sayings among you. Those who understand parables and riddles would penetrate the origins of knowledge. You must hold fast to the wonderful mysteries." Miles paused. His forehead creased as his eyes dully stared ahead.

Jake puzzled by Miles' behaviour turned to see what he was focusing on. A man crossed the dance floor with a slender, white-haired young woman in tow. Miles continued without taking his eyes off them.

"What good is a riddle to those searching the truth? You all know the secrets of sin. To all who'll listen, the angels of destruction know the difference between good and evil."

"What has this got to do with the box?" Caroline asked.

Miles seemed to look through her, and then screw his eyes shut as he rubbed his forehead. After a moment he broke into a wide grin. "Dearest Caroline, are you not listening to me? I was explaining that it's Pre-Christianity. Please, can you not tell me more about where these photographs came from?"

"Miles, you were talking about the angels of destruction. Can you tell us more about them?"

"Angels of destruction— really." Miles picked up Jake's glass. "I think you've had a few too many of these. Whatever next? I'm sorry, Caroline, it's been a most interesting evening, but for some reason I'm feeling very tired. Sorry, I cannot help you any further with your intriguing mystery. You'll let me know if you do find out more. I'll call you tomorrow." Miles left leaving them feeling a little stunned.

"I'm not sure what happened there. Miles is normally so clear-headed."

"Have you heard about these angels of destruction before, Caroline?"

"Let's go back to yours; I could do with a cuppa while we chat."

Back at the flat, Jake searched the internet while Caroline checked his collection of books for any references to the conversation they had with Miles. Caroline sat beside Jake on the settee. "It makes no sense whatsoever. Horebbah didn't even exist as far as the transcribers of the scrolls were concerned. I'll check a few things out in my books tomorrow and give you a ring. I'm done in, and my bed is calling me."

"Okay." Jake walked her to the door. "Thank you for a lovely evening."

***

Miles' phone call was still bothering Jake as he climbed out of the shower. He decided to pay a visit to Whitby Library. He thought he might have overlooked something in the back catalogue of local newspapers. He reached for a fresh t-shirt just as his phone rang. "Morning, Caroline."

"Morning, Jake. Did I wake you?"

"No, but Miles did. He apologised for not being helpful last night. Have you had a chance to take another look in the attic?"

"Not yet. Miles called me too. He must've called me first. Did he mention the murder last night at his hotel?"

"Murder! No!"

"Apparently, it happened while we were there. The local radio's been on about it all morning."

"Damn. I didn't have the radio on, too busy thinking. Any ideas on who died?"

"They haven't said. One of the guests, from what Miles said, but it could've been a heart attack. Who knows?"

"Well, it's a little odd. Miles didn't tell me when he called."

"He's vague about last night and was shocked when I mentioned his comments on the angels, and Horebbah's treasure. He didn't remember anything after looking at the photographs. Wondered if it was possible to have another look at them that's why he called me. Apparently a friend of his, Samuel Hieron, collects religious antiquities. He said it might be worth talking to him about them. Did he mention that to you?"

"Not a word. He just kept apologising for not being able to help us. Caroline, I hope you don't mind me saying but..."

"Go on. Say *it*." A hint of humour echoed in her voice.

Jake laughed. "Am I too easy to read?"

"Like a bloody cheap paperback." She giggled.

"I want to check a few things out first…"

"You mean the murder at the hotel?"

"Yes. But also a back catalogue at Whitby library. When I see Kate, I want to spend time with her. It'll be rude of me to disappear up into the attic. I promise I'll be over tomorrow." Jake was sure he heard Caroline *chuckle* down the line.

"All right. I understand."

"Do you, Caro?"

Her soft laughter echoed in his ear. "I do."

"Thanks. I get the feeling we should keep what we know to ourselves until we know what we're dealing with."

"I agree. At least until we fully understand quite what it is. I'll see you tomorrow. Oh, one other thing before I forget. Who did you see last night that spooked you?"

"Spooked me?"

"Yes, you saw someone exactly at the same time Miles started to act oddly."

"Hmm. I don't… Of course, the white-haired woman."

"An old woman? Not me." Caroline laughed.

"No, not you. And no not an old woman, but young and very beautiful girl with white hair. It's strange, but I know her. The first time I saw her was the same evening I found the body. The body was that of the man I had seen her with. Last night I saw a man leading her across the dance floor… That's interesting, especially if the dead guest turns out to be the guy, I saw her with."

"Jacob, do you think that's possible?"

"It does seem crazy. Twice I've seen her, and twice someone's landed up dead."

"Just a coincidence. But with Miles' odd behaviour too, who knows?"

Chapter Fourteen

Nothing To Report

As the news of another unexplained death spread, the media gathered to speculate. Among the jostling reporters and journalists, a lone wolf stepped away from the pack, allowing the masses to close in.

On the top step of the Grand Hotel's entrance stood the dark-suited figure of Detective Chief Inspector Martin. A solemn smile rested peacefully on his lips, one he'd mastered for such an occasion. Martin turned with the right amount of dignity and nodded. He was ready for the media volley of questions. As they fought for the juxtaposition, Martin held out his hands, palms down, gesturing to them. They lowered their voices as he began to speak.

"Please, I cannot answer all of your questions at once." He nodded as if to reinforce his words.

In amongst the mumbling masses stood a stocky built, bulldog-faced lone wolf drawing hard on his cigarette. He shook his head knowing the next few words off by heart as they tumbled from Martin's mouth. Jake Eldritch didn't bother to note them down.

"Yes, there's been another death, but at this moment in time, we cannot tell you how the person died. No, there's no links to any other deaths in the area. No, I cannot pass on any information about the person until the family has been informed. Thank you for your time and patience."

Jake recognised the same fixed smile on Martin's face. It was the same one he'd seen before at another time in another place. The flashing cameras lit the dark portico of the entrance and highlighted the silver in Martin's hair as well. They gave his face an unflattering look. He turned and disappeared inside.

Jake glanced around at the all too familiar faces. He knew most of them had only just joined the chase all were seeking for that elusive life-changing story. However, within the main pack of newbies there were a few old hands, like him.

"Hi Bill." Jake nodded to a tall, reedy man who stood scribbling down a few notes.

Bill Wicking smiled broadly. "Hi Jake, me old mate. How're you doing?"

"So, so. Do you know who that guy is over there?" Bill followed Jake's discreet gesture. A youth stood arrogantly leaning against one of the large modern sculptures that dotted the drive up to the hotel. The sinewy young man was dressed in an old army jacket, with jet-black hair and a goatee beard. He drew on a freshly rolled joint before nodding in Jake's direction.

"Him." Bill laughed. "That's Dog, our main drug supplier."

Jake studied the youth while Bill sorted out his camera. Dog wasn't what Jake imagined a hardened criminal to look like. "Deals in drugs?"

"Yep, known only as Dog, I'm afraid. Comes from Whitby, bit of a hard nut, by all accounts. No one of any real interest. What about this latest death then?" Bill said, losing interest in the drug dealer.

"Interesting. Want to know more about it"

"Wouldn't we all. The police are never very forthcoming, especially with us." Bill pulled his bag up onto his shoulder. "I'll be off then."

On realising Jake's mind was still on the drug pusher, Bill nodded in the direction of the sculpture. "Do you think he had something to do with the deaths? Selling bad stuff, maybe?"

"Who knows? The stupid thing was last night I was there, with a couple of friends. If only I'd stayed overnight, I would've been in the thick of it."

"Bloody typical. How are things with your great mystery? Uncovered anything new?"

"Not really, but who knows." Jake gestured towards the hotel. "Though, I do have a bit of a mystery.

"All ears. What's the problem?"

"Ever had the feeling when you meet someone for the first time, you know them?"

Bill put his bag down and took out a box of cigarettes. Out of politeness, he offered Jake one.

Jake shook his head and held up the one he was already smoking. Bill lit one and inhaled deeply before answering. "Well, it depends who it is." Bill exhaled a cloud of smoke. "If it's someone famous, you already think you know them, but often or not they're nothing like the image you have of them."

"No one famous. I saw her, last night for the second time, in a lift of all places. I felt she knew me, but she shot out of the lift, before I could speak to her."

Losing your charm with the fairer sex, are you?" Bill gave a cough.

"There's a certain something about her. I can't quite put my finger on it."

"Is she beautiful?" Bill nipped the end of his cigarette and slipped the dog end into his jacket pocket.

"Strangely…"

"I wouldn't be worrying about if I knew her or not. I'd just get to know her. If you do hear anything about this latest murder, let us know." Bill picked his bag up again.

"Of course. I'll be seeing you."

Jake watched as old Bill staggered away under the weight of his camera bag and flicked his cigarette butt into a drain. Overhead dark clouds were gathering, he decided it was time to give up the evil weed as he headed to his car.

In the cold comfort of his flat, Jake thumbed through a pile of newspaper cuttings and then did an online search for any links between the named victims. His journalist's nose twitched as he made a fresh list. Two names came up in the local area, a two-bit hustler Charlie Keys who died a few days ago in Middlesbrough, and John Blackstone who died eleven years ago in Whitby. Jake scribbled down, *unknown drug dealer, aka Dog of Whitby,* and underlined it.

Whitby library was no longer a haven of peace and quiet as Jake entered. A gang of youngsters huddled around a bank of computers that lined one wall. Some nodded their heads in time to music only they could hear, while others chatted noisily to their friends, none of them seemed interested in the books.

At the main reception desk, the librarian chatted to a dark-haired teenage girl who wore an array of silver rings on her fingers and in her ears. The girl thanked the librarian and took a seat by the window.

"How may I help you?" The librarian asked Jake.

"I'm interested in reading back-dated newspapers for Whitby 1996."

"Did you book one of the readers?"

"Book? No, I didn't."

"As we're not busy I'll check for a cancellation." In a moment, she was back. "If you can show me some id, and sign in here."

Jake signed the book then followed her over to the window where the young girl sat at another reader. The librarian showed Jake how the machine worked before giving him a box of discs. After a few minutes of scanning the pages he leaned back and glanced around. The young girl leant back in her seat, reading a book. He observed her for a while as she muttered something before scribbling in her notebook. Jake went back to his task and then stopped to change a disc.

"The more you find, the more you need to know," the young girl muttered. "But where do I begin?"

"At the beginning," Jake suggested.

"Sorry?" She glanced in his direction.

"I thought you were speaking to me. You're doing some research."

"Sorry, was I thinking aloud. I get very excited when I discover something new, but it always leads to a new question. Are you researching your family history too?" The girl motioned towards Jake's notepad.

"No, I'm just following up a few things. I'm a journalist by trade.

"I bet you're following the Middlesbrough murder. That's the second one. Do you think they're linked?"

"That's not why I'm here. I'm trying to solve an on-going puzzle. What are you researching?"

"It's my college homework. I'm studying art history. We have to research a little-known artist, so I'm trying to find out about an artist who painted a portrait of a family that lives in the house where my mum works. I'm working a bit backward in hope of finding out more about the artist by association." She chuckled. "That makes me sound clever."

Jake laughed. "So what have you found out so far?"

"The ship owner, Master Polidori Virosa, came from Albania and built the house where my mum works in 1778. I'm hoping to find out more about his daughter."

"Albania? That's interesting."

"That's where he came from?"

"I'm not questioning you. It's just a bit odd. You're the second person this week who has mentioned Albania to me."

The girl gave a sharp nod and picked up her book.

Jake took it as a dismissal and worked through the local events pages on the disc until he came to the births, deaths, and marriages.

"Oh, she doesn't seem to have aged in the censuses," the girl muttered.

"Sorry, who?" Jake placed his finger midway down the column he'd been reading.

"The daughter of the family I'm researching. She's not aging, though it could just be me. I'm bad at maths." She scribbled in her notebook.

Jake stared blankly at his screen. *It wasn't possible, was it*? He moved to the next page. The large headline on the front-page shouted at him. "Yes," he cried making the girl look up.

"You've found what you were looking for?"

"I think so." Jake scribbled a note on his pad as the girl came around the table and stood behind him. Jake glanced over his shoulder and saw the colour drained from her face. She staggered backwards.

"Are you all right?" Jake reached for her as her eyes

glazed over.

"Murdered?" She mouthed the word.

Jake turned to his screen. "Yes, I'm following up on one of several unexplained deaths on the moors, this one happened twelve years ago."

"I've got to go."

At her desk, the girl swept her belongings into a brightly coloured shoulder bag.

"Are you sure you're all right?" Jake asked again. Her brown eyes narrowed as she brushed her auburn hair back from her face. With pinched lips, she whispered, "Yes, I'm fine. Got to go, that's all."

"I hope I didn't say anything that's upset you?" Jake called as the girl hurried away. On her desk lay a large leather-bound dog-eared book lying open. He scanned the page she had been reading when a name jumped out at him; he pulled out his phone and took a couple of photos just as the librarian suddenly appeared at his shoulder.

"Have you finished with the reader?" she said tartly, ready to switch it off.

"Not quite." Jake smiled, hoping his winning ways still worked, "I'm sorry, but I got fascinated by this book."

She glared at him. "I told the young lady to tell me when she had finished with it."

"Well, I'm sure she would've if she hadn't been taken ill."

"Ill!" The woman sounded as though it could've been contagious.

"Yes, she went very pale, gathered up her things and left."

"Well, if you want to read the book, you'll have to sign for it." She picked it up and carried it over to her desk. Jake followed her.

The librarian brought the title of the book up on her computer screen and as she typed in his details. Jake saw on the screen what confirmed his suspicions. The girl's name was *Hope Blackstone.*

Back at the reader, Jake finished making notes about the death on the moors and turned his attention to the book. Apart from some small references to the ship owner from

Albania, the book mainly listed names of vessels. Jake took it back to the librarian and asked, "How can I find out more about a ship owner called Polidori Virosa?"

"Well, we do have a well-documented list of ship owners and the shipyards in Whitby through the years, so that might be of some help to you or, you could try looking at some of our early newspapers."

Back at the reader with a new box of discs, Jake worked his way through the earliest copies of the local newspapers. After about an hour and a half of not finding anything of interest the next article he had to reread twice. Surely it couldn't be the same man.

"Maybe it could be. Who's to say he didn't live to be a great age?" Jake muttered to himself while paging down to the article dated 1795.

The horrendous death of a Whitby ship owner Master Polidori Virosa, and his wife, Lady Ocreata Virosa has left the town in shock. The couple were attacked by persons unknown, while making their way home from Scarborough.

The article went on to say: *The family had lived in Whitby for many years, but an illness had stopped Master Polidori Virosa from conducting his business during the daytime.*

"Oh, my God, I don't believe it." He reached for his mobile phone, clicked the automatic redial button when a tap on his shoulder took him by surprise.

"I'm sorry sir, but you can't use the phone in here," the librarian said.

Jake apologised and carried on reading the old newspaper. After a moment, something caught his eye. "Now this is getting interesting."

Chapter Fifteen

Three's A Crowd

Jake was sure for the first time this was the evidence he was searching for. A small item at the bottom of the page ricocheted around his mind. The local newspaper reported that a man found asleep in a boathouse on the east side of the harbour was actually dead. Other than two small marks on his neck, there was no sign to explain how he died.

With difficulty, Jake contained his excitement and worked through another couple of months. A cold chill crept over him as the librarian announced, "The library will be closing in ten minutes."

"Damn it! Every time I make some kind of head way—"

"I know just what you mean," the man sitting on the next reader said as they exchanged frustrated nods and gathered up their notebooks.

Once outside, Jake switched his phone on. The late afternoon air was pleasantly warm as he strode towards the car park at the harbour side. A vision of Whitby in the 1700s was still clear in his mind. It was Master Virosa's ships could easily be pictured docked in the harbour, with screaming gulls mixing with the wind racing through the rigging, and the sounds of the men working on the newly-built vessels. Strong local accents mixed with the shouts and cries of the many languages from the hundreds of ocean-bound ships that dropped anchor in the harbour. Jake could smell the oakum and pitch, as well as the smoked kippers and the tannery on the sea breeze of those far away days. He became aware of his phone ringing.

"Hello?"

"Jake, where are you?"

"Sorry?" I can't hear you. Hang on!" He stepped into an empty shop doorway.

"Where are you?"

"Mariana. I'm in Whitby. I've made an amazing discovery. It's err…"

"There's someone here you should meet."

"I'll be over soon."

"Don't worry about dinner. There's something in the oven already."

"Okay. I won't be late."

Within the hour, Jake was climbing the backstairs in Mariana's apartment. As he buzzed to be let in, the smell of the roasting chicken filled his nostrils at the same time as a thought flicked through his mind. Had Mariana set him up with another blind date?

When the door opened, Mariana stood in a long silver dress, with her dark hair piled high and twists of auburn ringlets hanging around her ears.

"Stunning as always." Jake kissed her cheek.

"Thank you, Jacob. I'm pleased you made it." She leaned forward and returned his kiss. "Come in."

The apartment was spacious and modern. Exposed brickwork shouted out the building's history, along with highly polished bare floorboards worn down by the dockers' boots as they unloaded cargo from the ships that docked in the harbour. Mariana slipped her arm through Jake's as they went through to the kitchen area. "I think Bard might be able to help you," she said.

"Bard? Oh, so you haven't planned another blind date for me?"

"No silly." She patted his arm.

In the kitchen stood a tall man dressed in a white openneck shirt and tight-fitted, pale-blue denim jeans. His blond hair, cut short at the back, had a slightly longer fringe that hung over his dark green eyes. His jawline and chin were strong, his nose sharp and narrow. Jake guessed he was about thirty-five years old.

The man smiled broadly and offered his hand. A chill took hold of Jake as their hands met and he had the sensation of knowing him, but from where?

"Jacob, this is…" Mariana began but her phone rang and cut her off. "Damn. A new member of staff needs me." She rolled her eyes, annoyance marking her face

"Of course. We can manage to introduce ourselves," the man said to Mariana's receding back. "Hi, Jake. I'm Bard." His voice was steady, cultured and, to Jake's ears, artificial. "So pleased to meet you at last. Mariana told me so much about you."

Jake nodded in the direction of the window. "The view of the river is stunning, don't you think? Everything seems so crystal clear."

"Would you like a coffee, Jacob, or is it Jake. Mariana's just made a fresh pot."

"People who don't know me well call me Jake, though I've a feeling we've met before."

Bard continued to pour himself a coffee before sitting down. The silence of the room was shattered when Bard gave an eerie laugh and said, "I'm your worst nightmare, Mr Eldritch."

"Pardon." Jake unsure he had heard what had been said. The man was too good-looking, Jake decided. He knew that men like him were normally arrogant bastards. Why had Mariana let this arsehole into her inner sanctum? Jake wondered, under normal circumstances she never let anyone in. "Why has Mariana brought us together?"

"She thought you can help me with a problem I have…"

Jake wondered just what Mariana had said about him to this jerk. He opened his mouth to say something when she walked into the room.

"Talk about timing," she said.

Jake nodded.

"I'm pleased you're getting on so well. I knew you would."

Jake wanted to disagree but said nothing.

"So what do you think about it then, Jacob?" she asked, taking plates out of the oven. Jake realised she was still talking to him.

"Sorry, what did you say?"

She turned to Bard. "Didn't you tell him?"

"I was just about to when you walked in."

"Tell me what?"

"I'm Detective Inspector Bard Walker. Didn't Mariana mention I'm working on the latest murder?"

"You're Walker! Of course, now I recognise you. In this light you look different."

"I bet. I felt pretty grim. My first night in Middlesbrough and sent to investigate a dead body."

"You looked out of it when I found you."

"I wasn't quite prepared for that. Anyway, Mariana explained that we might be able to help one another?"

"I'm an investigative journalist"

"Yes, you told me as much. You said you were my worst nightmare." Walker's smile grew colder as a dark shadow crossed his eyes.

Jake wasn't sure what he had just witnessed. He'd seen it before, and not just in the alleyway. Aware Walker was still speaking; he focused on the man's lips.

"And for this reason, I've come to you," Bard said. "Nothing to do with my police work…"

"Are you saying you're *not* working for the police?"

"Not at all. I've seen some rather bizarre things. Not your normal random acts of violence. These are quite unexplainable which Mariana tells me is your speciality."

"My speciality!" Jake scoffed. "Mariana, that's not what you normally say either it's my *obsession* when she's being nice or my *insanity* when she's isn't."

"That's not true, Jacob Eldritch." Mariana denied.

Walker butted in. "Mariana said you would listen to me, unlike my superior officers…"

"Hey now, wait a minute. I'm not about to take sides. Your superior officers wouldn't be happy about the fact you've been discussing your case with a journalist."

"I haven't come to speak to you as a policeman but a friend. Mariana said you would jump..."

"At the chance to get some inside info," Jake finished the sentence. "But not by bringing the whole police force down around my ears. I'm strictly a one-man band."

Mariana placed a roast dinner in front of Jake. "Give the guy a chance, Jacob. Listen, while you eat."

"Okay." Jake smiled softly at her.

"Now I'm leaving." Mariana placed another plate in front of Walker. "I'm needed downstairs. You can sort yourselves out. Don't forget to do the washing up."

As they tucked into their dinners, Walker said, "You scrape, I'll stack." Jake nodded while chewing a large chunk of roast potato. After a moment, Walker broke the silence. "So what made you become a journalist then?"

"My father." Jake picked up his mug of tea, uncomfortable at being asked the questions. To his relief, Mariana returned. Once their plates were in the dishwasher and their mugs refilled, Mariana poured herself a coffee and joined them at the table.

"Is everything okay?" Jake asked.

"New staff. Sometimes I wish there was two of me." She gave a beguiling smile.

"Was your father a reporter too?" Walker said. "Only I've been reading some of the reports and found these unexplained deaths go back over quite a few years. So I wondered if your father was involved with the early cases."

"He wasn't a newspaper journalist."

"So what's your take on these recent cases? Are they like any of the other ones you've investigated?" Walker lifted his mug to his lips.

Jake saw him furrow his brow as his hand shook slightly causing droplets of his drink to splash the table. He looked down at his mug as a confused expression slid across his features.

"Why are you asking me?" Jake said. "Surely you're privy to more information than I am."

Walker set his cup down and dabbed at the spilled drink

with his napkin. "I'm interested in an outsider's viewpoint, that's all." He broke into a wolfish grin.

"My viewpoint?"

"Yes. The reports say not by natural causes, or even an act of God." He laughed, letting his smile grow cold.

"No idea." Jake glanced at Mariana, who returned his smile.

"I think you have. Try me?"

"Okay. It's a woman." Jake waited for a dismissive remark, but it never came. Walker leaned back in his seat, his eyes closed. Jake waited. The skin around Walker's eyes rippled as though something moved just beneath the surface. It altered his face, causing it to take on a sterner look. Walker opened his eyes and locked onto Jake's. Jake blinked. It was as though something physical had passed between them.

Walker's eyes darkened into flat discs, seeming to become unblinking. His lips thinned, and as he spoke, his voice became richer and had a heavier tone, like an accent.

"So you think there's a link between the two crimes?" Walker asked.

"Probably, but I'm not privy to the full facts of the hotel death. In my opinion, there are similarities between the two crimes. What's the police's view?"

Walker laughed. "They have none. They can't see any further than the end of their nose. To them, it's random. I agree, it's a woman. I've been trying to figure out how she selects her victims?"

"They're definitely not random. There's a pattern. These men are more or less of the same type." Jake reached for his cup.

"In what way?"

"They're your normal everyday adulterous bastards found in any nightclubs, bars and other places where young women gather."

"Yes, but what about the mysterious woman reportedly seen at both crime sites?"

Jake detected a hint of sarcasm in Walker's voice. *So, here's the real reason for his interest.* "Sorry mate. I can't

91

help you as I said the police know more than I."

"Worth a try." Walker's shoulders slumped.

"Can't believe your lot need help from a journalist," Jake scoffed.

"If you're looking for adulterous bastards, I know a great place to find them," Mariana said.

"My main interest is in finding the woman," Walker snapped.

"Just trying to help," Mariana said.

"Where's that? Jake asked.

"A web site called *ManWatch*, for unfaithful lovers and husbands. I can show you, Jacob."

"Can't do any harm."

They followed her through to a small office where Mariana sat and punched a few computer keys. Jake watched over her shoulder as she typed in the title.

"How did you hear about it?"

"A customer. She checks out any guy who shows an interest in her, just in case he has a family or lover in tow. One of her friends had a bad experience. She said the site's quite a revelation. I've checked it for fun really. Here it is," she added with a wink.

Mariana let Jake sit down. She leaned over his shoulder so she could guide him through the web site. "Go to *Rogue's Gallery*, that's it. Then click on the cupid. Right, you're there."

A long list of men's names appeared with photographs. Jake paged down the screen and then stopped and clicked back a couple of shots. "Are there any more details about the guys?"

"See the 'Golden Rat' there?"

Jake moved the cursor across and clicked. "Oh, that's clever." The photograph turned over to reveal all the details."

Jake read aloud. "Anthony Sharp, a quiet little louse, with big ideas and no money."

"Did you just say Sharp?" Walker turned from the window.

"Wasn't he the one who died at the hotel?" Jake said

turning in his seat

"Yes." Walker pulled up a chair. "Let's see if any other names pop up."

"His death was accidental, so the news reported," Mariana said. "Something to do with magic mushrooms."

The men ignored her comment as they paged through the photographs. She gave a heavy sigh. "Okay, if you need me, I'll be downstairs." On getting no answer, she left them to it.

Chapter Sixteen

A Dead Dog

A slight vibration woke Amanita from a deep sleep. Her eyes sprung open as the sound travelled through her body, alerting her senses. She threw back the heavy covers. The cool night air touched her skin as she swung her legs off the bed. She padded over to the window and looked out.

The shimmering light of the moon lit up the garden below and the harbour beyond. Her senses more alert now, she licked at her dry lips and acknowledged that something wasn't right. On the landing, she inhaled deeply. A strange scent rose up from below. She knew it wasn't her housekeeper, Elizabeth.

A loud bang echoed throughout the house. Tiredness and hunger weakened her. Sleep gave her neither peace nor rest. With heavy limbs, she went back into her room and gathered up a pale blue silk wrap. Slipping it on, she made her way up to the attic. Before a bank of small closed-circuit screens, she switched her computer on. Hidden within each of the rooms a camera allowed her to search for the intruder.

In the dim light of the kitchen she watched him ransacking the cupboards, and tossing everything to the floor.

She zoomed in on her unwelcome guest. He was tall, slender, with cropped black hair, and a neat goatee. The man wore a white t-shirt and tight black jeans, which emphasised his lean, toned body. He leaned forward to retrieve a small box he'd just discarded. Amanita was surprised to see he wore a small black cross.

The intruder kicked the detritus to one side and made his way along the hall to the parlour at the front of the house.

She followed him on the next screen as he searched for anything of value. He took his time to study each item before crushing it under foot.

Her heart held a beat, for in this room was her most precious object. It hung over an ornate marble fireplace. The oil painting depicting a man dressed in a white high-collar shirt with a white cravat, under a crow-black dress coat. He stood with his hand resting lightly on his seated wife's shoulder as she sat before him on a chair. Together they both stared serenely out. At the man's feet stood a little girl, aged about four, wearing a white muslin dress that mirrored her mother's. She leaned with her head resting on her arm, on her mother's knees. In her other hand she held a cross which hung down at her side. Her mother rested her left hand on her daughter's head. All three of them had pale skin and white hair.

The unwanted guest muttered while kicking aside broken china. He turned his attention to the wall and pressed his ear to it as he began to tap. Amanita, puzzled by his strange behaviour, watched. He moved slowly along placing his ear to it and again tapping as he made his way towards the painting.

Within a second, Amanita was at the parlour door just as the man was pulling a knife from his back pocket.

"It's just a painting. Nothing behind it." Her words were barely whispered.

At first, she wasn't sure whether he had heard her as the knife moved towards the canvas.

"Well, what do we have here? Miss Virosa, I believe." He turned; a cold smile played across his lips.

"You have me at a disadvantage, sir."

The corners of his mouth curled.

In the dimly lit room, Amanita was aware of his thoughts, sensing his emotions, from the blood coursing through his veins, to the changes in his breathing as he became aroused. An odd odour lay between them in the tense air. It wasn't the scent of fear she was familiar with, but something destructive, unchangeable, and final.

He stepped closer, his gaze faltering. He turned his head, averting his eyes and, within that split-second, the knife was at her throat, his hand was around her waist.

"Now my little lady, we'll have some fun!" He pressed his body against hers and she felt his hardness against her thigh. He slid the knife across her throat. "Don't get smart with me. My speciality is killing."

She inhaled, closed her eyes, and relaxed against him. The man sensed something and pushed the blade harder against her throat. The thin, cold metal sliced into her skin and she stopped struggling.

"Dog's me name, bitch. For someone who doesn't look well, you're a feisty little thing. Let's take a look upstairs." He dragged her out of the parlour and across the hallway. Amanita fought to stay upright as the long silk wrap caught around her legs.

"Hold the fucking thing up, you silly cow!"

At the top of the stairs, he sent her sprawling. "Treat them mean and keep them keen." Dog knelt beside her, using the tip of his Bowie knife to lift the hem of the wrap. "Nice pussy. Come to Doggie." He leaned forward, moving the knife along the inside of her thighs until the tip touched her essence. "Just a little prick for now. Later I'll give you something hard so you'll never forget."

Amanita met his cold, glassy eyes and said nothing. He yanked her up, and hauled her along the landing, pushing open doors as he went. He stopped at her bedroom door. "Ah, ain't this pretty?" He shoved her towards the bed, and she fell backward, hitting the floor with a thud. "Move a muscle and you're dead!"

Dog's face lit up at the sight of her mother's jewellery box. He crossed to it and emptied the contents onto the dressing table. Necklaces of ruby, diamond-encrusted bracelets, and earrings glinted in the half-light as he held them up one at a time to make his selection before pocketing some.

Amanita pulled herself up onto her knees. If she didn't keep her breathing steady the hunger would take control, travelling up from her abdomen, it washed over her. The urge to kill him was strong. "Not here, Not yet," she murmured while imagining sweetness of his blood filling her mouth.

Dog rounded on her, waving the knife. "Don't! Don't think I won't kill you." The veins in his neck pulsated angrily at her. She turned away and Dog laughed. "That's right, bitch. Know your place." He continued to empty the drawers.

"I do not keep money in the house."

"Lying, rich bitch!" Dog bared his yellowing teeth and grabbed a handful of her hair, wrenching her head back. "Don't waste my time telling me that shit!" With a backward sweep of his hand, he caught her across the face. She fell narrowly missing the corner of the bed. Amanita cringed as her fingers found the damage to her cheek and swallowed the bittersweet taste of her own blood.

"Get some fucking clothes on!" Dog yanked her up by her hair. "No bloody funny stuff, either?"

She nodded.

"Good. We understand each other." On opening her wardrobe door, he flung her clothes to the floor until he found something he liked. He tossed a short red silk dress in her direction. "Here put this on, bitch."

With modesty, she turned her back to him.

"Don't bother trying to hide anything from me. I'll soon be enjoying it." He laughed and dropped into a chair and picked at his nails with the tip of the knife while waiting for her to dress.

Amanita hesitated.

"What are you waiting for princess, a servant?"

"I need my underwear." She pulled the wrap tightly round her,

"Honey, you won't need any tonight. Just put the fucking dress on."

She dropped the wrap and slipped on the dress. It came to the middle of her white thighs, hugging the curves of her hips and buttocks. The soft neckline draped over her firm breasts.

"Fuck me. I'll have some pussy now. Unfortunately I've some pressing business to take care of first. Some nasty men will enjoy your company once I've finished with you in exchange for my outstanding debt. You've got a car, haven't you?" He pointed the knife as if to remind her.

She nodded.

He grabbed her arm, dragged her towards the door. "Let's take a little ride and have some fun."

"I need some shoes!" She struggled free and picked up a pair of flat pumps.

Dog snatched a handful of her hair. Amanita raised her hand, trying to free her hair from his grip but caught a thin silver chain around his neck. His eyes narrowed to black slits as he prised her fingers from his neck. Pointing the knife, he said, "I'll think nothing of killing you here."

"We need my bankcards if its money you want!" Amanita opened a drawer and fumbled in the back of it, releasing a hidden drawer, while Dog mesmerised by the shape of her buttocks through the red silk dress caught his breath.

"Come on, bitch. It's time to go!" He snarled at her. She held out the cards to him, but he grabbed her arm and dragged her down the stairs. In the kitchen, Amanita unlocked the door into the garage.

"Fuck me. A midnight blue Aston Martin Vanquish V12. Nice touch, bloody tinted windows." He opened the driver's door. "Get in! Let's get you to the bank."

Amanita slid into the passenger seat and belted up. "The door opens automatically when you start the car."

"Fucking brilliant!" Dog caressed the steering wheel as the car burst into life, filling the garage with a cloud of blue smoke.

Chapter Seventeen

Then There Were Two

After about an hour, Walker's excitement was uncontainable as he became hyper babbling on about how the two photos on the *ManWatch* website matched Andrew Hull and Charles Keys. Jake wasn't convinced about Keys, but his gut told him it was the man he'd seen laughing with the white-haired girl.

"Do you recognise any of the men?" Walker pointed to the screen.

"Nah, sorry mate. Keys wasn't with the girl I thought." Jake recalled Walker saying something about Andrew Hull couldn't describe the woman either. "So, do you think she uses this site?" Jake asked.

"It's the only link we have so far."

"You're forgetting that Andrew Hull was just a witness."

"But his picture is on the site."

"Yes. In his statement, he described how he accidently knocked a glass of wine onto the lap of the woman seated next to him at the bar. They got talking, and when he went to say goodbye she'd changed, but how, he couldn't put his finger on it. He was adamant that she *was* the same woman Keys was with. But how?"

"He said her looks had changed, not her clothes. The red wine stain should have been on her skirt, but it wasn't."

"If it wasn't, then it must have been a different woman."

"But he must have seen her to know whether it was the same woman he'd been talking to all evening, so why couldn't he describe her?"

"No idea. Let's leave Andrew Hull out of it for now. All the witnesses described the woman as strikingly beautiful, but no one could say in what way. You would think it should be easy to describe her, but none of them can say what made her stand out. Some said her hair, her eyes and her mouth…"

Walker's brow lifted. "Why her mouth?"

"Don't you find women's mouths beautiful?"

"Never really thought about it."

"Just me then. The way they apply lipstick. Funny thing is that other women tend to notice if a woman is wearing the wrong shade."

"What's lipstick got to do with any of this?"

"Women pick up on these things far more than men. Yet none of the women I spoke to saw an outstanding woman. That's odd, don't you think?"

"Maybe." Walker continued to scan the photographs. "What about the security cameras? Mariana and the buildings around here must have them."

"Didn't the police check them?"

"Yes, but only the men are on them by themselves."

"Walker, think about this. Let's say the woman's time is limited. She has to find a victim, draw them away from the masses, feed and then get home before sunrise—"

"What?" Walker roared with laughter.

"You explain the missing blood then."

"You're expecting me to take you seriously? The woman's a vampire." Walker's lips curled slightly. "Are you sure it's just blood that's missing?"

"Were there other body parts missing?" Jake knew the reports and witness statements all said the victims looked as though they were sleeping. Walker was lying. The body in the alley showed no signs of disturbance, apart from the fact that the guy's flies were undone.

Walker's hand on the desk started shaking uncontrollably. He threw himself forward and clutched at his head.

"Are you okay?" Jake touched his arm.

Walker lifted his head. His eyes darkened and bulged as though under a heavy pressure.

"Walker?"

The police officer fought to focus on him as a spasm tightened his face. Walker rubbed his forehead as his eyes rolled back into his head. He struggled to lift his hand as his head shook violently and then he crumpled into the chair. Whatever had caused the spasm was gone as the tension in his face seemed to drain away. Jake fetched a glass of water, and Walker let out a stifled groan, then pushed his hair back from his eyes.

"Wow, glad to see you're getting some colour back, mate. Here, sip this."

"What?" Walker straightened in his seat. "What the hell do I need water for?"

"You had some sort of fit!"

"Nothing of the sort!"

"Okay." Jake set the glass down. "Right, are you ready to continue with the problem of how she finds these men?" He pointed to the screen.

"Of course. That's why I'm here."

"Then we'll need Mariana." Jake picked up the phone in the kitchen, a direct link to downstairs. It rang twice before she answered.

"Mariana, could you spare us some of your time, please?" He nodded, and then hung up. "Right while we're waiting, we'll need to decide which of us is to be the bait. I'm sure Mariana has a few nasty things to say about us."

The lift door opened and Mariana floated into the room. Walker sprung to his feet. "Jake has a plan. You're needed to write something wicked about one of us on *ManWatch*."

"Like what?" she teased. "You're lousy in bed, can't cook, and hate doing the dishes?" Mariana stroked Walker's face and then blew him a kiss.

"Please concentrate. It's very important." He turned to Jake. "Which one of us?"

"As you're married, it's more believable you're the adulterer." Jake was amazed by the change in Walker as he flirted with Mariana.

"To start with, we need a photograph." Mariana pulled her phone from her pocket. "Now, Bard, let's have you on the sofa." She winked, leaned over him, and slowly unbuttoned his shirt to his waist, pulling it free from his jeans to reveal his toned stomach. Stepping back, she admired her handy work. Walker winked with dark, smouldering eyes, playfully spreading his legs, resting his hand near his crotch.

"My darling, I want you to be alluring to women, not to gay men."

Walker rearranged himself into a position Mariana was happy with and then she snapped a couple of shots.

Jake became aware of his phone vibrating against his leg and took the call. "Hi, Caroline. How can I help?" He watched as Walker and Mariana loaded the pictures up on to the net.

"Where are you, Jake?" Caroline asked.

"I'm at Mariana's. Why?"

"Can you meet me at your flat? I've something to show you."

"Okay, give me about half an hour. I'll be walking."

"Jacob, come and see," Mariana said, gesturing at the screen. "I can't believe for one minute this will work, but as they say, '*Show the mouse the cheese and who know*s?'"

"So I'm not a dirty rat then," Walker said.

Mariana giggled and smiled up at Walker, her eyes shining bright.

"She's very excitable, isn't she, Jacob?" Walker slipped his arm around Mariana's shoulders and kissed the top of her head.

Jake watched, uncertain of what he was witnessing as Mariana relaxed, and leaned back against him. Suddenly three had become a crowd.

"I'm sorry Mariana but I need to go. Thank you for another wonderful meal. It's been a pleasure to meet you, Walker. Just let us know if anything happens with your picture."

Walker pushed Mariana away and joined Jake at the lift door. His eyes, wide and dark, bore into Jake's. "It's a shame you have to leave, my dear friend. I've so much more to share with you, but still, you'll be seeing more of me, if I'm to be the bait."

Jake sensed a disturbing memory and tried to recall what it was that had unsettled him, but it was gone. "Bye, Mariana."

Chapter Eighteen

Across The Wild Moors

The deserted streets were awash after the heavy rain. The short drive took them to the cash point at the quayside. Dog gripped Amanita's knee as she opened the car door, his nails digging in.

"Fucking wait until I get out first!"

He rushed around to her side and yanked her from the car, banging her head. She tried to straighten her dress, but he gripped her arm and frogmarched her to the cash point. He pressed himself against her, watching over her shoulder as she keyed in her pin number.

"How much do you want?"

"Get as much as you can!"

On the way back to the car, Dog stopped, released her arm and yanked her closer. He placed a finger to his lips and nodded in the direction of the car. In front of them, two young men stood trying to peer in through the windows. Amanita held her breath at the sight of Dog's blade glinting in the streetlight. Frightened of what he might do, she leaned into him, trying to keep his attention on her. She felt his arm tighten around her waist as his breathing increased. The men lost interest and moved on. Amanita heard Dog swear under his breath as he pulled her over to the car.

Once inside the car he relaxed and patted Amanita's knee as if she was his girlfriend. "Let's take this baby for a spin!"

The car roared across the moors. The night sky exploded above them with a myriad of sparkling stars. Dog screamed wildly as he drove at a break-neck speed, allowing the creature its freedom. The car hugged the contours of the road. Amanita studied the man. He sensed her watching him and gave a nasty snort. She read his thoughts. *Silly bitch*! *She's no idea what I have in store for her.*

She knew the glow of the dashboard had intensified the paleness of her skin, adding to his arousal. Without warning, he turned off the road onto a rough farm track. The car bumped and jarred over potholes before coming to a halt. The moon highlighting the landscape made it dance with shadows and half-shadows.

Dog leapt from the car in a rush of adrenalin. He snatched her door open. "Get out!" he snarled while roughly unclipping her seat belt. He pulled her against him and fondled her breast. "Out here, it's just you and me babe. We're gonna have such fun. There's nothing for miles so you're free to scream."

Amanita leaned into him, allowing her eyes to adjust to the darkness. An ache in her jawbone alerted her to her strength returning. She licked at the numbness in her gums, moaned softly, and arched her back, inhaling the cold air. Her senses tingled with the sweet smell of rain-soaked earth and decaying leaf mould. The overpowering smell caught at the back of her throat with each breath she took.

In a sweeping movement, Dog slammed her across the car bonnet and pushed hard onto the small of her back. He kicked her legs apart as he pulled the dress over her hips, exposing her bare buttocks.

"Just right," he laughed. With a single thrust of his hips he entered her. "Doggie gives it to you, hot, hard, and fast!"

With each thrust from Dog, a pain like hot needles ripped through her gums, filling her mouth with blood. Amanita moaned as the agonizing pain rippled through her body and she shook her head as her teeth sliced through her gums. The more she moaned the greater Dog's frenzy as he rode her. He slapped the tops of her thighs, crying out, "Old Doggie knows how you rich bitches like it!" His breathing deepened with his climax. On closing his eyes, he lessened his grip on her hips.

In a synchronized movement, Amanita contorted. Springing backward and snarling, she tore into him like a wild animal.

Dog's eyes flew open as a pair of bloodied snarling jaws confronted him. The full force knocked him backwards. His jeans dropped to his ankles, hindering him as he struggled to free himself from the weight of the animal. Blood trickled down his arms onto his face while he tried to protect it with his arms as the creature tore chunks out of him.

The creature's weight lifted, but Dog could still feel its breath on his face. He opened his eyes and saw in the car lights the whiteness of the creature's teeth against the red of his blood.

His mind froze. *Bare, white skin and eyes, an unholy shade of blue.* A woman sprawled at his feet, staring up at him with those same amethyst-blue eyes. The two images merged, and his scream echoed across the moors. He gulped in air, trying to push her away, but the more he struggled, the harder it was to breathe.

Amanita bared her teeth at him. An unearthly sound rang in his ears as she slipped the needle-like incisors into his jugular vein, filling him with a venomous secretion.

Dog lay whimpering on the blood-sodden grass. In the headlights of the car he saw what the woman had become. The soft white hair was now wet with blood. Her face altered by her extended jaws with snake-like incisors arched over her human teeth.

Amanita sat on her haunches, licking at her lips, the hunger now satisfied. Dog tried to speak, his eyes unblinking.

"You left me no choice," she said. "You broke into my home and violated me. Now you must pay for your sins."

He whimpered.

"You made your choice." She stroked his hair, caressed his face, and ran her fingers across his lips and then licked the blood from them.

He flinched.

"You've taken from me, so I must take from you." She sunk her teeth into his throat and finished him off. Once done, she stretched, arched her back and sniffed the air. She picked her way across the moors until she came to the small creek. She stripped off the dress and bent to wash between her legs, her battered face and body in the icy water. An unexpected pain ripped through her abdomen, dropping her to her knees. The fast-flowing water carried her dress away. She clutched at her stomach, waiting for the pain to subside before looking for her dress and was relieved to find it had caught on a rock. A second pain cut across her belly as Amanita scrambled onto the bank and made her way back to the car.

Dog lay staring towards the heavens. Amanita pulled at his jeans, fingers probing for her mother's jewellery. She encountered the knife and tossed it to the ground, gathering up her bankcards and keys. She made it back to the car just as the first droplets of rain started to fall.

On turning into St Hilda's Terrace, Amanita relaxed as the pain subsided. While waiting for the garage door to open, a wave of nausea washed over her. In desperation to keep it under control, she panted, sucking in gulps of air. Once the door lifted enough, she eased the car in.

Clutching her stomach, she used the garage wall to support her as she made her way into the kitchen. Her shoes crunched and slid on the scattered contents from her cupboards. At the breakfast bar, she pulled the telephone by its lead from the floor. Relief ebbed away when she heard no dialling tone and tossed it aside. With her head resting on the breakfast bar, she reached under and released a hidden drawer. From it, she took a mobile phone and pressed the automatic dial key.

"Sorry to call you so early, Mrs Blackstone. I... need you. Please come at once?" Amanita dropped the phone and snatched a tea towel off a hook. She held it to her mouth, climbed the backstairs and made it to the bathroom. She dropped to her knees and retched, a crimson wave spread across the tiled floor as the next spasm of nausea hit. She heaved up more blood, spraying the wall.

Chapter Nineteen

Dead Or Alive

D.I Walker bothered Jake. He turned his collar up against the chilling night air as he entered an alleyway with its overflowing dustbins and skips. An unsavoury air of despondency hit him as he hurried on, ignoring his gut feelings as the badly lit alley had never bothered him before.

The maze, known locally as the rat run, was divided into two main thoroughfares plus several short paths that led to the rear of the shops and businesses. Anyone unfamiliar with the area would soon find themselves disorientated by the indistinguishable surroundings walking along the interconnecting footpaths. In the shadowy half-light, the mind could play tricks as the surrounding darkness seemed to descend into the alleyways from the adjacent buildings.

Jake tried to make sense of what he'd witnessed a few days ago. Confusion clouded his mind as he tried to recall the event clearly. How easily the flickering streetlights could've played tricks on him. Further along, vandalism had taken out some of the lights completely. Even in the daytime, an air of discomfort hung over those who bravely travelled the shortcut to the main street. Jake wondered if ghosts of the stevedores still travelled the routes to and from the docks. The sound of their hobnail boots echoed off the old warehouses now converted into new apartments and office blocks, eradicating forever their once familiar surroundings. Now all that the alleyways seemed fit for was to dump rubbish.

Jake turned the corner. Before him the only visible sign to what had happened, a couple of days ago were the tattered remains of the crime scene tape fluttering from a drainpipe. He knew for certain he had seen a man standing over the prostrate body. Of course, he hadn't known it was Walker, nor the standing man was actually dead. The image had been clear in his mind, but so impossible. Then there was the noise. A high-pitch squealing that had rooted him to the spot. It penetrated deep into his skull, bringing him to his knees. After the sound subsided, Jake lifted his head expecting to find that the whole of Middlesbrough had descended on the alleyway, only to find he was alone. The flickering streetlights made it hard to see anything clearly. He picked the abandoned torch up, deciding to investigate. The standing figure was sprawled in the doorway, looking very dead indeed. *More asleep*, Jake thought, casting the torch beam across his face.

"Oh God. It's the guy I saw with the white-haired beauty."

Jake pulled out his pencil and moved the man's shirt collar. On his neck, in the torch light, Jake saw two distinct marks. "I knew it." He took a couple of photos with his phone, and then leant in to fire off another couple for luck. A low moan caused him to turn. The other body wasn't a body. He shone the torch beam across the man's face, revealing a mop of thick blond hair.

All of a sudden, a deep melodious tune filled the darkness. The source came from a mobile on the ground between the man's legs. Jake used the tip of his pencil to pull the phone towards him and was shocked to see the local police station number flashing up on its screen.

"Oh shit! An unconscious police officer…and a dead body." Jake checked the officer's pockets, found his ID card, and photographed it before carefully pushing it back into place.

At the time, Jake couldn't quite put his finger on it, whether it had been a smell of the alley, or his gut feeling, something had unnerved him.

"Don't like Walker!" Jake invoked the man's name in the place where it all began hoping for an answer. Jake tried to imagine what Keys' last thoughts might've been as he realised the inevitable was about to happen. He recalled what he and Caroline had witnessed on the video, his father knowing that he was unable to protect his wife from what was about to happen.

The screeching of brakes followed by the honking horn shattered his train of thought. He turned from the crime scene, crossed over the main thoroughfare, and entered another semi-dark alleyway. What happened two nights ago merged with his parents' execution caused Jake to tremble at the thought that somehow the two parts of a puzzle were interconnected. Doctor Cula's face slowly merged with that of DI Bard Walker in Jake's mind. "Maybe…" Jake quickened his step. "I need to do a little digging. Who is Doctor Cula? More to the point, what's known about Walker?"

Taking the steps two at a time, Jake arrived at his flat to find Caroline sitting on the wall. "Hello. Aren't you cold out here?"

"A little, but I didn't want to be in my car with the engine running. Talking about running, it sounds like you've had your engine more than just ticking over."

"Very funny! All I get is abuse after worrying about leaving you waiting too long." He kissed her lightly on her cheek.

"A nice hot cup of tea wouldn't go amiss. If you open up, I'll make it."

As Caroline made her way through to the kitchen, she called to Jake. "Isn't it about time you sorted your heating out? I'm sure its warmer outside."

"I'll switch it on then, Boss." Jake heard Caroline laughing as the heating rattled and gurgled into life. He switched the computer on and sighed at the thought of writing another article to pay for the heating bill. He cleared a pile of books and folders from a chair before moving it up closer to the desk. By the time Caroline carried the drinks through he'd cleared a space beside the screen for the cups.

"Wow, that's much better already. If the heater isn't broken why don't you keep it on low to take the chill out of the air and get rid of the smell of dampness?"

"Forever the practical, Caroline."

"Who did Mariana set you up with this time?"

"Not so much who, as what."

"I'm intrigued." She sipped her tea. "Tell all."

"Before we start, does this man remind you of anyone?"

Jake clicked on the *ManWatch* site.

Mesmerised, Caroline read out some of the posts. "*My boyfriend tells me he's faithful, but I'm not so sure. Could anyone tell me the truth? He's good looking with wonderful blue eyes and his name is Michael Thomas, age 27. As soon as I get a photograph of him, I will post it. Susan Dailey.*"

"Is this for real? Are you telling me women really do post their unfaithful lovers, husbands, and partners on the net?"

"Yes, and Bard Walker is on there too."

"Bard Walker... Mariana doesn't think you're gay just because you've never been on a second date with any of her female friends?"

"No, of course not." Jake frowned. "Let's just forget about me and my lack of hot second dates. Walker is a police officer. He's working on the unexplained deaths. Two nights ago I came across him in the alleyway. I thought he was dead. Last night Mariana introduced him to me and posted his picture on this website to see if she could lure the killer to strike again, but I want you to see him."

Jake clicked on to Rogue's Gallery and scanned along the new photographs until he found the pages of new golden rats. Caroline gasped.

"So I take it, it's not my imagination then."

"But how's that possible? He doesn't look a day over thirty-five."

"I know. It's uncanny."

Caroline placed her hand on the screen covering Walker's mouth and nose leaving only his dark green eyes. "He's definitely got Doctor Cula's eyes."

"Couldn't they be from the same gene pool?"

"You mean... not to be trusted and watch your back at all times."

"Yes, that's the sort of thing. So why are you here again so soon, or are you missing my company? You sounded insistent on the phone."

Caroline blushed. "Actually, I've been up in the attic again. You really must come over."

"I know. You keep saying. So what couldn't wait this time?"

"It's in my car."

"Okay, I'll fetch it. You put the kettle on again."

"It's in the boot. Be careful, it's quite large."

Five minutes later, Jake returned, struggling with a large box. "What the hell's in it?"

"Wait and see. You'd better bring it through here. I've cleared the coffee table."

Jake followed Caroline into his smallest bedroom where she'd put the fresh drinks.

"Hey, you haven't been moving my stuff around have you? It's all in order." Jake laughed when he saw the coffee table minus his clutter.

"Oh, do shut up and set the box down here. Carefully does it!"

"All right. Do you know what's in it?"

"No idea. I don't think it's been opened since arriving from Albania."

On opening the cardboard box, Jake lifted out a large metal container. "No wonder it was heavy. Don't tell me you carried that down from the attic."

"No. Kate's friend George helped me."

"Do we have a key, or have I got to break in?" Jake studied a small padlock.

"Wait until we've looked at what else the box has to offer." Caroline handed Jake a collection of photos. He laid them out on the table. Most were pictures of the team at work. Some showed the trenches at varying levels, and different stages of uncovering the skeletons. A set of photos showed a series of close-up shots of a skull. The colour drained from Jake's face.

"Are you all right?" Caroline placed her hand on his arm.

"This might be in this box."

"What?"

Jake held up the photograph.

"It could be almost anything. There's six more like it in the attic."

"And you never opened them? I would've done."

"They're not mine to open. Ahh, what do we have here?" Like a magician pulling a white rabbit from a hat, Caroline produced a set of keys.

Jake contemplated them. They looked to be about the same size. The first one didn't turn. Caroline laughed at the disappointment on his face.

"In all good films, it's always the last one they try."

"Okay, let's skip to the last one then." He slipped the key in and still nothing.

"I can't be right all the time." Caroline shrugged and took another sip of her tea.

Jake tried another, and the padlock sprung open. They stared at each other as Jake rose, took a deep breath, and lifted the lid gingerly. A musky smell filled the room as the past met the present. Caroline placed her cup on the table.

"Is it the skull?"

A look of disappointment reappeared on Jake's face as he lifted out a set of hard-back notebooks once held together with a rubber band that had perished. Each had the name of its owner stuck on the front with a strip of tape. Jake shuddered as he read out the names. One by one, he passed the books to Caroline.

"There's one missing, Jake."

Chapter Twenty

The Call

The incessant ringing shattered Elizabeth Blackstone's slumber, leaving her wondering whether it had been part of her dream or not. Blearily, she reached for the phone. "Hello."

"I'm sorry to disturb you, but..."

"Amanita, what's happened?" Elizabeth leapt out of bed at the sound of retching followed by a loud crash. "Amanita!" Elizabeth tossed the phone onto the bed and pulled on her jeans and jumper from yesterday. She grabbed her keys, and mobile and headed downstairs. Halfway down, her daughter's bedroom door opened.

"Mum, where are you going?" Hope called down.

"Darling, go back to bed. Nothing to worry about and I won't be long."

"I'm coming with you." Hope turned back to her room letting her door bang.

"No. At eighteen you're more than old enough to stay on your own," Elizabeth called up to her. "Please just go back to bed. I haven't got time to argue with you."

Hope was dressed and ready to go by the time Elizabeth reached the front door.

***

The night still held sway over the day as they drove along the wet and deserted streets and passed over the swing bridge before turning towards Bagdale. Just before Pannett Park, Elizabeth turned into Brunswick Street.

"Who was it on the phone, Mum?" Hope asked, worried by her mother's strange behaviour.

"Miss Virosa."

"Oh, the lady you work for?"

"Yes." Elizabeth turned into the back of the St Hilda's Terrace.

"Isn't it late for her to call?"

"I think she's hurt herself. I need to check. Thank God. The garage door is shut." Elizabeth reversed into a space at the back of the house.

"I'm sure everything's okay, Mum."

"Me too. Keep quiet. Don't want to disturb the neighbours. Have you got your phone?"

Hope held it up.

"Right, stay here. Once I know everything's okay, I'll call. You know how Miss Virosa doesn't like anyone to wander around her house."

"I know, Mum. I don't like the idea of you going in on your own."

"I won't be long."

"Couldn't we just phone the police?"

"No, we can't. Please, Hope, I must go." Elizabeth pulled her bag off the backseat and then leaned back into the car. "Please stay here until I call."

"For how long?"

"I'm not sure." She tossed Hope the car keys before closing the door and hurried across the street. Hope watched as her mother disappeared through the gate into a small yard.

The moonlight cast deep shadows across the high pillars and gargoyles on the roof of the garage, reminding Hope of a mausoleum with its high, central temple-like structure that held the garage. As the chilling night air penetrated the warmth of the car, Hope checked the time and found only fifteen minutes had passed since her Mum left, but already she wished she hadn't been so hasty in coming, or at least put on a thick jumper instead of the denim jacket, or even both.

Years ago, as a child, while her mother was busy cleaning, she had the freedom of the downstairs rooms, but not allowed

114

to go upstairs. She had no recollection of meeting Miss Virosa.

When her art college teacher set the assignment to research a little-known artist, Hope had been reminded of the painting she'd seen as a child in the house. For days, she had wondered how she might be able to get back in to photograph the painting after all these years. Her silly dream was to discover that it was a long-lost masterpiece.

Hope pulled her jacket collar up, and checked her phone, wishing her Mum would hurry up. Trying not to think about the cold, Hope focused on what had happened in the library. So far, the only fact she had uncovered had nothing to do with the painting, but with the death of her father. According to the journalist, he was murdered. Hope wondered whether her mother knew. The only memories she had of her father was seeing her mum's tear-stained battered face and then he was gone. She remembered fondly the time spent in the eerie green light that glowed in every room, and the huge family portrait of Miss Virosa with her parents which made a huge impact on her. Miss Virosa's father looked like the kind of father she would have loved. He stood like a guardian angel watching over his family.

"Maybe," Hope muttered. "This is the opportunity I've been wishing for. Just one quick snap is all I need." She locked the car door and slipped the keys in her pocket. "Anyway, it's too damned cold to be sitting around."

Hope opened the gate into the small yard and paused. Where was the security light that normally came on?

The small window in the back door was broken and the eerie green light flooded out. Hope's light touch caused the door to swing open. Cautiously she entered the kitchen and something crunched under her foot. Even in the strange light, she could see it was broken glass. She moved more slowly and turned on the torch on her phone. More broken glass and crockery crunched underfoot and then Hope saw drying dark red liquid on the tiled floor. "Oh no... blood!"

Had her mum cut herself? She wondered. In the hall, she listened. The house remained silent. "Mum, where are you?"

On hearing no answer, Hope went into the parlour. The beautiful room lay in chaos, with shattered china figurines, bookshelves empty of their contents, and upturned drawers scattered across the floor. Among the destruction, Hope smelled something familiar that hung in the air as she picked her way over the strewn papers and books to the ornate fireplace. "Please, God. Not the painting."

It hung undamaged at a slight angle. Hope straightened it and then took a couple of photos before a close-up of the signature and date. On her way out of the room, she picked up the hall table, which lay on its side. On retrieving its cloth, she saw among the debris something she recognised. The small jet cross was the one stolen from her. It was out of place and should never have been in the house.

Chapter Twenty-One

"My cross! That bastard Dog, did this!" Hope shivered, remembering too well the night she agreed to go with her friend, Mary-Anne to Gatekeeper's Cottage.

Most of the youngsters in Whitby knew about Gatekeeper's Cottage. It was less of a *cottage,* in the romantic cosy sense, and more of a boarded-up, burnt-out wreck of a house. After slipping under the security fence, they entered the building via the kitchen. A narrow hallway took them into a large open-plan room.

At the centre, a wooden staircase descended into the squalid heart of the house, with peeling blackened paintwork and wallpaper it slumbered in semi-darkness. The only light illuminating the chaos was a multitude of thick, coloured candles that dotted the room in various stages of use. Some looked new, while others were just a pile of blackened wax. A collection of grimy furniture comprising of several stained mattresses, a sofa, and two battered armchairs littered the room.

Hope followed Mary-Anne into the smoky room, stepping over the freshly discarded remains of the latest rave that littered the floor - beer cans, silver paper, needles, glue bags, and the ubiquitous cigarette butts.

"This place is horrible. Let's go." Hope tugged on Mary-Anne's arm.

"No! Stay and have some fun."

A group of youths gathered around a battered sofa. A man lay sprawled out, eyes closed, lazily smoking a joint. The three youths and the girl called Candy acknowledged Mary-Anne with a nod, but not Hope. In the half-light, their pallid complexions showed their allegiance to the man as they waited for him to speak.

"So this is the legendary Dog," Hope muttered under her breath.

No one seemed to know anything about Dog. Not that any of them were interested. All they wanted was his one-way ticket to heaven as his drugs gave their lives purpose.

Somehow, Dog managed to keep himself so clean, with his freshly washed black hair and snowy, white t-shirt. Going by the state of the building, and the flickering candlelight, there hadn't been electricity or running water in the house for years. Yet his pale skin seemed to emphasise his neatly trimmed goatee and his tight black jeans showed off his long muscular legs and highly polished black Doc Martins.

Dog half opened his eyes, aware he had an audience and grinned. He swung his legs round while tossing the end of his joint into the disused fireplace, already overflowing with rubbish. His bright blue eyes darted from one to another as an eager smile crossed his thin lips. From a small table, Dog picked up a bottle of water and drunk thirstily.

His band of thieves waited, with bated breath. He replaced the bottle on the table, and gestured to a tall, skinny, spotty lad with long oily hair. The anxious, twitching lad stepped forward and laid his offering before him.

"Is this all you could get, Manny!" Dog snapped. "The fucking town's full of bloody tourists."

"Sorry, Man. I'll try harder next time." The boy stepped back from his offering. Three cans of beer, four mobile phones, and thirty pound in cash. The scene reminded Hope of Charles Dicken's Fagin as Dog received the stolen goods and signalled to the next boy. "Let me see what you've got, Woody."

The youth stepped forward. Clearly on his face and arms was his devotion. Like the first lad, his glassy eyes twitched nervously whilst he endlessly scratched the skin on his arms and neck.

"You've done well, lad." Dog picked up the two bulging wallets. Without looking, he slipped them into the pocket of a grubby army jacket slung over the back of the sofa. "Now, my dear Mary-Anne, what have you got for me?"

Hope's friend placed the handbag she had been carrying on the table.

"Well, you're such a shining example of how to be light-fingered." Dog checked the contents of the bag. Satisfied enough, he delivered some of his magic to brighten their dark world and handed Mary-Anne some joints. She grinned with pride and glanced over her bony shoulder at her friends.

Dog dropped the bag at his side and turned his attention to Hope. "Who's this? A new recruit, Fish?"

Hope found herself being propelled forward by a heavy-set youth with dark curly hair. She glared over her shoulder at him. Under her breath she had cursed Mary-Anne. *So much for fun, the lying, thieving bitch.*

"So what's your name?" Dog rolled a joint, lit it, and inhaled before his bright blue eyes made contact with hers.

She held her breath, not wanting to breathe in fumes.

"Hope." He let the word out slowly, along with a thin ribbon of smoke before plucking a bit of tobacco from his lip.

Hope's stomach turned as the sickly-sweet pungent smell of the tobacco mixed with the scented candles. She tried not to pass out as her head started to spin and her throat felt dry. Everything took on a weird aura as flickering candlelight distorted the faces around her. The sight of Fish and Mary-Anne sprawled together on a stained mattress in the far corner mesmerised her. Mary-Anne had stripped off her t-shirt exposing her large breasts that glowed in the dancing candlelight.

Hope turned back to the man. He gestured for her to sit and she did, only because it stopped her from falling down. Dog took a small, battered tin from his jacket pocket and signalled to Manny. Eagerly, Manny held his hand out. Dog grabbed the youth's arm, yanked him down, and then whispered something into his ear. The boy glanced over at Hope, and then beamed at Dog. "Yeah, sure Man."

Dog counted out the five oval pills into Manny's palm. Manny winked at Hope and then went back to the others, said something and handed out a pill to each of them. They stood unsteadily, thanked Dog, and went upstairs.

"I think I should be going." Hope stood up.

"Sit!" Dog snapped. "I haven't finished talking to you!"

Hope sat and, to her horror, became aware of grunting noises and creaking floorboards above. That's when *he* asked about her mother.

Hope took in the damage done to Miss Virosa's home and put her head in her hands, sobbing. *How could she have been so bloody stupid?*

Dog had grinned insanely at her as she heard herself telling him that her mum worked as a cleaner in a big house. "Tell me something I don't know, love." Shocked, she stared at him. He drew long and hard on his joint, letting out a smoke ring. "I make it my business to know."

Mary-Anne had told him. Her stupid friend had sold her out for a pill.

"So your daddy fucked off like all good daddies do, leaving your mum to work all hours as a cleaner for some rich bitch."

"Whatever," Hope had said, smugly.

He tossed a fresh bottle of water at her and then leaned back in his sofa.

"Doesn't it piss you off knowing your mum is nothing, but a cleaner while the rich have everything?"

"Why didn't you get an education instead of living in this shit-hole?" She had retorted as she stood and tossed the bottle back at him.

Within an instant he jumped up. "Don't fucking speak to me like that you stuck up little bitch!" he said, and smacked her across her face.

She froze for a second, as a wave of anger swept over her. "How dare you hit me! No one hits me." She pushed past him. He followed her into the kitchen and grabbed her arm. She tried to pull away. Dog pushed himself into her as he brought his lips close to her mouth, almost touching. "Where do you think you are going?" He whispered.

"Home! You can't stop me!"

"How fucking dare you come into my home, without bringing me a little something in exchange."

She struggled to pull away. He released her and she fell back against the filthy kitchen cupboard as Dog reached out and snatched her jet cross. Stunned, her hand flew to her neck. In the flickering candlelight, his dark glassy blue eyes narrowed as an evil smile crossed his pale face. Dog held the cross up; the silver chain glinted in the subdued light. "Thank you for my little gift." He rubbed himself. "Be fucking thankful I didn't take a bit of pussy."

In the chaos created by Dog, she wished she had told her Mum instead of thinking she had a lucky escape. Her mum had always said that *actions created reactions so always think carefully before you react.* Her only question now was, what had he done to her mum and poor old Miss Virosa.

Chapter Twenty-Two

A Dying Angel

"It's my fault…" Hope sobbed, making her way along the hall to the stairs. Halfway up, she saw a bare footprint visible on the carpet. "Oh god, it's blood. What if Dog is still here?" She took out her phone and called her mum. A faint ringing began in one of the rooms off the landing. "Answer it, Mum. Please."

She brushed aside the tears, switched off her phone, and edged closer to the door. A low moaning emanated from within. "Mum, is that you?" She pressed her ear to the door and heard something. Someone spoke in whispers. Excited, she flung open the door. "Oh, Mum, I was so…" Hope covered her mouth.

Elizabeth stood wearing long plastic gloves covered in blood that ran down her arms, and pooled at her feet. "Oh, Hope. Sorry I forgot all about you…"

The stone-tiled floor was awash with blood. At the centre, a woman lay on her side, naked, in the foetal position. One arm stretched out in front of her while the other hung awkwardly over her back. Stunning purple eyes stared blankly out of her pale face, and from the corner of her blue lips, a trickle of blood seeped. Her hair was matted with congealing blood.

"Mum. So much blood."

"I'm so sorry, Hope. Only I couldn't leave her. Once she has calmed down, I can clean the mess up."

"She's not dead then?"

"Oh, no dear. The new blood has to fight the bad."

The woman moaned softly. Elizabeth knelt and gently

stroked her hand before turning back to her daughter. "We got here just in time. She'll be all right in a few hours and then hopefully she'll be able to tell us what has happened."

"Mum, it's my fault, if I hadn't..." Hope's voice trailed off.

"Oh, don't worry, dear. She's all right." Elizabeth ran the hot water and began to wash the blood off her gloved hands.

"Where's the blood come from?" Hope saw no wounds on the woman's body. In answer to her question, the woman pulled herself onto her knees, arched her back and lifted her head. At the same time, her bottom jaw dropped to allow a gush of evil smelling blood to erupt from her body. After a brief second, she shook her head, fell weakly on to her side, and began to whimper again. The stench of the blood made Hope cover her mouth, and she began retching.

"Put these on." Elizabeth gave her a pair of rubber gloves. "I'll need your help while you're here."

Hope frowned.

"We have to help Amanita, otherwise she'll die." Elizabeth shook her daughter gently by the shoulders.

"That's Miss Virosa."

"Yes, it's Amanita. Who did you think it was?"

"She's so young."

Elizabeth knelt beside Amanita and brushed the hair away from her face. "Amanita, can you hear me, dear?"

Amanita didn't respond.

"How can I help, Mum?"

"Can you watch her for a moment? I need to check on how much more fresh blood I have." Elizabeth turned to leave the room.

"Fresh blood?"

"Yes. And don't get any blood on your skin," Elizabeth said over her shoulder.

Hope took in the surreal scene. It looked like something out of a terrible horror movie. "Gone to get more fresh blood?" Hope muttered. Just an hour or so ago she was snuggled down in her warm bed, now alone in a cold, stinking room with a half-dead naked woman bathing in her own blood. "Maybe I'll wake up and it'll be just a bad dream."

"Not a dream," the barely audible voice said.

Hope looked towards the door, expecting to see her mother. On turning back, she noticed Amanita had rolled on her back.

"Where's Elizabeth?" She stared up at Hope with wide, unblinking dark eyes her thin lips scarcely moving.

"Err... she'll be back soon." Hope glanced longingly at the door.

The large purple eyes studied Hope for a moment, then they began to blink rapidly before rolling backward and snapping shut. Hope, terrified she had died, was on the verge of rushing to find her mum when Amanita spoke again. "I am hungry." Relief washed over Hope and she reached out to stroke Amanita's arm. "Mum will be back in a minute. She's gone to get something."

The thin white hand clawed at the floor exposing the pattern of sandstone beneath the congealing blood. "Please help me. I'm dying," Amanita cried. Her energy seeped away, and her hand stopped moving.

"No, please don't," Hope sobbed. She rushed to the sink and started to run the hot water. She took a fresh face cloth, rinsed it under the tap. On returning to Amanita, she washed the dry blood from around her eyes and mouth and noticed some dark marks on the side of her face. "Did he hit you?"

Amanita's eyes opened, and she mouthed the word, "*Yes*."

Suddenly the bathroom door burst open. Hope jumped up. "Mum, it's all right. She's..."

A piercing scream echoed around the room as the silhouette of a man stood in the doorway. "What the fuck's going on here?" he snapped. In the eerie light, Hope saw a horrified expression cross his face.

In answer to his question, Amanita rolled onto her side and heaved up more blood. A dark stream of stinking blood raced across the floor as Hope rushed screaming at the man to get out. He grabbed her wrists and started to shake her. "What the bloody hell are you doing to her?"

A pair of hands grabbed the man's arm from behind and yanked him back.

"Let go of her and get out of the way!" Elizabeth shouted as she pushed past him and rushed to Amanita's side. The man let go of Hope and stepped back.

"You're the journalist... from the library. What are you doing here?"

Elizabeth's eyes flashed with rage. "I don't give a fuck if you're the Pope, mister. I need to get her to bed, otherwise she'll die. Help me or piss off. The choice is yours!"

Amanita let out a low moan as her eyes blinked open.

"God, it's her!" Jake uttered and turned to Elizabeth. "All right, what do you want me to do?"

Elizabeth snatched a pair of gloves from her apron pocket and thrust them into his hands. "Please put these on and be prepared to get wet. You too, Hope."

Jake removed his jacket, tossed it onto the landing, rolled up his shirtsleeves, and pulled on the gloves. Hope knelt beside Amanita stroking her arm. "Elizabeth is here now so we'll soon have you well again." She looked up at her mum and said, "She's fine, Mum. She just wants something to eat."

"What! Oh, sweet Jesus no." She pulled the showerhead from the wall. It burst into life, soaking everything. "Quick. We must get her washed down and into her bed. Stand back." Kneeling beside Amanita, Elizabeth said, "Please my dear, keep your eyes closed." Elizabeth started to wash away the dried blood from Amanita's body, face, and hair. The floor, awash with dark red water, faded to a pale pink, and then began to run clear. "Do you mind getting wet, mister?" Elizabeth asked.

"The name's Jake. What would you like me to do?"

"Can you lift her up?" Elizabeth let the showerhead continue to wash the clots of congealed blood down the drain.

As Jake's fingertips made contact with Amanita's upper arm, a rush of electricity swept over him, filling his mind with the image of the dead man in the alleyway. An icy chill engulfed his fingertips, travelled up his nerve endings, through his blood vessels, and penetrating into his bone marrow causing data overload and confusion. As his mind cleared, Elizabeth's voice came into focus, and the words rushed in.

"Can you hold her, Jake while I fetch some clean towels?"

"Yes, of course." He slipped his arm under her waist and lifted her from the floor, clasping her to his broad chest. Amanita rested her head against his neck and moaned softly as the warmth and the sound of his blood coursing through his body echoed in her ears. Unaware of her needs, Jake studied the woman in his arms, comparing the two images of her, the dying woman he held to the one in the nightclub.

How had she managed to cough up so much blood and not die? There wasn't any sign that she had suffered an injury. If the blood wasn't hers... the thought sent a wave of nausea through him.

Elizabeth emerged carrying some bath sheets and wrapped them around Amanita.

"Right, which car are we taking? Mine is parked just across the street, but I think we should wrap her in some blankets too."

"Car?" Elizabeth frowned. "Please bring her through to her bedroom."

"You said she's dying. We need to get her to a hospital, now!"

Chapter Twenty-Three

Bring Death To My Door

"We need to get her to the hospital." Jake clutched the dying woman to him. "Now!"

"You're not taking her anywhere but to her bedroom." Elizabeth pointed across the landing to an open door.

Jake lifted her slightly, trying to make her more comfortable in his arms. She let out a low groan, and he felt a shiver go through her thin body.

"Please. She'll die in your arms if you don't." Elizabeth's voice softened.

Jake was aware of the woman's open lips against his neck, her tongue probing his skin like a butterfly caught in his hands. A cold chill entered his body, and suddenly he felt the need to put her down. Nodding to Elizabeth, he crossed the landing and laid her on the four-poster bed.

"Right, you can go now" Elizabeth removed the towels before pulling the covers over Amanita's shivering body.

"I'm not going anywhere." Jake stood, dripping onto the carpet. "I'm not leaving until I know what's going on."

"Thanks for your help. But this is of no concern to you."

"If you won't take her to the hospital, you should at least phone the police about the break-in."

"Why don't you just mind your own business and go?"

"By the state of this woman and the house, I think I've every right to be concerned."

"Stay, but don't interfere with things you don't understand." Elizabeth leaned down, opened a drawer in the bedside cabinet, took out a blood bag, suspended it from a hook over the bed, slipped the cannula in the vein on Amanita's arm, and began to massage it slowly.

"What the fuck are you doing?"

Once she was sure the blood was flowing down the tube into Amanita's veins, she turned to Jake. "What I've been trained to do. Be patient, then I'll explain things to you."

The door opened and Hope entered carrying Jake's jacket and a ruffled neck shirt. Though, her hair hung damp around her shoulders, she had changed out of her wet clothes and stood dressed in a large shirt identical to the one she was carrying. She wore it tied at the waist with a wide belt and it just about covered her bare knees. Smiling, she said, "I've brought you one too," and handed Jake his jacket and the shirt. "It should fit all right. They come up quite large."

"Oh, thanks." Jake took it and then he realised he was holding something else. He held up a pair of knee-length breeches.

"I thought you could wear them until we get your jeans dried," Hope said. "How is she, Mum?"

"We'll have to just wait and see. Coughing up all that blood has drained too much of her energy. It's left her weak and vulnerable, but this should help her." Elizabeth tapped the side of the blood bag.

"Oh yuck." Hope screwed up her face. "Would you like me to watch over her while you change into something dry?"

"All right, but I won't be long. Then you and I need to talk." Elizabeth eyed Jake suspiciously.

He nodded. "Is there somewhere I can change into these?"

"If you follow me, I can take your wet clothes with ours, and put them in the dryer." Elizabeth headed out the door. After a few minutes, Jake came back, and Hope stifled a giggle.

"I know I'm not exactly Mr Darcy, Miss Blackstone," Jake said. The breeches fitted him a little too snugly, but he'd reasoned after looking in the mirror that at least the shirt covered his paunch. "Your mum said our clothes won't take too long to dry."

"How did you get in here?"

"I followed you. Don't worry. I made sure the door was secured behind us. Would you like to tell me what's going on?" Jake gestured to the corpse-like shape on the bed. The white satin sheets hadn't improved her funereal complexion. Elizabeth had pulled them up to the base of her throat, leaving her left arm free to have the cannula inserted. Jake studied the painting over the fire and then asked, "Can you tell me the name of the artist who painted it?"

"I've no idea. This is the first time I've been allowed up here," Hope said, joining him beside the fire.

"It's a picture of the woman, isn't it?"

"Amanita. Yes, I guess so."

"Would you say she was…about twenty-five in the picture?" Jake gazed at the painting then towards the bed.

"Hmm, yes."

"Don't you find that a little odd?"

"Why? Oh, I see what you mean. It could've been painted yesterday, because she looks to be about the same age as the painting."

"That's what I thought. But this was painted in 1700." Jake gestured to the date at the corner of the picture.

"No way!" Hope stood on tiptoes for a closer look.

In one sweeping movement, Jake knocked her to the floor and began to smack the top of her legs.

"Get off me, you bastard!" Hope shrieked, fighting to push him off, just as Elizabeth walked in.

"What do you think you're doing with my daughter?"

Jake pulled himself off the floor with as much dignity as the breeches would allow. "Stopping her from going up in flames."

Hope looked at the hem of the shirt and saw the edge was singed. "Oh my God. I didn't think about the fire. Too busy looking at the date on the painting, Mum."

"Well, instead of worrying about the painting you should be thinking about, Amanita. Can you make some drinks please? I know I could do with a cuppa. What about you, Jake, do you drink tea?"

"Please. Love one. No sugar for me."

"Two teas. Please be careful. There's broken glass everywhere. Your trainers are wet, but you'll find an old pair of my shoes in my apron cupboard."

"Shall I give your daughter a hand to tidy up while I wait for my clothes?"

"She's fine on her own. I want you here."

"Where you can keep an eye on me, Mrs Blackstone?"

"So you know who I am?" Elizabeth raised an eyebrow,

"You'll want to know why I'm here at this unearthly time."

"Did cross my mind."

"*ManWatch.*"

"Oh…"

"Your husband… John Blackstone found dead on the moors, twelve years ago."

"I should've guessed knights in shining armour only turn up in storybooks."

"I'm a journalist, Elizabeth." Jake studied her face for any reaction. Elizabeth was leaning over Amanita, rubbing her arm, and trying to stimulate the blood vessels. Jake noticed some discolouration to Amanita's face.

"I guess you've lots of questions you want to ask, but now isn't a good time." Elizabeth met his stare." I've a question for you, and then you'll have to be patient because saving Miss Virosa is far more important than you having a great story." Elizabeth tapped the blood bag.

Jake picked up Amanita's other arm and started to rub it.

"Come on." Elizabeth willed Amanita to show a sign that she was responding to her treatment. Gently, she stroked Amanita's forehead and found it was cold to the touch. She choked back her tears. "Please don't give up on us yet. We need you."

Amanita's blue lips moved slowly. "You don't think that I would give up so easily, do you, Elizabeth…?"

Jake saw relief spread across Elizabeth's face.

"No, my dear child, I didn't think you would. Can you tell me what happened here?"

"He was… in my home." Amanita struggled to find the words as agony marked her face.

Elizabeth looked at Jake. He shook his head. "It wasn't me. I followed your daughter in."

130

"Do you know who it was, Amanita?" Elizabeth asked.

"I do not know… Looking for money, I think. Too weak, I could not…" Her voice trailed off.

"You must rest then we'll talk again later."

"Hungry. Too hungry…"

Elizabeth knew by Amanita's shallow breathing that the hunger was deep rooted. "I know you are, but at the moment there isn't anything we can do. For now, all we have are these." She tapped the blood bag. "I know they're too pure for you, but they're your lifesaver."

"I do not know what I would do without you. Thank you."

The housekeeper brushed a strand of hair back from Amanita's face then kissed her on the cheek. "It's nothing I owe you far more. I had better help Hope. We'll stay here for now, if that's all right with you. There's a hell of a mess to clear up downstairs, and a window to fix too. After a few hours sleep we'll make a start."

"I am glad you're staying. Thank you. What about you, Mr Eldritch? Are my secrets safe?"

Jake turned to Elizabeth who smiled back at him.

"She knows all there is to know about you. For now, we must let her sleep. I want you to stay here while I go and see how my daughter is doing. You can make yourself comfortable, while Miss Virosa sleeps." Elizabeth pointed to a chair beside the bed.

Jake settled into the armchair, his eyes closing as his body relaxed. It had been a wild idea to check out where Elizabeth Blackstone worked so late at night before going to question her at home. Now he was glad he had. As he drifted off to sleep, he thought he heard someone say, "Can I trust you, Mr Eldritch? Can I, Jacob?"

"How do you know my name?" He opened his eyes to see Amanita struggling to sit up.

"I know enough." She remained where she was, allowing the blood to continue to drip slowly. "You came here for two reasons. Firstly, you wondered whether there is some sort of link between the death of your parents and me. You've

131

always had a sense of losing them twice. First they abandoned you to follow their dreams, and then they died, leaving you for good."

Jake said nothing.

"*ManWatch* brought you here. You discovered a link between Elizabeth and me."

"How do you know that? And what about all that blood?"

"My father."

"Your father?"

"Mr Eldritch, are you going to keep interrupting? If so, I shall never explain anything. I do not have the strength or the time to keep repeating everything. The forces are working against me."

"What forces?"

"Let me finish..."

"Sorry, but how? Your parents died in 1795, so how could your father know anything about my parents' deaths?"

Amanita inhaled deeply. The pain in her head had begun to subside though her ribcage still throbbed. "Your parents and mine are part of a delicate chain of events which are unfolding as we speak. Can I trust you, Mr Eldritch?"

"I'm a journalist. Can anyone trust a journalist?" Jake leant over the bed so she could see his face. "You are in a lot of pain."

"That's a bit of an understatement, Mr Eldritch." She tried to smile. "It comes with the job. Like you, I work freelance. The pay is shit, but I enjoy what I do."

"At least you've kept your sense of humour. Me..." He shrugged and saw her flinch as she tried not to laugh. "Sorry, you were saying about your parents?"

"So I can trust you?"

"If you can give me more insight into my parents' death then you can trust me."

"Then I must first explain why we've been hunted to extinction."

"Extinction! That's an inappropriate word. Vampires just bite someone else to turn them into one."

"That maybe so, if we were such creatures."

Chapter Twenty-Four

Heal Thy Self

As Jake listened, he noticed the bruises on her face were changing. The colours were fading. The cut under her left eye that looked as though it required a stitch or two fifteen minutes ago had closed up, and her swollen right eye looked less puffy. He leaned in for a closer look. The corners of the cut were a fraction tighter, as though it was days old, maybe even a week rather than half an hour since he found her lying covered in blood on the bathroom floor.

"It's rude to stare, Mr Eldritch."

"Your face. It's healing...."

"I should hope so. It would make my job far harder if it did not. Perhaps you would rather I lay in agony for weeks waiting for it to heal. Would it make me seem more human?" She lifted her free hand and touched the swollen eye. Wincing slightly, she let her hand drop on to the sheets.

Jake leant against the bedpost. "So if you're not the creatures of horror, what are you?"

"Please sit, Mr Eldritch, because it is a long story."

Jake dropped into the armchair.

"Are you ready?" Amanita gave a lopsided smile.

"Yes, only if you're up to it."

"I can assure you I shall be fine. I will begin on the night I lost my parents. My father...."

"Polidori Virosa..."

Amanita blinked her good eye at him. "You have been doing your homework, Mr Journalist."

Jake smiled. "Sorry I interrupted."

Amanita closed her eye and inhaled. "When my family

moved to England, my mother's family remained in Albania, believing they were safe. After a while, the lack of news from our homeland worried my father. A few days before they died, he seemed more impatient, which concerned my mother. My people are from prehistory. We first settled along the Adriatic Sea in 950BC. As we expanded, the elders decided for the sake of our people, and to fulfil our task that we all didn't remain in one place but spread throughout the world. Since losing my parents, I have lost contact with the rest of my kind."

Jake detected sadness in her voice. He reached out and wrapped his hand around her long, slender fingers. He expected her skin to burn with a fever, but instead, a chilling pain raced up his arm. He withdrew his hand, sure that his heart had frozen, as an icy chill overwhelmed him.

"Not a good time to touch me, Jacob, but I thank you for your concern. My body is fighting the unnatural toxins in the blood I consumed tonight. To do this it has to close down all of my unessential functions. I should be asleep really as this speeds things up."

"What about the blood Elizabeth has given you?"

"Too pure. My system cannot feed on it. I need to go out hunting as soon as possible. But for now, I have my story to tell."

"Are you asking me to shut up?"

"No, telling you."

Jake found himself beaming.

"In 1795 the moon was high and the night was still. Father received news that a ship from Albania was returning on the next tide. Together with my mother, he made plans to travel to Scarborough. They wanted to meet it at the dock, hoping for news from their families. Most nights I travelled with them, but mother insisted I remained at home. It is important for you to understand that I would have remained with my parents until we returned to our father's kingdom. All of this is lost to me now, and our task remains incomplete."

"Your father's kingdom? Has Albania got a king?"

"My father's kingdom is not in Albania."

Jake poured a glass of water and offered it to her. After taking a sip, she handed it back and nodded.

"Their journey to Scarborough had been full of promise but turned out to be a trap I later learnt from William."

"William?"

"Yes, our manservant."

"He knew what your family were?"

"Do *you?*" There was a hint of sarcasm in her tone.

"Not really. I suppose if I shut up, you'll have chance to explain."

Amanita blinked both eyes slowly then continued. "Throughout our long existence humans have worked for us. Many have shared their whole lifetime in our service. We are indebted to the likes of William and Elizabeth. We entrust ourselves to them at our most vulnerable times. William and his wife Kathy spent their lives looking after me until they died, after them, their children and grandchildren until Elizabeth took over.

On the day I lost my parents, I remained at home with Kathy. She fussed over me all evening, unaware that I knew things were about to change forever."

"Surely if you knew, why let them go?"

"When they left, I did not know the balance of the war was not in our favour."

"What war?"

"I am jumping too far ahead." She closed her eyes and in a low voice, said, "William always whistled. The gentle rhythmic swaying of the landau lured my parents to sleep, wrapped in each other arms as they headed home. William knew the night sky brought the promise of a bright, spring morning, and he needed to get my parents' home as soon as possible.

On reaching the rise that brought Whitby into view, William stopped whistling. Father sensed a change in his manner and called to him through a small window behind the coachman's seat. The carriage slowed and, in the soft candlelight of the interior, father spoke softly to mother. "Ocreata, my love, be still."

"Master Polidori—be on your guard, sir!" William called, while encouraging the horses to go faster. My father held my mother close as the landau swung violently back and forth. William fought to keep it under control, but the sudden shift in weight of the passengers caused the carriage to topple. A loud crack echoed across the moors as the swingletree broke, freeing the horses. The landau finally came to a rest on its side. "Jesus Christ, what's that...?" were the last words father heard William say.

"We need to get out of here, Ocreata. Soon it will be light."

Now the landau laid on its side and the door was above them. Father struggled to open it. "William, come help."

"Polidori, where is William?"

"I do not know. He may be hurt. First we must get out of here, my love. Are you ready?"

"I do not think anything is broken." Mother straightened her bonnet.

Father climbed out and then leaned in to lift mother out. Once on the ground, he embraced her, kissing her passionately.

"Well ain't love grand, boys?" A dark, sarcastic voice echoed.

In the moonlight, seven unknown men held William slumped between two of them. He was bleeding badly from the side of his head.

"Are you all right?" Father feared the worst. Having both fed well, they needed to sleep until the hunger overtook them again. "My fine gentlemen, I'm so glad you are here. We've had a bit of an accident. You will be greatly rewarded for your services."

Well isn't that just grand, Jack? We'll be rewarded by this fine gentleman for our services." The leader's laughter rang out. "We've planned that already boys, didn't we just?"

"Polidori, they are going to kill us," Mother whispered.

"I know my love, but William is badly injured. We have no strength. Be at peace, my darling. Remember, I love you."

Ocreata lifted her face to the man she had loved all her

life, only to have him snatched away as three of the men pulled them apart. They dragged Polidori to the ground as an ear-splitting scream split the night.

"Please leave him alone! We've done nothing to you."

She struck one of the men on the back of the head, but he held her away while others punched and kicked at the prostrate figure.

"Leave them be!" William cried, struggling to free himself from the ropes that bound him. "You've no idea who you're dealing with."

"What'll yer be doing about it, old man?" a blackened-tooth youth said.

Mother rushed to William's side and freed him only to watch as the blackened-tooth youth hit him across the back of the head. William dropped and keeled over.

Now all eyes turned to the small kneeling figure. She pleaded incoherently for father not to leave her. The tallest of the Jackleg, a band of thieves, stepped over father's body and grabbed her by her hair, pulling her to her feet.

"Me and t'mates, we ain't ever 'ad a real lady. So as yer old mester is out of it for a bit, t'lads and I 'ould like to see 'ow the rich like it."

"Oh no, sir. Please no!"

The Jackleg leader struggled to get a better grip on mother, but she broke free and ran. The youngest of them let out a yell and went after her. He grabbed her bonnet, but it came away in his hand. Mother tripped on her full-length cloak and he rolled her over.

"Please, no…" she begged

"I ain't going to hurt thee, missus. Be as gentle as lambs in the field." The young lad's eyes widened with excitement.

Amanita paused. Her chest ached, but not from the beating she suffered. She hadn't spoken about what had happened to her parents for over two hundred years. Pain tore through her in the same way as the bad blood had done.

"Are you all right?"

"Just painful memories."

"If you'd rather not talk about it, I understand."

"You have too many unanswered questions for me to stop.

"Yes, I have. Like how you know so much about the events of that evening if you weren't there. Did William survive?"

"Yes, but he had no memory of what happened. Kathy had stood most of that evening by the front window waiting for the sound of William's carriage. She knew my parents would never be late. As the sun rose, Kathy dropped the heavy velvet curtain aware that I knew already. I wanted to comfort her, Jacob, to tell her they were fine, but in the end, all I could do was give her hope.

"How could they be dead, mistress? They're immortal."

I sent her to fetch help for William. In those days, all our neighbours knew and understood about the illness, which affected my family, so Kathy went to rouse our good neighbour, Richard Moorsom.

Chapter Twenty-Five

Destruction Of The Virosas

The sun climbed slowly in the watery blue sky by the time George and his master, Richard Moorsom, together with a few of his men from the shipyard, set off for the standing stones. The wet winter had left deep ruts in the road though the surface was dry now. The party of rescuers moved slowly following the directions William had given Kathy in case of such an emergency. The servant, George, rode alongside his master.

"How much further do thee think it will be?" George asked.

"It depends on what time they left Scarborough. I am sure something must have befallen Master Virosa. He would never stay out at this time of the day."

Over the next hill, they heard yelling and whipped their horses into action. As they descended, neither was prepared for the sight that met them. The landau lay half buried, on its side, among rough heather and scrub, with one horse that had broken front legs.

"Please may the Lord God be merciful," George whispered.

"This is the work of Jacklegs," Master Richard said. "The Justice of the Peace and the parish constable will be told."

"Over here, Master Moorsom!" One of Richard's men shouted. Swinging down from their horses, George and Richard raised their hand to cover their nostrils. On a light breeze came the smell of hell. They reached where the men had gathered. All had pressed their neckerchiefs to their noses and muttered the Lord's Prayer while crossing themselves against the devil's work.

Richard reached the spot where William lay on his stomach in the damp grass. He bent and touched the side of William's face. He felt cold to the touch. William suddenly convulsed and rolled on to his back. "My dear God, William. You're alive!" Richard shouted.

"Master Virosa, you be all right?" William whispered.

"William, its Master Moorsom. Can you tell me what has happened?"

William reached to touch the side of his head, but Richard stopped him. "Can you hear me?" Richard said. "What has happened?"

"Scarborough, Master Polidori. Don't you remember?"

George knelt beside Richard. "He's taken a bash to the head, sir. It's messed his brains up. Ye won't get much out of him for a while. Thee best come and see what they did to Master Virosa and his good lady. They're not pretty sights and that horrendous smell comes from them."

"What do you mean, George?"

"Best thee see, Master."

Richard gestured to his men. "Be gentle with him. We need to get him home safe and pray he will remember who has done this terrible deed."

If it had not been for William being found close by, Richard would not have recognised his much-respected friends. My parents lay spread-eagled on their backs with their clothes intact, though the top of my mother's legs was bare for all to see. Her dress and petticoats covered her face while her hand reached out for my father.

"Oh, dear God. The bastards raped her!" George crossed himself. "Please forgive my language, master."

"Under these circumstances, your language is justified, George."

Richard called to the men to bring the wagon over. George knelt beside mother's body and very carefully pulled her dress down to cover her legs.

"What in heaven's name made them set fire to their bodies, master?" George asked.

"I have no idea. But I pray whoever is responsible for such

140

a terrible deed will hang for it."

George described my parents' bodies as having boiling oil poured over them as blisters covered all the exposed skin. Their mouths hung open in some eternal scream for forgiveness from our unhearing Father. No peace, or an eternal life in heaven for them. The good men of Whitby offered silent prayers before removing the soulless bodies from the bleak moorland, with its grey standing stones that seemed to point the way to our unattainable kingdom above.

By the time they returned my beloved parents and William home, the sun was high above the church on the cliff. From the dark shadows of the hallway I watched them carry the two coffins out of the sunshine into the darkness of my home. Kathy with George and Master Richard's men helped take William up to their rooms at the top of the house. Richard's face told me all I needed to know.

"I am so sorry, my dear child." He held my hand in his. "I shall do all within my power to punish those who are responsible. May God deliver your dear parents into his eternal peace and free them from their earthly suffering."

I bowed my head. "May our Father be merciful." I knew we were losing our power over the dark ones.

"Amen to that." Richard took his leave. At the gate, he turned briefly. "If you need anything, my dear child, I'll always be here for you."

As soon as the doctor had left, Kathy came to find me in the back parlour with my parents.

"How is William?"

"The doctor said we won't know until he's had a good sleep."

"Please may I see him?"

"Yes, of course. But he's asleep. I've been told that the parish constables will speak to him once he's awake."

"Yes, of course they must. But I need to see him now."

I waited on the landing outside their rooms, while Kathy drew all the curtains and lit the lamps. Once seated on the bed beside William I took hold of his hand while Kathy sat on the other side.

"Kathy, would you like to see what happened to them?" I asked.

"But how can we?"

"You must be strong for William's sake and do exactly what I ask."

"Mistress Amanita, this isn't the devil's work, is it?"

"How long have you lived in this house, Kathy?"

"I'm sorry, Mistress Amanita. When I go to the shops, they say…"

I cut her off. "You, of all people, should know what the Lord's book says about tattlers and busybodies, speaking things which they ought not."

"William tells me off for being foolish. Oh, my poor William, please don't leave me," she sobbed.

"Kathy, please be strong. Time is against us. Do you want to find the men who did this to William and my parents?"

She wiped her eyes on the back of her hand. "I'm sorry for being so selfish when you've lost your parents. Of course I'll help."

"You must trust me as much as I have to trust you. If William dies I will have no one I can trust. You will be my eyes and ears when I cannot go out. You have lived with us long enough to understand my life here."

She grasped my hand. "I'll always be here for you. Tell me what I must do."

"Take hold of William's hand. Whatever happens, and whatever you see, do not be afraid. You will see pictures like in a book though they are moving, nothing will touch you, nor see you. I am here with you." I squeezed her hand. "Are you ready?"

She nodded.

"The language I will use next will be the language of my people. It is not the Devil's voice. I will ask for God's guidance."

"I'm ready." She squeezed William's and my hand.

"Close your eyes and remember whatever happens we're here together with William." After a few moments I called to my father, he answered me with the all-seeing eye of my

142

people.

I heard Kathy gasp and whispered, "Can you see what I can see?"

"Yes, I can." We found ourselves standing high up on the moors bathed in silver light. William shuddered.

"Look, Mistress, can you see what those men are doing?" Kathy said.

We watched as the men pushed and rolled boulders into the path of the oncoming carriage. "Look at their faces, Kathy, and remember them, that's the most important thing."

"Are you sure they cannot see us? For I'm sure I know one of them. He works at White Hall Shipyard."

The seventh man stood back from the rest, encouraging the others, not that they needed much. There was something about the tall, well-built, rugged man, with crow-black hair and a lazy way that unnerved me. I could only read what is in a man's mind when I was close to them. Over time and distance, I could not pick up, or engage his feelings or emotions. He stood in the shadows, watching as the others took their turns with my mother. They egged on the youngster called Jack as he gratified himself. With deep throaty screams, my mother cursed but they just laughed and tore at her clothes exposing her pale breasts as she kicked her legs.

Jack pulled himself from her and then slapped her hard, splitting her lips open. Tasting her own blood, she became silent and closed her mind to them.

One of the older men pushed Jack away. "Aye, me lad. Let the rest of us have some now," He dropped to his knees and unfastened his breeches. His manhood hung like a dead skinned rat between his skinny white thighs. He rubbed himself. "Come on, me old man. Don't let me down now."

The others laughed. "Come on old Bert. We ain't got all bleeding night you know."

With a deep thrust, he grunted and fell onto mother's body.

"Out the way old man. It's my turn now." A man with black teeth pulled Bert clear. Laughing, he dropped to his knees.

"No it ain't. It's mine." The man with filthy breeches said pushing Black-teeth away. Black-teeth swung a punch catching Filthy on his right cheek. Filthy touched his face, his hand came away covered in blood, enraged he turned on his friend. As the punches flew, the others joined in.

My mother rolled over and pulled herself toward Father. She reached for the hand of the man she had loved since the birth of time. Suddenly it was gone from her grasp.

"Where you be going?" The grinning face stared deep within her eyes. "It ain't nice to leave the ball early, my lady, especially when we ain't finished with you." He knelt beside her and rubbed the tip of his finger over her split lip until the blood ran free. Through her swollen eyes, she watched as his tongue shot out and licked her blood off his fingers. "Pure angel's blood that be."

"My God, he's like you, mistress." Kathy's voice broke the silence.

William moaned and Kathy squeezed his hand. "It's all right my beloved."

The pictures vanished. I slumped onto the chair the mind link was broken as my energy drained away.

"How was it possible with William being unconscious?" Jake asked.

"Though he was not aware of what was happening, his mind drew in all the vibes and energies. This is what I was able to read."

"If your parents died, then you're not a vampire?

She flashed her teeth at him. "We do not feed on blood, Jacob. We feed on sin. We are the Sin Seekers. To survive in your world, I feed on the sins of the sinners. My people cleanse the souls of the wicked in order to free your world."

"What happened next?"

At first, Kathy was nervous about being out with me. Nowadays I have more freedom to hunt alone, but back then, things were very different. We made our way down Church Street on a bitterly cold night. There was always plenty of hustle and bustle from the taverns and inns. We dressed warmly in thick woollen cloaks, keeping our hoods up to protect us from the cold winds and prying eyes. Men sheltered where they could talk and smoke while women plied their services for tuppence along the narrow alleyways and yards.

"Where are we going?" Kathy asked as I linked arms with her.

"We're going to the Golden Lion Tavern."

"Why…?"

"Kathy, take a look at the man in the doorway. Is he not one of them?"

She looked over my shoulder. "He is. That is the young one they called Jack." In the half- light, Kathy sauntered over to him, flashing her large, bright eyes.

"Hello, what's a pretty little thing like thee doing out on such a night as this?"

With peals of laughter, Kathy played her part and took his arm in hers. "Why, sir, I'm looking for a fine gentleman like your good self to warm my cold bed."

He laughed and slipped his arm round her petite waist as she led him down an alleyway and through to a small boathouse on a jetty. When he tried to kiss her, she held him back, whispering, "Soon my love. You'll have such pleasure, my master. The wait will be worth it. I know somewhere we can go to get out of this cold wind." Kathy opened the door of the boathouse and stepped back. Within, the boathouse candles burnt brightly. Jack could not believe what he saw. Still greedy for more, he turned, only to find that Kathy was gone.

"Wait until the lads back at the shipyard hear about this. They'll never believe me." He laughed, pulling off his clothes.

I held my cloak open so he could see the fullness of my breasts.

"Wait… you're too eager, my little bitch. Jack here can last all night, me lovely." He dropped the front of his breeches as I pulled him down onto the sacking before climbing on him.

"Thou are a pure maid," he cried. "I'll make you into a

wild bitch, hungry for more." He pulled at my breast. I moved, allowing him to taste the pleasure. He stretched his neck to reach my nipple and closed his eyes as his mouth eagerly reached for its reward. Out of the indescribable pleasure, he felt an equal indescribable pain shoot down the side of his neck and course through his body. His eyes sprung open. A wave of numbness overtook his body as an intense coldness moved through him. His head set at a strange angle meant he was unable to see me back away from him. Pure pleasure coursed through my body as the heat of his blood began to work its magic, changing the colour of my hair to its natural mid-winter white. "Hello, Jack," I murmured.

Jack tried to move. In his head he screamed for his mother and God almighty.

"It's too late to turn to God now. Not after what you did to my parents."

He stopped screaming as the fear took hold. Now his mind filled with questions. How was it possible that I knew his part in the terrible deed? He tried to move again. I leaned over him and whispered in his ear. "Do not worry. You're not the only one who will pay for your crime. I shall hunt you all down. For your wickedness is food for my soul."

Then, in the lamplight, he could see the gift I was offering him as I slipped my teeth into his white neck and drank deeply on his sin. After a minute his eyes became frosted glass as he sank into damnation.

The next morning, we found William sitting up in bed with a sore head and no real memory of what had happened that evening. In time he recovered and together they looked after me." Amanita sat up and pulled the cannula out of her arm.

"You hunted them all... And more?" Jake fixed his steely-grey eyes on hers.

"It's what I do."

146

Chapter Twenty-Six

Hunting The Hunters

Jake paced the floor at the end of Amanita's bed. "I understand why you want revenge after what they did."

"Not quite all of them. We never found Isaac Blake, the White Hall Worker. William made enquiries and was told he had returned to Albania."

"What happened to the rest of your people in the city of Amantia? My parents only uncovered a few graves."

"They found graves, but what of the boxes?"

"You know about the boxes?"

"Yes." She raised her hand. "Please let me finish. There's a bigger picture, Jacob. Blake's family lived in squalor. His wife told us that he had changed since his return from Albania. He spent what little money they had on fine clothes. He spoke differently too. She described him as a well-dressed man with glossy jet-black hair who did not like to dirty his hands. She thought it was because he had spent time abroad, but after his disappearance she stopped worrying deciding the man wasn't her husband."

"Did she explain what she meant?"

"I asked her. She said the man had green eyes."

"Green eyes?"

"Blake might have looked like her husband, having the same shaped mole on his back and hair colour, walked the same way, and in all sense be her husband. But it was his eyes that gave him away. Her husband's were dark blue."

"That's incredible. I wondered why no one else has picked up on the change in the eye col—" Jake stopped mid-sentence. The cut under Amanita's eye and bruising was completely gone. Her eyes shone radiantly, and her limp hair now shimmered.

"Jacob, you're staring again." She smiled her lips free of cuts and bruising.

"I take it you've recovered."

"Not quite. My full strength only returns after I have fed."

"Right, little sin seeker. The missing blood."

"Jacob, it is your blood that carries your sins. This is what infects your mind and everything you do. To you, they're dead, but I have freed them from their sins."

"So your people are soul cleansers."

"Soul Cleansers— I like it. Yes, our task is to return humanity to its pure state before the Great War of heaven passed on the knowledge and the dark ones walked the earth."

"What knowledge, what war, and what are the Dark Ones? And what has it all to do with the death of my parents?"

"First I need to get dressed. Then I must feed. And then I might explain."

"Okay. I'll tell Elizabeth you need her."

In the kitchen, Jake cradled a hot cup of tea, while Hope busily made scrambled eggs and toast for everyone now that the house was tidy.

"Don't you find this all a bit odd?" Jake put his cup down.

"What, having breakfast so late in the evening, or…?" Hope put a finger to her lips mockingly and cocked her head on one side. "Is it too early in the morning for a cooked breakfast?" She said brightly.

"No. I meant—"

"She knows exactly what you mean, Mr Eldritch." Elizabeth stood in a doorway Jake hadn't noticed before. "Amanita would like to see you before you go." Elizabeth motioned to the staircase behind her.

Jake nodded his thanks for the breakfast to Hope. He followed Elizabeth up the backstairs and they emerged onto a landing before Amanita's bedroom. Elizabeth guided Jake away from Amanita's bedroom and through another door, which could be easily mistaken for a cupboard too. As she opened the door, Jake was amazed to see the back wall was missing and in its place was a narrow passage. They climbed another set of steps and arrived in the roof space, where heavy velvet curtains covered narrow dormer windows. Jake wondered whether these were Kathy and William's suite of rooms.

Amanita sat on an antique chair, before a matching desk, which seemed at odds with the hi-tech computer and surveillance equipment. She greeted him with a smile, her face soft and pale in the half-light. It showed no signs of the beating she had suffered, while her white hair crowned her head like a halo. She was dressed in a short, pale lilac skirt and matching jacket. Her smile never left her face as she gestured to a low chair beside her desk.

"I am so glad you are still with us. Please, sit down."

The small chair, more fitting to someone of Amanita's delicate size, Jake found uncomfortable for his large frame.

"I am sure there is much you would like to ask me. But I wish to know more about your parents' deaths."

"Okay, my parents died in Albania twenty-six years ago and yours nearly two hundred and twenty-four years ago in England. What possible link could there be?"

"In your line of work, you know that anything is possible. Have you ever wondered why they died?"

"If you read minds, then you'll already know."

She nodded slowly. "Then I shall ask you another question instead. Where are the gold boxes, Jacob?"

"Hang on...you know about them? Oh, stupid question, you read my mind."

She nodded.

"They were killed for those boxes..."

"No, not greed, for power, a power so strong you cannot begin to understand."

"Try me. I've waited long enough. Why were they taken from me? Don't bother sparing my feelings."

"I understand your anger, Jacob. There are no such things as vamps, but there are such things as the dark forces."

Amanita licked her lips and ran her hand across her throat. She closed her eyes, her voice deepened. "The Dark Betrayers are growing stronger as your society breaks down. I am sorry, but it is hard for me to stay focused on what I must tell you when I am so hungry."

Amanita hit the computer keys and her website appeared. "Are you not curious to know about *ManWatch*, Jacob?"

"Well, actually, I know about the site and what it's supposed to do. It's the reason I'm here. I wanted to question Elizabeth about the death of her husband. The police hadn't been able to find any connection between any of the men. My own research hadn't found a link between any of the victims until I saw the *ManWatch* site. Not only were there several photographs of the victims on it, but the site was run by Elizabeth Blackstone."

"So *ManWatch* is the missing link." Amanita tapped a few more keys.

"You could say that."

"You did not inform the police?"

Jake shrugged. "No need. I was in the company of a friend who is a police officer."

Amanita lifted an eyebrow slightly and Jake wondered whether she was reading his mind. He continued. "I wanted to check out where Elizabeth worked as I met her daughter in Whitby library the other day."

"You met Hope by chance?"

"Yes."

Jake watched the route Amanita took as she moved her cursor over the photographs checking out the latest additions to the *Rogues Gallery*. She let out a low howl, sounding like a wounded animal. Her hand flew to her mouth as she turned to him. Her amethyst eyes widened and darkened as fine lines rapidly appeared across her forehead.

Jake rose as her eyes locked with his. He stepped back, caught between fascination and horror. Amanita's lips curled back exposing two rows of perfectly formed white teeth. Then two dots appeared in her gum line directly over her maxillary canine teeth. The area changed from white to pink in seconds, and her nostrils seemed almost to fold back on themselves. The sound of her snarling increased steadily as the lines across her forehead deepened. The two dots on her gum began to trickle blood as the tips of two needle-thin white teeth appear out of it and curve down over her front teeth.

Elizabeth burst into the room. "Amanita, what's the matter?"

"It's him!" She turned to Jake. "You've brought death to me." Her voice ripped through him. "He has spent an eternity searching for me, and now I'm lost forever."

"No one knows I'm here. I came by myself." Jake backed towards the stairs. "Who are you talking about?"

"Isaac Blake. The White Hall Ship worker!"

"That's impossible. He's been dead for years. If he was alive when—" Jake stared at Elizabeth.

Amanita's smile hardened. "You were saying, Mr Eldritch!"

"You can't begin to understand, Jacob." Elizabeth shook her head.

"Let me see who you are looking at." Jake moved slowly around Amanita, his eyes not leaving her until he was close enough to the computer. "Oh, him— that's the copper, Bard Walker. Mariana and I put his photograph on your site yesterday because we found photographs of the other men that had been murdered—" He paused and looked up. Amanita's eyes portrayed her distrust of him.

"She doesn't kill them." Elizabeth pointed to the screen. "She releases them from their imperfect state unlike this man."

"He's just a copper, though I thought he looked a bit like the man that shot my parents, a Doctor Cula."

"That's because he is!" Amanita's face distorted. "You do not understand, Mr Eldritch even with all his charisma and charm, he isn't human. He's a predator feeding on human weaknesses. He moves from one body to another, and so does the evil within him."

Chapter Twenty-Seven

The Return Of The Dark

"Calm down my dear." Elizabeth touched Amanita's arm lightly. Amanita's snarling face softened as the lines that crossed her forehead, and her unusual teeth, disappeared. She dropped into her chair, emotionally drained.

"You do not understand," Amanita whispered.

"Mr Eldritch wasn't to know, Amanita," Elizabeth said, wiping her hand across her weary face. "Bard Walker is the Whitehall Worker, and was Doctor...Err."

"Cula," Jake said.

"Thank you. Doctor Cula is an entity who enters a person's soul to control their mind and body. They've existed for as long as the Sin Seekers have."

"No, Elizabeth," Amanita interrupted. "The Dark, as we know it, has existed only since man was given the knowledge. I must leave here if I am to complete the task my parents started and those before them."

"Look, it was only by chance I found you," Jake said.

"You will tell him all without uttering a word. He will read your mind, pick up on your senses and emotions and will plant thoughts and beliefs in your head. If you are more beneficial to his quest to hunt me out, he will leave Walker as a husk, and transfer to your body. You would not be able to lie to him, or hide your true feelings."

"So I would become a dead man walking?"

"Yes."

"What can I do to help you?"

"Can you call me friend?"

"Do you bite your friends?" he asked with a smile.

"Only if I need to," she said. "What I need now is your trust."

"I take it you've read my mind and know my thoughts."

"Of sorts. But I understand human nature far better. What is important is that we find the whereabouts of the gold boxes."

"You're talking about the ones from my parents' archaeological dig?"

"Yes." Amanita turned to Elizabeth. "Do you have another bag please?"

Elizabeth touched Amanita's forehead. "I'll fetch you one, but no more. You really need a fresh feed tonight."

After Elizabeth had left, Amanita said, "My takeaway isn't to everyone's choice, but it helps me to survive. Are you surprised, Jacob?" She moved to an old armchair as the last of her energy slipped away. Elizabeth returned and hooked the blood bag over Amanita's head. Once more, Amanita seemed to take on a golden aura and settled again.

"I'm off to bed now. Is there anything else you need?" Elizabeth directed the question to Amanita. She shook her head.

"Thank you for your help this evening, Elizabeth."

Elizabeth bent and kissed Amanita's forehead before turning to wish Jake goodnight. He nodded. After Elizabeth's footsteps faded and the sound of a door closing was heard Amanita said, "Now that it is just you and me, Jacob, I shall ask you again about the boxes."

Jake pulled the picture from his pocket and passed it over. "This was in amongst my parents' things."

"This is what you were showing the gentlemen at the hotel."

"Yes, but— you stopped him from telling us."

"No, he told you what they were, but you didn't understand. Do you have any idea where they are now?"

"None. Are they important?"

"You have no idea what these are?"

"No. I'm not even sure if my parents knew, but I expect Doctor Cula did, and that's why he killed them."

"Please sit." Amanita gestured to a chair.

Amanita studied the soft lines of his face, taking in his steely grey eyes and decided he was a man who was at ease with himself. When he set his mind to something; he gave his all, a blind commitment to family and friends. As the blood dripped slowly into her veins, she studied the photograph, running her fingertips across the picture. "These are soul boxes, Jacob, designed to protect our souls from the impurities of your world until we complete our task."

"Soul boxes. I didn't think you were human."

She laughed. "Only humans are worthy of souls. Maybe it would be easier for you to understand the word, Angel."

"Angels! But what about the missing blood."

"You're willing to believe in vampires and believe I have all the characteristics of a fictitious creature, but not to believe in angels. I am the last of the Sin Seekers, humanity's ticket back to redemption. My race and yours has the same creator. At the end of the Great War my father in his wisdom cast out those who had betrayed him…"

"A war in heaven?"

"Yes. Have you not studied your Holy Scriptures? The Sons of Light battled against the Sons of the Darkness. Your parents must have been aware of the old text known as the Dead Sea Scrolls if they went to Albania."

"Of course."

Amanita rubbed her arm where the cannula was attached. The blood bag was half-empty now.

"Are you all right?" Jake asked.

"The people who donate their blood are too good for me. Now if they were wicked, I could live quite comfortably."

"The Sons of Darkness. Are you talking about Satan?"

"No. Your word, *Satan,* is an abbreviation for the Hebrew word meaning adversary. Satan is an Old English word via Latin and Greek, from the Hebrew *to plot against.* Our father, your God gave Lucifer the title of adversary, or Satan as you called him, because he betrayed his trust. Lucifer was known as the light of heaven and was an angel who fell into the darkness."

"You are a fallen angel?"

Amanita straightened in the chair. "First, I'm a vampire and now you see me as a fallen angel. No, not fallen. You see only devils and demons, but the forces of evil are much more cunning than that. Devils and demons would be recognisable to you with ugly malformed features, with fork tongues, tails, leathery skin, like the smell of food when it is rotten. It's bad and evil. But what if evil is a thing of beauty? Looks can be deceiving, is that not what they say. How much sweeter your fall would be. Evil comes in many forms, Jacob, most of the time it is unrecognisable."

"You're beautiful."

"Am I? How can you be sure of what you see before you, Jacob? Is this the real me?"

Amanita's appearance slowly slipped effortlessly into his Aunt Kate and then Caroline as a young girl, and then back into herself.

"How did you do that?"

"Are they not the people who have made the biggest impact on your life? By knowing your weakness, and your desires, I can get you to do anything I want. Our father gave you the right to make choices, to choose between what is right and wrong, and not only for yourselves, but to help and guide others around you. After the war in heaven, our father cast out all those who had betrayed him. Their numbers were many. They overran your world, so he created a new race, known as the destroying angels.

"These destroying angels are Sin Seekers?"

She nodded. "Our task was to eradicate sins from your world. The forbidden knowledge the dark betrayers created. Until we've completed our task, we are unable to return to heaven. Your parents uncovered the site of the first colony of destroying angels. My parents were among the first to establish themselves at Amantia, on the Adriatic Sea. Over the next two thousand years the colony grew to the point where many of the angels had regained their soul boxes but chose to remain on earth to help the rest of their family reclaim theirs. The ones that left their earthly remains behind replaced their spirits with their souls within the gold boxes and returned to heaven. My parents died a painful death without their boxes, so are unable to return to our father's kingdom.

The earth entered into its golden age, the power of destroying angels seemed to be winning the war against sin, though some lost sight of the joys of heaven and succumbed to the pleasure of sin, allowing the power of the dark ones to regain a foothold. Once an angel has chosen the dark side, there's no return for them. They lose all memory of their family and our father's kingdom. The fallen angel then becomes a dark betrayer and is able to walk in the daylight unlike the destroying angels that can only walk in the light of God once they have regained their true spirit and left their earthly body behind. The dark betrayers' destiny is to seek out and destroy the Sin Seekers.

In an attempt to make it harder for the Dark to find the sin seekers, my parents with the remaining sin seekers decided to spread out across the world. The Dark knows that whoever owns the gold angel soul boxes have control over an angel's destiny. If the angel has their own box, they regain the freedom to choose how to live out their eternal life. Some chose to continue helping those angels who have not regained their freewill, while others chose to return to heaven.

If the Dark finds a box, they can do one of two things, destroy it, and destroy the angel, thus diminishing our father's army of sin seekers, or they find an angel without a soul box and take control by turning them in to a dark betrayer thus increasing the strength of dark over the light."

Jake picked up the picture and studied the gold box. "If it's true, then my parents were killed to stop them finding out about these."

"Doubting me already, Jacob?"

Jake rubbed his face. "Maybe I'm just tired. Just too much to take in. I need to talk to my aunt first. She knows far more than I can tell you about what happened to my parents' things. I'll be seeing her later. If I find out anything which will help us..."

"Us? So you are willing to help me."

"I guess I am. How do you feel about travelling to London?"

"Interested."

Chapter Twenty-Eight

Angels And Kings

Jake headed out across the moors. The vast open sky, even on the dullest of days, lifted his spirit. Its blueness, in the height of the summer, could make him forget everything, even his problems. Today the gathering grey clouds hung low, blocking out the sun. Jake opened his car window, hoping the chilling air with its smells of peat and heather would clear his mind of its accumulation of puzzles and unanswered questions.

As Whitby and the sea came into view, the sun broke free from the clouds. On the brightest of days, with the sunshine reflected off the ruins of Saint Hilda's Abbey, the place seemed to sparkle as proudly as any jewel set in the English crown.

Jake drove through the town and headed out on the main road towards Scarborough. He mulled over the questions he needed answered. Surely the police would've gone through everything to find out who had killed the team of archaeologists. Could he possibly find out more about the mysterious Doctor Cula? If the entity was responsible for the deaths, then what happened to the real doctor?

Jake's laughter echoed around his car. "My news-breaking story isn't one I can share," he shouted, as he passed through the sleepy village of Raw, with its open rolling countryside of patchwork fields enclosed by low stone walls. In the distance, the blue of the sea seemed to touch the sky.

Jake pulled onto his aunt's drive, killed the engine, and sat for a minute staring at the house he'd grown up in. Above the guttering, he could just make out the dormer windows in the roof. The front door opened, and Aunt Kate stepped out. She stood straight-backed, looking years younger than her seventy-four years, dressed in pale-blue jeans, a crocheted jumper of pale blues and soft pinks with her long white hair hanging in a single plait down to her narrow waist.

Jake greeted her with a hug. He noticed that she looked a little drawn, but she smiled brightly, and it dismissed any concerns he had.

"Good afternoon, Jacob. I thought I recognised Mary-Bell. Glad to see she's still going strong." Kate ran her hand lovingly over the bonnet of the Morris Traveller before kissing him lightly on the cheek. "Caroline said to expect you today, so I invited my friend George over. I've wanted you to meet him for ages now."

"That sounds a bit ominous."

"He's a good friend, so be nice." Kate touched Jake's cheek.

"As long as he's a gentleman to you he has nothing to worry about, Auntie." He slipped his arm around her shoulder and kissed the top of her head.

Kate put her arm through his and led him around the side of the house, up on to a raised patio. In a large warm conservatory, seated at a green cast-iron table, was a white-haired man. As they entered, he broke off his conversation with Caroline and stood up.

"George, here's my nephew, Jacob."

George extended a slender hand. "Hi son. At last we meet properly, Jacob. Or do you prefer Jake?"

"Jake is fine. I'm Jacob to family and close friends." Jake smiled warmly at Caroline, who nodded back.

"Please let's all sit down and have a cup of tea," Kate said.

When Caroline and George went to fetch the tea things, Jake sensed there was more to George than just being his aunt's friend.

In the past, Jake pretended he could see his mother's eyes smiling back at him through his aunt's, desperate to keep something of her alive. Since watching the film, he found his parents' smiling faces were much clearer to him.

"Aunt, Caroline tells me you still have most of my parents' things here."

Kate took his hands in hers. "Yes, I do. Sorry I haven't spoken to you about them sooner. Please don't think I was hiding them from you. It's just that…" She paused as George and Caroline returned. Once the tea things were set out, she poured the drinks and passed a cup to Jake. "I had always planned to tell you. At first you seemed so young. Then it was never the right time."

Jake looked towards George. He was smiling at Kate as though some knowledge or understanding had passed between them. Kate nodded, and George took his cue. "I'm not just your aunt's gardener, Jacob. We've been friends for years. In a way it was your parents that brought us together."

"My parents?" Jake looked to his aunt.

"George was the police officer assigned to investigate what happened to them in Albania. We kept in touch." Kate hesitated and looked to George.

"I took early retirement to become a gardener after giving thirty years of my life to the force. Albania was my last case." George picked up a slice of homemade cake.

Jake sipped his drink while trying to decide what question to ask first. "So what did you find when you first got there?"

"Look, son, I understand your need to know. In your shoes I would feel the same. But none of what I'm about to tell you can be reported, or published."

Jake looked to his aunt. "Is this the real reason you've never told me because I became a journalist?"

"No, of course not." She reached for his hand. "I've always wanted to tell you." She took a sip of her tea. "I couldn't face talking about it. I was so angry when the photograph of Charlotte and Robert, dead in each other's arms, was splashed over the front of the tabloids. George tried to find out who had taken the picture, but to no avail. We couldn't grieve in peace because your parents were so well known. I had persuaded my sister to keep you out of the limelight, and I brought you up here while they worked and travelled abroad. Your father wanted you to travel and experience all the places and history with them, but your mother agreed with me, saying they had plenty of time for you to travel with them once you had finished your schooling."

Tears rolled down Kate's cheeks. "When the news broke of their deaths I was relieved you hadn't gone with them otherwise I would've lost you all. Then the guilt hit. I was devastated to think how selfish I'd been keeping you to myself all those wonderful years."

"I don't understand."

"You missed out on getting to know your parents because of me."

"No, you and my parents did what you thought was best for me at that time. You didn't kill them. All I want is to understand why they had to die and who killed them. I need to look at their things because I hope it will bring them closer to me. Maybe help me see why it was so important for them to travel to the site in the first place. I'm not looking for a story, just answers. I blame only the ones that pulled the trigger. So, George, what happened when you arrived in the country?"

"It wasn't a pleasant job for us when we got to the hilltop settlement. More of a salvage job to recover the bodies and get out with as little fuss as possible. We'd been warned to tread lightly and not to go in stomping about upsetting the local police who'd already carried out their own investigations. It was discovered that neither your parents nor their team had the right be at the site, or in the country. It wasn't their fault, I know. They were digging at a historical site without the proper permits. As they were so well-known, the programme makers were willing to pay out a large sum of money to keep things quiet with the British government in agreement. The last thing anyone wanted was to be known as supporters of tomb-raiding tactics, especially as your mother had links to the British Museum. After all, the Greeks were very vocal about getting their marbles back and the last thing anyone wanted was to trigger international plundering of the world's museums as other countries started to demand back what they saw as stolen treasures. So it had to be swept under the carpet."

Jake opened his mouth, but George stopped him from speaking.

"I'm sorry, but don't think for one minute I would stand up in court, swear an oath, and repeat what I've just told you, because I won't. I've a pension to think about and nothing anyone can say or do will bring any of them back now."

Jake nodded. "Don't think I don't understand, George. It must have been difficult for you."

"It was. Kate wanted to know what happened, and I understood her pain. I'd lost my wife three years before I met her. She'd been left devastated by the sudden loss of your parents and I wanted to help. I did all I could, but I had rules to follow, otherwise I wouldn't have been of any help whatsoever."

"Has Caroline told you about the DVD she'd had made from one of Mum and Dad's films?"

Kate looked across at Caroline.

"I'm sorry, Kate. It was meant to be a surprise. But after Jake and I watched it we decided not to show you."

"What was on it?" George asked.

Jake held Kate's hand. "It shows exactly what happened to Mum and Dad. The camera must've been left running. It witnessed everything."

Kate's hand flew to her mouth. "Dear God, the answer was in my loft all this time."

"Please don't get upset, Aunt. George, do you know what happened to Lisa?"

Chapter Twenty-Nine

Turning Tides

Walker wondered, as he looked out of his office window at another grey day, what Eldritch had been up to since they met at Mariana's. He hadn't heard from him. Back at his desk he switched on the computer and paged down to study the picture of himself that Mariana had posted on *ManWatch* two nights ago.

His fingertips tingled with anticipation at the thought of lovely Mariana, with her silky dark hair. He inhaled deeply, imagining the fun he could have watching her die. But for now, he needed to focus on finding his prey.

Did Eldritch realise he wasn't the copper, Bard Walker? Dark wondered was this the reason he was avoiding him. He tried so hard to keep within Walker's normal behaviour, a weak, broken man before he had succumbed to the darkness. Okay, so he had his odd little moments, but he was sure Walker's family and colleagues were much happier having a stronger man in their lives, especially after the way he'd dealt with the first assignment when he stumbled across a dead body. It was a bad time for Walker having to deal with the fact his wife, a couple of days prior, had walked out on him, taking his kids too. His superior officers hadn't expected him to return to work straightaway, but he was needed to complete the task of finding the girl.

The door opened, and Charles Brookbanks entered. "Morning, Walker. Glad to see someone's working hard."

"Morning, sir." Walker stood. "Just going over some of the case details to see if there's anything we've overlooked."

"Very diligent of you. Glad to see you've returned with

more vigour. Have you heard the latest? Another body found on the moors this morning. It's in the morgue. I'm just going over there. Would you care to join me?"

"Yes, thank you, sir." With Brookbanks on his side, maybe he didn't need Eldritch after all.

Brookbanks shivered noticeably as they entered the morgue. If Walker had learned one thing about the human race, it was that they feared death. Heather Easton sat at her desk and looked up as they entered.

"Morning, Easton. Hope you've something new to tell us. The body count isn't to my liking," Brookbanks said.

Easton threw him a sideways glance, before ushering them through a pair of heavy swing doors. Walker sensed the pathologist's dislike of Brookbanks and smiled to himself knowing Brookbanks would be far from impressed if he knew just what a pathetic individual she thought he was. She acknowledged Walker with a smile as he held the door for her. She led them to where the body of Joe Edmond lay on the mortuary table.

"There are signs that Edmond, aka Dog, tried to fight off his attacker," she said. "Police records showed him as a possible hard drug dealer. I found no signs that he was a user himself. However, marijuana and phencyclidine did show up in his test samples. Apart from that, he was well-fed and a fit young man with his life ahead of him.

"You sound sorry for the bastard," Brookbanks said.

"I feel sorry for any wasted life."

"I don't. Whether he was a user or not is unimportant. He was a menace to society. He dished out hell to other kids, PCP or peace pill to give their fancy street name, and they have plenty of other names too."

Easton shook her head. "I'm fully aware of what damage these drugs can do."

"I'm sure you are, but you're not the one who has to explain to the kid's parents that their son or daughter believed after popping a pill they could stop a train with their superhuman strength." Brookbanks stared at the pale body on the slab.

"No, you're right. I'm the one who has to make sense of why they're dead and how they died, but still, it doesn't stop me from feeling sorry for such a waste of a young life. Your colleagues gave me this young man's police records. They showed me that, unlike you, he never had the same opportunities in his life. The difference between you and him was that someone believed in you. I have seen many young people from good families land up on my slab, under my knife, very dead, after encountering drugs, guns, and knives.

I'm not here to pass judgement on Edmond, but to tell you how he came to be here. To start with, you can clearly see these lacerations." She pointed to his arms, face, and neck. "Unlike our other victims, Edmond struggled with his attacker. While the others show signs that they had sex before they died in their sleep, our friend here had put up a fight. He has the same toxins in his body as the others, but unlike them, I found traces of our other victims' DNA on his body and in it too."

"How's that possible?" Brookbanks stared at the body as though it would answer his question. "Did he have any contact with the others?"

"Not in here, if that's what you mean." Easton's eyes narrowed.

"So there's no chance of cross-contamination?"

"None! From where the samples were taken, the body needed to have been in physical contact with the other victims, or some other source."

"What about the attacker? Any leads this time to who this person might be?"

"As before, none."

Surely the killer's DNA would've been all over Edmond's body, under his nails, if he had fought off his attacker. There must be some trace evidence."

"None. Like I said, only the other victims' DNA." Easton sighed.

"We're getting nowhere."

"May I make a suggestion, sir?" Walker cut in.

Brookbanks nodded. "Anything that can help, lad."

165

"There's a possible link. It's a slight one." Walker gestured to the body. "A victim who died twelve years ago named Blackstone."

"Twelve years ago! Highly unlikely."

Walker ignored the glaring looks and flicked through his notebook. "The victim, John Blackstone, had a daughter called Hope and she knew Joe Edmond."

"Now that's interesting— his daughter. Was she involved with drugs?"

"She doesn't show up on any reports, though it has been reported that she hangs around with a girl who has been linked to a group of youngsters known as Gatekeeper's Cottage Gang."

"Maybe it's worth questioning the girl. Good work, lad."

"I would need a DNA sample from the girl to eliminate her from the test results." Easton studied her notes. "The most puzzling results are the toxins found in each of the victims. My team have now identified it as a fungus, *Amanita Virosa*, commonly known as the *Destroying Angel*."

"So are you saying that a new street drug caused the deaths of these *Dead Men Sleeping* and is nothing more than a drug poisoning from a deadly fungus?"

"Hard to tell at this point as we need to run more tests, but it's a possibility. The timeline has me puzzled. Their reaction from consuming the toxins to the time they were found dead is too short. If consumed, the toadstool should've taken up to sixteen days for them to die, normally a slow and painful death. They would've suffered a mixture of vomiting, bloody diarrhoea, and stomach cramps causing rapid fluid loss and intense thirst.

After twelve hours, they would've felt fine until the next stage hits them. Starting with watering eyes, slow and difficult breathing, followed by delirium, and confusion leading to seizures and then a coma and death. There would've been signs of jaundice in their eyes as the toxins start to affect the liver and kidneys. I would have expected to see signs of loss of fluid in the tissues as the liver and kidneys start to break down, but the amount of missing blood is unexplainable. I had expected to see a certain amount of damage to the red blood cells, but not blood loss."

"What could've caused the body to break down so quickly then?"

"There are two small punctures on the hotel victim's neck. I wonder if they might be needle marks instead of bite marks as first thought. If the poison was injected into the blood stream this may account for the process being speeded up, but not from days to a few hours."

Brookbanks raised his hand to signal he'd heard enough, and turned to Walker. "Best go and see this girl, Hope Blackstone. Also find out what drugs Edmond was dealing. If we have something new on the streets, I want to know."

Back at his desk, Walker returned to the *ManWatch* site. He paged down to the bottom and found what he was looking for the perfect excuse to speak to Elizabeth Blackstone without drawing any unnecessary attention to himself. A tap on the door disturbed his thoughts. Brookbanks entered.

"Walker, haven't you gone yet to check out this Blackstone girl?"

"I'm just off now, sir."

"When you get back, let me know if you uncover anything."

"Yes, of course."

The overcast sky still hadn't lifted as Walker crossed to his car. His body tingled with excitement; his prey was in sight. He thought about the last conversation he had with Eldritch at Mariana's. Maybe it was time he paid him a visit at home. On pulling out of the car park, he headed towards Jake's flat. Maybe he could persuade Eldritch to come with him to see Blackstone. *Sweet is the revenge, which is mine, said the Lord.*

Walker laughed and pressed redial on his phone. "Nope, it's all mine. Fuck God. Eldritch will be in deep shit once I've finished with him. Fuck it. His phone's switched off." Walker concentrated on the road ahead. "Still, it's worth checking out where he lives anyway." He turned into the residents' car park and was relieved to find it was a quiet cul-de-sac.

Walker checked the numbers on a small plaque, found Jake's on the first floor, and took the steps two at a time. He knocked on the door, while glancing up and down the balcony, before inserting a small probe into the keyhole. A hard push, with a slight twist of the wrist and he was in.

In the small hall, Walker took a deep breath, allowing all his senses to kick in and tell him what he needed to know. The place smelled of Eldritch, though he could pick up the scent of a woman who had been here, and not so long ago. But she wasn't his prey. He placed his hand against the wall. Interestingly enough, there was a sense of peace. Humans, he had found, were too wrapped up in themselves to worry about anything other than enjoying their short lives. A pain shot through his head and down his side.

"Don't bother trying to fight me, Walker. It'll do you no good." The entity spoke from within, and Walker felt himself take hold of his head. The pain instantly stopped.

"Good. Now keep it that way. Enjoy what life you have left. You and I will have such fun when we find her."

Walker opened the nearest door and found Jake's notes about the crime scenes covered the living room walls. It didn't surprise him how thorough Jake was in his research. He sensed that as soon as they met. In amongst the cuttings were reminders of things Jake needed to check out, one said, *'John Blackstone's wife: See if she knew whom her husband had been with on the night he died.'*

"So he knew!" Walker headed towards the front door when a shiver passed over him. He pressed his hands against the wall. A loud rushing noise filled his eardrums and exploded into his mind. He distilled the mixture of sounds and emotions from the other tenants in the adjoining apartments, and siphoned off the stronger, more powerful energy. Something familiar hovered on the periphery of his senses and he forced his human host's thoughts out as he tried to revive some of his memories from before. Now and then, he caught flashes of experiences amid his deep-rooted obsessions.

Walker opened the next door in the hallway and found himself swamped by a surge of energy in every fibre of his corporeal being as the past and present collided. The entity within Walker ran his fingertips across the surfaces like a bat hunting its prey. The source of the energy was within the room somewhere.

Thousands of images flooded Walker's mind with blood, gore, screams and fear.

"Shut the fuck up!" the entity cursed. "These are my memories, not yours. We've work to do!"

The nauseating pain subsided, allowing the entity to infest Walker completely. The entity reached for the box on the coffee table and inhaled. The sweetest of memories returned and he felt the familiar weight of a gun in his hand. The rich smell of death filled his lungs along with the music of suffering and loss.

Oh, it was good to be alive again. To be able to recall the fear in the woman's eyes as she leaned over the edge of the trench trying to pull the man up. He had questioning look in his blue eyes on seeing him, Doctor Cula raising the gun. There had been a stunned expression on the woman's face before the bullet sliced through her head sending hair and grey matter in every direction.

"So they were Eldritch's parents that I killed." Walker opened his eyes as the memories faded. "Was it possible that Jake recognised him, but how?

Walker dropped the picture showing a gold box resting next to a fanged skull and left the apartment. *Maybe time wasn't on his side after all*, Walker thought as he climbed into his car.

Chapter Thirty

Angels And Demons

"Lisa? You don't mean Lisa King, one of the archaeological team members?" George asked.

"Yes, she's on the film, but her notebook isn't with the others in the box Caroline had brought over to me. Another thing I don't understand, why does Aunt Kate have everything in her loft?"

"I've told you already, neither wanted to own up to what happened to your parents. There's more I have to tell you, but it mustn't go any further."

"No, don't, George. Please." Kate reached for his hand.

"The lad has the right to know." George kissed the back of Kate's hand. "The Albanian police left it as killed by unknown rebels. At that time, there was an uprising in the country. The programme makers should've taken this into account before your parents and their team went, but they were too interested in getting top ratings to miss out on a great scoop. A diplomatic decision was taken by both countries."

"George was told to back off when he started to ask questions on behalf of the devastated families. It wasn't a good idea to push too much. Maybe we should have tried harder." Kate inhaled deeply. "It was Lisa's idea that we brought everything here. What we hadn't taken into account was her state of mind."

George continued. "That young girl had been through hell. Nowadays she would've had some sort of trauma counselling. Her family insisted, with the compensation they received, could take care of her, but they hadn't taken into account survivor's guilt. I was too busy worrying about you and Kate."

"So she survived the massacre?"

"God only knows how."

"Did your team question Doctor Ahriman Cula?"

"How did you know about him?"

"The film showed he pulled the trigger."

"That's impossible, Jacob. He was dead."

"You can see for yourself. Though it isn't nice viewing." Jacob pulled his phone from his pocket.

"His body was found at his home. He'd been dead for some time, about eight weeks they reckoned."

"That's incredible. No one noticed? Unless, of course." Jake paused.

"What?"

"Well, I was told…No." Jake remembered what Elizabeth had said about the entity. No point in trying to explain that to George. If the entity had taken over Cula looking for Amanita when had it gone back to Albania? Was the history of the hillside settlement the reason it was drawn back to the place? How had it tracked her down this time? Was it through his parents' link to Yorkshire that it had returned?

Aware the attention was all on him, Jake smiled. "Sorry, just thinking about a comment Mum and Dad made on the film, but it doesn't matter. So how did the doctor's death go unnoticed for so long?"

"A scholarly old gentleman who enjoyed the company of books more than people. His house was situated miles from anywhere. His name was among Robert's things. The problem was that Doctor Cula never worked for Butrint Museum in Albania."

"Jacob, let them see the film." Caroline pointed to his phone. You can see someone called Doctor Cula murdering them."

George shook his head. "I believe you. The man known as Ahriman Cula died two weeks before Robert and Charlotte arrived in the country. He never worked for the museum and was some sort of independent historian. The programme makers employed him to do a background research on the site before your parents arrived in the country. Admittedly, his body was found two weeks after the killings, but he'd been dead for eight weeks."

"And no one missed him?" Jake said.

"It happens. There wasn't anything suspicious about his death, just old age. It was only when the death of your parents and their team came to light that his death was uncovered too.

"How did the television company make contact with him in the first place?" Jake asked.

"No idea. Once we got Lisa, the bodies, and all your parents' things out of there, we didn't ask too many other questions."

"Hang on a minute. On the film, my father said there had been a change of plan. Digger Mike commented on the fact that there wasn't a team from the museum on the site while they were working."

"Maybe that's why Cula didn't like to be filmed," Caroline added. "Did the local police question Lisa?"

"They weren't able to as she was incoherent. We found her clutching what remained of her dead twin brother. The top of his head was blown off. The Albanian police didn't find her, we did. We reckon she'd been sitting like that for days, just talking to him."

"So police weren't thorough in their search?"

"They did their best under difficult circumstances, Jacob. We found her sitting in some sort of temple surrounded by trays of finds and other data. The rebels hit while she was busy hiding the trench finds. It must've been awful to come out and find everyone was dead. We think she dragged her brother's body to her hideaway and sat waiting."

"Is she still alive now?"

Kate turned to George.

"She is." George gave Kate's hand a squeeze, "She isn't the person she was…"

"If you want to have a look in the attic, Jacob, please do." Kate stood. "George and I are off to the garden centre. I hope

172

you'll stay for dinner when we come back."

"Of course I will. I'm looking forward to tasting some of Caro's cooking," Jake said, trying to ease the tension in the room. After George and Kate had gone, Jake followed Caroline up the narrow stairs to the attic space. "How much is there of my parent's things, Caro?"

Caroline opened a door half the size of a normal one. "You'll be as surprised as I was. Oh, and mind your head too."

The attic was light and airy with a high roof. The skylights as well as the two dormer windows to the front of the house gave the attic a feeling of space.

"Kate is finding the stairs a bit tiresome. That's why she asked me to sort things out."

"I don't remember coming up here before. To think I've lived in this house all of my life and wasn't aware this was their workspace. I must take after both my parents for untidiness."

"No, you're worse." Caroline laughed.

The space, fitted out with shelves, was full with piles of files, folders as well as books. There were stacks of black VHS tapes. Under each of the dormer windows was a desk. On each of these were framed photographs of a toddler with his parents.

"I think that's Mum's desk and the other's Dad's."

"How can you tell?"

"Well, it's elementary, my dear Watson. You see, but do not observe. On observing the books over there, they're all on filmmaking and photography. While these here are all are on history, ancient chronicles, and poetry, as well as child-rearing."

"And there was me thinking you're clever. So your Dad was a bit of a male chauvinist, unlike you."

"How do you work that one out then, Watson?"

"Well, I know your methods, Mr Holmes. Your mother's shelf has the child-rearing books."

They both laughed.

Jake sat in his mother's chair and started to go through the drawers. In the first, he found the usual collection of pens, pencils, paperclips, and writing pads. The next one, under some letters, he pulled out a diary dated two years before they died. His mother's handwriting was small and very neat. It didn't surprise Jake to find that both his parents were methodical in their record keeping. On opening the diary, he read, and then reread the entry. "Listen to this, Caro."

'*Today I've been to London, to the museum. My friend was right. I'm very interested in what they had to show me. Robert said its mind blowing. (His new catchphrase makes me love him more.) My new catch phrase is <u>Chasing Angels.</u>*'

"Chasing Angels?" Caroline looked over Jake's shoulder.

"She's even underlined it."

"I wonder who her friend was, and what museum was she talking about.*"*

"It can only be the British Museum. As for the friend, no idea."

"Of course, your mum worked there until they became celebrities and had to leave. On the film cases I found the programme's title, *Timelines*. I vaguely remember that they researched old documents and followed their trails."

"That's right. I remember that too. Mum went to see someone about an old document at the museum."

"Maybe we'll find the answers to what Charlie saw in these." Caroline gestured to the files and folders.

"Are these more of the films that they made?" Jake pointed to the unmarked tapes.

"Yes. There's also some other metal boxes at the back too, but I haven't found the keys for them yet."

Chapter Thirty-One

Secrets Told

Jake and Caroline moved the heavy-duty grey metal box onto his mother's desk. The ex-army surplus store lockbox was unmarked apart from a sticker on the top, which had a number printed on it.

"Do you think Kate and George know what's in these?" Jake knelt beside five other similar boxes that stood in a neat row under the eaves of the house.

"I don't think so." Caroline sat on Charlie's chair. "The proof you've wanted for your theory on vampires might be in these boxes." She grinned at him.

Jake stopped studying the small padlock and glanced over his shoulder. "It might, Caro, but it'll be inappropriate to mention my wild ideas, especially as Kate finds them so upsetting."

Caroline's smile dropped. "You're right. I'm sorry. I've mentioned to George that Kate had asked me to sort out the attic. He said he'll give me a hand whenever I need it. It took me by surprise when he told me he had helped Kate move her sister's things up here."

Through the window, Caroline saw only the fields stretching off into the distance. "It must have been hard for your aunt when she lost her sister so soon after losing her husband and to bring up a young child too.

"Hey, I wasn't so difficult to bring up." Jake scoffed. "Anyway, I'm a bloody useless journalist and not very observant, am I? Did you have any inkling that George was anything other than Kate's gardener?

"None whatsoever. George was just George. He just appears in the morning and potters around the garden for an hour or two then goes. Though, just lately, he'd been coming more often. I thought that was because Kate was redesigning the flowerbed down by the beck."

"Have any idea where we might find the keys to these boxes?"

Caroline shrugged. "Nope. Try looking in the drawers. When I first came up here, all I did was a bit of tidying up and some dusting. It felt wrong to snoop through everything, but now you're here, it's okay." Caroline dropped to her knees beside Charlie's desk and pulled open the drawers. In the third one down she found not the keys, but another journal. Originally it had been a diary, but Charlie had crossed out some of the dates and scribbled over two or three days so even the months were out of order. Caroline passed it to Jake.

"We know your mother thought she was looking for angels but was shocked to find they weren't." Caroline sat on the chair again. "I apologise, but I did read some of it while I tried to decide what I should do." She gestured to the room. "If they weren't Angels, what were they? I know we saw they had fangs, but seriously, I can't believe they were vampires."

Jake glanced up from the journal, and wanted to say, *Well, Caroline actually I was nearly right, they're a sort of vamp, but don't worry they're on our side. It's the Dark ones; we should be worrying about.* In reality, even though he knew he could trust Caroline, it wasn't safe for her to know.

"You surely don't think they are vampires!"

Jake tossed the journal onto his father's desk and sat down in his chair. "Please explain why you're quick to believe in angels with wings, yet you can't believe in vampires or demons."

"Nephilim," Caroline said.

"No need to use that sort of language." He grinned. "Okay, what's *Nephilim*? Sounds like some sort of a pop group."

"Well, I know who and what it was believed the *Nephilim* were, but why your mother should've underlined the word,

I've no idea. Maybe, she believed they would uncover the truth behind the mythology. Nephilim were believed to be the Sons of God and the Daughters of Men as spoken about in the Dead Sea Scrolls."

"Isn't that what Miles spoke about the other night when he said '*Horebbah* and the Dead Sea Scrolls?"

"Maybe. But *Nephilim* were sometimes known as *The Watchers*. The explanation behind the story has a threefold aspect to the Sin of the Watchers."

"Sin?"

"Yes. Not just the human everyday sort of sin, white lies included. This was a bigger sin…"

"You learnt all of this at university?"

"After studying Latin and the ancient languages of the bible, I used to transcribe old church documents, until I came back to look after Mum and Dad."

Jake nodded. He remembered all too well what his aunt's thoughts had been when Caroline returned home to look after her aging parents. *What a waste of a young girl's life.* Kate didn't think of Caroline as her carer as they'd lived next door to each other for years. To her, she was more like a daughter, or a close friend. Jake, like his aunt, often wondered why Caroline had never married. He had been briefly married a long time ago, though no one was surprised, least of all him, when it had come to an abrupt end, due to his love for his work rather than her affairs.

"Anyway, back to the sinning," Caroline said, bringing Jake out of the past. "According to the records found by the Dead Sea, the first of the three big sins was the defilement of the essence of the angels to marry and engage in sexual acts with human women. Second, the union between the angels and mortal women created evil, because of the Nephilim. Finally, the angels sinned by revealing the secrets of the natural universe to humanity against the wishes of God."

"Are you saying that the graves my parents found weren't of angels at all, but of evil incarnate?"

"That's one way of putting it. Vamps are supposed to turn to dust, but these were graves with skeletons in them. Though it does make sense if we believe what the Dead Sea Scrolls tells us."

"If Mum had seen copies of the scrolls then she might've followed up on them."

Caroline began to hunt around. She pulled out box files and looked inside.

"It doesn't make sense. Surely Kate and George would've found the keys in amongst the personal belongings." Jake opened and closed the drawers. "What about those set of keys you brought over to mine?"

"Oh, of course. I'll get them."

Caroline went to fetch the keys, closing the door behind her with a bang. Jake turned and saw the attic door hid a small cupboard with a key in its lock. He found a pile of notebooks inside and at the back of the cupboard a row of keys, each numbered. One read 4Q184. Jake lifted the key, took the pile of books back to his father's desk. He started to read. Soon the rattling of cups on a tea tray alerted Jake to Caroline's return as she nudged open the door.

"You're ready for a cuppa? I know I am. Oh, you found the key."

"When the door closed, it revealed a cupboard. These were inside too." Jake held up the book, he was reading.

"Anything new?" Caroline handed Jake the bunch of keys.

"These look to be duplicates."

"Maybe one set was Charlie's, or perhaps they kept a set here for safety." Caroline poured the tea. "What's in the books?"

"Well, Digger Mike from the film, as we know, wasn't at all happy. Now we know why. My father knew about the unrest in Albania, because Mike had voiced his opinion, saying he felt it made the site vulnerable."

"If your father knew it was dangerous, why go ahead with the filming?"

"According to what the others had said, they were all excited about the whole thing. Julie Wakefield and Lisa King were amazed by how excited Digger Mike was, usually he worried about cost, but as the programme makers were covering the expense, he seemed more relaxed about the whole thing."

Caroline picked up one of the books and started to read. "According to the others, Stewart Ward was superstitious about the numbers, and was happier with even numbers than odd, but the one thing he wasn't happy about was Doctor Ahriman Cula."

"We need to find out about him. Does Stewart say why he wasn't happy about him?"

"Only that the doctor joined them at the last minute, bringing with him two other colleagues."

"It's crazy to think that an archaeologist was spooked by the number 13," Jake said. "Was that the only reason he wasn't happy about Cula?"

"No, and I quote. *"Doctor Ahriman Cula wanted to know everything that was going on. He wasn't happy about appearing on television. We're led to believe that he was interested in our progress as he was working on another site. I tried to talk to him about the other site; he pretended not to understand me. Yet I've heard him talking perfectly good English with Charlotte. I tried to voice my opinions but wasn't listened to. The other members of Doctor Cula's team kept away until we had uncovered the skeletons"*. That's interesting. Other members of Cula's team, surely they should've been questioned about the death of your parents and what had happened to the real Doctor Cula."

"That's an interesting point. If we can get a photograph of the real Doctor Cula, we can match him to the one on the film. Didn't Charlotte say he was from some local museum?"

"George said he was an independent historian."

Jake began to make notes. "I wonder where Cula's worked before he retired. If his main area of research had been the settlement at Amantia, Albania, then it's obvious why the *Timelines* producers made contact with him, and why the doctor was killed."

"Murder! Are you sure, Jacob? George said he was an elderly man, implying he died of natural causes. Anyway, early on you suggested that the policeman Bard Walker looked like Cula."

"Logic tells us the *Timelines* producers must have made contact with the doctor before they went. They would've discussed the aims of the programme, and what their chances were of uncovering something amazing at the site."

"That makes sense. They must've called in some sort of expert."

"Someone must have known Cula well enough to suggest him to the programme makers. The police's story about him is rubbish— lonely old man only interested in his books and papers! Who were the doctor's colleagues and are they still alive? There must be records in the programme archives."

"But Jacob, Stewart said he was brought in at the last minute."

"If that was so, then who was he a substitute for, and why? I'm sure my parents have a contact list of those they were travelling with and meeting there. Some sort of itinerary. Tomorrow we'll go through everything in here." Jake looked at his watch. "No wonder I can't think straight. I need a bite to eat. If Kate doesn't mind, I'd like to stop over tonight. My best thinking time is in the morning."

"Wow, she'll be amazed. After seeing you for the first time in six months, now you want to stop over. I better go and sort out your old room."

Chapter Thirty-Two

Dark Betrayer Stalks

As the door opened, Walker leaned forward and smiled broadly. "Hello. Are you, Mrs Blackstone?

"I am. Who's asking?" The woman smiled back though her voice betrayed her nervousness.

"I'm DI Walker. May I come in and talk to you for a moment?" He held out his badge.

"A policeman?" She opened the door a little wider. "Is my daughter in trouble again? Tut, I've tried speaking to her. I knew no good would come, if she hung around with that lot. Now one of them has wound up dead. I just knew it."

"Are you talking about Joe Edmond? So your daughter knew the victim?"

"You're talking about Dog, the drug dealer, whose body was found by a hiker. I hate to think how he came by such a name. My daughter isn't here, so you'll have to come back some other time." Elizabeth started to close the door.

Walker put his hand out and was shocked to see her flinch away from his touch. "Actually, it isn't just your daughter I've come to see. I've a few questions for you. Please can I come in, Mrs Blackstone?"

"Me? Sorry, I can't help you with your enquiries about the body on the moors."

Walker leaned on the door. "It's about your husband."

"My husband isn't here either."

"I know he's been dead for twelve years, Mrs Blackstone. Are you not worried about what your neighbours might think with me standing on your doorstep?"

"DI Walker, you're new to the area, aren't you? If you

weren't, then you would've known my husband's behaviour towards me gave my neighbours plenty to talk about."

Walker studied her face. Within her hazel eyes he saw strength of character, but what surprised him most was the control she was keeping over her emotions. She pushed the strands of dark brown hair away from her face. Her eyes remained locked with his as she started to close the door again.

"Our conversation is finished now, DI Walker."

"You know who I am." Suddenly he wasn't sure whether he had been playing her, or whether she still had the upper hand.

Elizabeth nodded, stepped back, and ushered him in. "Please don't take up too much of my time. I have an evening job working at the local hospital."

Walker tried to read her mind and was shocked to find himself standing in a woodland scene. The picture kept rerunning as a small oak leaf floated over a waterfall and then returned to the top to make the same journey again. As he passed her in the narrow hallway, she said, "I was just making myself a cup of coffee, would you care to join me? Please go through while I shut this door, it has a nasty habit of sticking."

Walker stood by the window, looking down onto Whitby harbour.

"That door is such a nuisance. It doesn't close properly, if you don't give it a hard enough push. Did you say you would join me in a cup of coffee?" Elizabeth disappeared from his view and stepped into the small kitchen area off the sitting room.

Walker leaned against a brick arch that separated the kitchen from the sitting room to answer her question.

"Please."

Elizabeth turned and smiled.

"I noticed you don't have any photos of your husband on show." Walker said, not acknowledging that he had seen her slip her mobile into her pocket.

"Are you really checking up on whether widows are still

grieving?" She laughed, but it didn't reach her eyes. "Is it a new way for the police to waste taxpayer's money?"

"Don't women normally keep a picture or two of their spouse about, especially as you have a young daughter? Mine's black, please."

Elizabeth poured hot water into the mugs. "Call me a callous bitch if you wish, but you didn't have to live with a man who only spoke with his fists." She handed him his mug and then took hers through to the sitting room.

"The night your husband left, did you know where he was going?" Walker brightened his tone.

Elizabeth took a sip of her coffee, and then sucked on her bottom lip as though forgetting just how hot it was. "No idea. My husband didn't believe I had a right to know about his comings or goings."

"It was normal for him to stay out overnight?"

"Why, all of a sudden, are you interested in him? I've already stated that fact. My dearly departed husband wasn't the kind of man you questioned too often, unless you enjoyed being knocked about. I didn't, so I didn't ask." There was venom in her voice.

"A man you claim hated you so much named you as the beneficiary on a life insurance policy."

Elizabeth threw her head back and laughed. "My husband didn't do it out of kindness, DI Walker. He had one because he also had one made out in my name, and our daughter's too. What's a little accident between loved ones? Only I didn't know about it at the time. I just did what my husband told me to do, without any questions. Anyway, his death was accidental. All of this was decided at the time. So why a new investigation?

"But was it?"

"Was it what?"

"Accidental."

"Are you saying you lot didn't do your job properly. Is that why you are here?"

"I'm here to tell you it was murder."

"Murder!" Elizabeth's eyebrows lifted. She pushed her

hair back over her shoulder. "What makes you believe that?

Walker smiled at the sight of two small red pinpricks on her throat.

"I'm glad you find it amusing. You come into my home, accuse me of murder." She rose and took her empty cups into the kitchen.

"I'm not accusing you, but I think you know who did it."

Her laughter floated through to Walker. "If you read his death certificate, you'd know that he died of fungus poisoning."

"And you believe that, Mrs Blackstone?"

"My husband enjoyed taking drugs and drinking. Do you know about the other women in his life? Now, I need to get ready for work."

"One more question, and then I'll leave."

She nodded.

"What about your website?"

"Oh that. My little hobby. I started it a few years ago. Silly really, but it caught on. I shouldn't have been surprised. There's many other women suffering in silence like I did."

"You might be able to help me, Mrs Blackstone. A few of the men who've appeared on your website have suffered the same fate as your husband."

"Oh, dear me. And you think I'm somehow linked?"

"That's what the evidence shows us. Did you notice anything odd or strange about anyone who came online or posted messages?"

Walker noticed that Elizabeth was beginning to relax.

"Not that I can think of. What has this got to do with John's death?"

"When did you set up the website?"

Elizabeth crossed to the window and looked out. "You'll already know if you found my name on the website."

"The killer has been using it to select their victims."

"I can't be responsible. The site is open to the public. It means any number of women could use the site for that purpose."

"So you think the killer is a woman then?"

Elizabeth turned to face him. Walker wondered whether she was aware of the shock inadvertently registered on her face. "Thank you for your help," he said smugly.

Elizabeth smiled, but it didn't reach her eyes. "Sorry, I can't be more helpful."

Walker headed towards the door but suddenly turned back. "Just one more thing."

"What?"

"Where's your computer? I don't see one here."

"It's..."

"I'll be off then. But I'll be back to talk to your daughter another time."

Chapter Thirty-Three

Truth Is Out

The sun shone brightly, reflecting off the sea in Robin Hood's Bay as Jake walked into the conservatory to find his aunt and Caroline already up and having breakfast.

"Good morning, Jacob. Did you sleep well?" Kate asked.

"Out like a light." He kissed her cheek, sat down, helping himself to a slice of toast and buttered it. "No George today, Aunt Kate?"

She gave a girlish giggle. "He's still asleep. Yesterday we bought some new plants, which he wants to put in the new flowerbed this morning, but I don't want him tiring himself out too soon. Did you have any luck in the attic?" she asked as though to change the subject. She turned to Caroline. "Can we have more fresh tea, my dear?"

"Yes, I think so, Aunt." Jake bit into his toast. "We've made an interesting discovery, but... I know you're not happy about this, Aunt. I do need to talk to Lisa King."

Kate took a small sip of tea before answering. "Don't think I don't understand your need to know, Jacob, but she suffered terribly. I don't wish her to have to relive it after all these years."

George followed Caroline into the conservatory. The cup he was carrying filled the conservatory with the aroma of coffee. "Good morning, Jacob." He placed a hand on Kate's shoulder and leaned in to kiss her cheek. "Morning my dear."

"As we said last night, George," Kate whispered.

"Aha, we thought you might, Jacob. Well, we can't stop you. Tread carefully."

"It's been twenty-six years. Time heals to a certain

degree."

"Not when you've been to hell and back."

"I'm interested in finding out what happened before they went to Albania. She's the only one who can tell me."

George took a sip of his drink and then added two spoonfuls of sugar, stirred it, and took another sip. "I take it you've found something up there." He nodded in the direction of the roof.

"We read that Cula was a last decision. I'm curious to know who their original choice was. You said that Cula was an elderly man, but the man we saw on the film was tall, 5'9 with jet-black hair and piercing dark green eyes, and aged about thirty-five to forty-five at the most."

George nodded.

"Why was there a change of plan? Who was Doctor Cula, because he wasn't the old man? The boxes, were they checked by either you, or by the Albanian police?"

Jake sensed George's hesitation as he eyed him. It was as though he was unsure of how much he could say, or even was willing to say.

"Look George, I'm a journalist. It's how I make my living. I'm fully aware that you know I'm on the hunt for a brilliant story, but this is my parents we're talking about here. From what I understand, from what you've told me. Either my parents or the programme makers messed up big time and the *Timelines* team landed up dead because of it. I have nothing to gain from digging up the past, but for me to have closure; I need to have answers to a few questions."

"Then let me start. But I'll be truthful with you, the Albanian police didn't know about Lisa, or the finds she was protecting."

Jake turned to his aunt.

Kate shook her head. "George was only doing what he thought was right."

"Our brief was to bring back the bodies, and that's what we did. We were left to get on with it by the local police. The excavation covered quite a large area, but what astonished us most was what we found at the campsite. It was untouched as though any moment, the team would walk in, sit down and chat about the day's work.

"Surely if it had been rebels…" Caroline said.

"That's what made us suspicious," George interrupted her. "Someone had slaughtered them. Vehicles stood with their keys in them, tents with personal property untouched. It didn't make sense. Like you, we knew if it had been rebels, they would've stripped the place. The day the local police took us there, they seemed uncomfortable, as if spooked. Maybe the rebels felt the same. It was while I was exploring the site on my own that I heard a whimpering coming from the ground."

"From the ground itself?" Caroline asked.

"Yes. I called some of my team over to listen. Just to be sure, I wasn't going crazy." He laughed, though there was no humour in it. "The place was starting to get to me. The smell along, with an eerie silence, it was though nature had died along with them. No bird song, even the insects were quiet. It seems absurd now, sitting round this table, but in my head, voices screamed at me to get the hell out of there.

That's when we found the hidden chamber." George lowered his head. His voice strained as though he was holding back his emotions. "I was the first to enter. The strangest part of it all was that the odd little ruin didn't seem much at first. The underground chamber must have been part of a temple. We walked around it twice. In my eyes there wasn't much to see apart from a small hole at the bottom of the wall. I shone my torch in. There wasn't any sign of it being anything other than a rat hole. We listened. We heard the sound of running water like a beck but there was another sound too, a low mournful crying.

One of my men found a narrow hole within a recess, set low down in the wall. It might've been a fireplace in the past. He pulled at the sides of the hole and found it was made of clay. He enlarged it, revealing narrow stone steps that led into an antechamber. It was pitch-black. As my torch beam fell on her face, it was like something from hell. She sat in the middle of a stench-ridden hole, rocking back and forth clutching her brother's maggot-infested body to her. Her wild eyes stared fixedly at us as she snarled like a wounded animal."

"Oh, how awful!" Caroline's hand flew to her mouth.

"Once we'd rigged up some lights in the chamber, we found she had a generator running at one time, giving her heating and lighting but the oil had run out. Your parents must have known about the chamber and used it as storage."

"How on earth did you get her out of there?" Caroline asked.

"Once we'd been able to calm her and removed her dead brother, she seemed to come out of a sort of trance, though she wasn't communicative. We bagged up bodies and placed them in wooden cases ready for transportation. The paperwork was for ten bodies. It was just a case of making up the empty wooden case with finds from the site. Lisa already sealed the metal boxes, so we had no idea what was in them. The one she opened to show us just had a child's skull and some bones. That was enough for me to see."

"So you saw one of the skulls?" Jake asked.

"Just the top. The box was padded out to protect it. Lisa said the burials contained family graves."

"Did she explain what happened?"

"Not really. I didn't want to question her, not there, not at the site. We cleared the site, got her cleaned up and headed back to England on a private plane before I had time to talk to her."

"Did she tell you anything?"

"Nothing—not another word. It was as if she was on autopilot, going through the motion. You put food in front of her and she ate, tell her to drink and she would. Time for bed and she would close her eyes. It was as though her soul had died with her brother and her cousins."

"We all hoped that she would regain her sanity, but on the few occasions we went to see her, she seemed to have deteriorated further," Kate said.

"When did you last see her?"

"About ten years ago, Jacob. We're not what you could

call caring friends, are we? We've tried to keep in contact, but the last time we saw her…" Kate shook her head. "She never made a full recovery. Her cousin Rita looks after her since her parents passed away. If you are thinking about paying her a visit, don't expect too much Jacob. You might be lucky and see her on a good day when she makes sense."

George patted Kate's hand. "Kate blames herself for not making sure she got the best care."

"You can't, Aunt. You weren't responsible for her going out to Albania."

"I should've made sure she had the best help available in England, but her parents wouldn't listen. I could've done more. I always hoped by staying in touch with her, when she recovered enough, she could've thrown some light on what happened."

"Then give me the chance to see what I can find out, Aunt."

"99 Lansdowne Road, London. But you might not be invited in."

"What do you mean?"

"You'll soon find out," George said.

Back in the attic, Jake pulled the padlock apart and opened the box. The tension tightened on Caroline's face as he pulled the wrapping out bit by bit. Jake lifted a glass box out, and gently placed it on the table.

"I can't believe it's real."

"Of course it is. You saw it on the film."

"I know, but it's not the same as seeing it with your own eyes."

Jake opened the lid.

"What are you doing?"

"Just checking." Jake lifted the skull and carefully tipped it slightly forward.

"Your mother was right. They're not an angel, but vampires!" Caroline said, as the needle-like teeth appeared.

"That's settled it. We really need to speak to Lisa."

Chapter Thirty-Four

Trip To London

Amanita used the end of her bed to support herself as she made her way to sit beside the fire. Jacob watched her. There was nothing about her appearance that told him anything other than what she had told him. Devil or angel? Was it possible, she was a vampire? The skull and the missing blood reinforced that possibility.

"You have nothing to fear, Jacob. I have no desire to sink my teeth into your neck." She looked up and smiled, flashing her pure white teeth as though making a point. "If we're going to work together, we must trust each other. The entity Bard Walker is closing in on me. I must survive and complete the task my parents started."

"Surely your parents wouldn't expect you to risk your life."

"But I must." She stood the loose garment she wore shimmered as she crossed to her bed. "I hate to lose. You have much to learn. There's danger for you too. He will not let anyone stand in his way. What drives him is the same as what drives me, a need to finish the task. Unlike me, he reads your mind as well as your emotions. He feeds on your fears and anxieties. It makes him grow stronger."

"Why me? What danger am I to him?"

"At the moment, none, but you are useful to him. Through you, he has found me. He sought you out, Jacob, as he has me. After destroying our parents, we are his unfinished business. I should have trusted you sooner."

"You knew who I was, when I first saw you at the nightclub?"

She nodded. "Now we must talk about how we are going

191

to stop Bard Walker from finding the missing gold boxes."

"I have an address for Miss King. I'm just off to London as I believe she's still in possession of the boxes."

"Then I shall come with you. Please do not look so surprised, Jacob. I promise not to turn to ash in the fading sunlight. You really need to forget your preconceived ideas."

While Jake waited in the kitchen for Amanita to get ready, he pondered the relationship Elizabeth had with Amanita. He tried to imagine what it must be like knowing the person you're caring for isn't aging but you are.

"I am ready, Jacob," a voice behind him called.

Jake let out his breath slowly. She was stunning and he was lucky enough to be out on a date with her. Amanita was dressed in a charcoal-grey cropped-jacket trouser-suit with flat shoes. He grinned at her as they made their way through to the garage.

"Is there something wrong?" She picked up her small shoulder bag and keys.

"Nothing at all."

She cocked her head to one side and studied him.

"Hey, no cheating," Jake said, aware that she could be reading his mind. "Please allow me to have some thoughts to myself."

"All right, but only if you drive." Amanita tossed him the key to her car.

"Me drive that?" The slinky inky black Aston Martin V12 Vanquish gleamed before him.

"Yes. I need a little longer to recover." She opened the passenger door.

Jake eyed her suspiciously. "Are you sure you'll be all right?"

"I'm tougher than I look."

"Can I ask you a stupid question?"

She nodded.

"Please explain why donated blood is so bad for you, when you drink it anyway?"

Amanita fastened her safety belt.

"Sin, Jacob." The blood Elizabeth supplies has been purified. I feed on sin, and the donated blood doesn't contain enough for me to feed on. Digesting it leaves me weaker than normal, so I need longer to rest."

Jake started the engine and the garage doors slid open. As sunlight filled the space, Amanita seemed to blink through the windows were tinted. It took Jake a moment to adjust to the car's interior. Driving at night was one thing, but to drive in a stygian interior while sunlight bathed the exterior seemed odd even to him.

"Don't worry. You'll soon get used to it. This Lisa we're going to see, what can you tell me about her?"

Jake handed some photos to Amanita before driving out of the garage. "She survived the attack which killed my parents. Somehow she hid herself among the ruins with the finds from the dig."

Amanita flicked through the snapshots of the team members and stopped at the picture of the gold boxes. "Do you think she'll still have them?"

"No idea. We mustn't expect too much from this visit. But we might get lucky."

Late afternoon moved swiftly into early evening as they travelled south. The roads were clear of any delays until they hit the outskirts of London.

"This is why I hate coming to the city— too much bloody traffic! Jake sighed. "Keep an eye out for junction twenty-five."

"What's the name of the road we're looking for?"

"Lansdowne Road. What the hell?" Jake swore as another car pulled out in front of them.

"I hope it doesn't take us too long to find it," Amanita said as the sat nav barked out its commands. "Ahh, is that the road there?" she pointed.

Much to the annoyance of the other drivers, Jake slowed as Amanita studied the house numbers.

"Now what's that idiot trying to do?" Jake shouted as the car behind them lost patience, flashed and sounded its horn before squealing past them.

"I think this is it, Jacob. How odd. It doesn't look inhabited."

In the fading light, on the noisy street, they studied the large Victorian town house. What once stood grandly out from the rest of the houses, with its ornate stonework and cast-iron decorative balcony, now stood in need of attention. Grass and weeds filled the paint-peeling guttering. The front door and the boarded-up windows were covered in graffiti showing gothic, ghostly images of shadowy figures emerging from a mist interspersed with symbols and Celtic signs.

Amanita opened the gate into a weed-choked garden. "You're sure you spoke to someone that lives here?"

"Yes."

At the door, she searched for a bell, gave up, and then tried knocking. Jake moved away from the doorway when an upstairs window in the house next door opened. A large, rough hand pulled back the billowing, faded curtains, as a huge, black, middle-aged woman's face appeared. "You'll have no luck there, love. Them ain't Jehovah Witnesses, just a couple of bloody weirdoes."

Jake beamed at the woman. "May I ask, are you a believer? We've travelled many miles to spread the good Lord's name. May we come and speak with you instead?"

A shocked expression appeared on the woman's face and her head disappeared as someone in the house shouted something at her. The window suddenly slammed shut.

"What a welcoming place London is. What would you have done if she had said yes?"

"I would've gone round to see if I could find out anything about our friend Lisa."

Amanita knocked again and bent to listen at the door. "Someone's coming this time."

The sounds of keys and the rattle of chains echoed through the door and then it opened to a sliver. A single, red eye blinked slowly at them.

Jake smiled at the eye. "Hello, are you, Rita? I'm Jacob

194

Eldritch. We spoke last night..."

The eye blinked, narrowed, and then cut him off in mid-sentence as the door slammed shut.

"I don't know about you, Amanita, but I could murder that woman for a cup of bloody tea," Jake said with a heavy sigh. "I'm beginning to think her neighbour was right."

"No, she isn't," said a sharp voice. "I'm more than happy to make you a cup of tea. Would you like to come in?" A petite, dark eyed woman held the door open.

Jake and Amanita entered a large, vividly painted hallway. The light was almost blinding with its brightness. Amanita slipped her hand into her bag and brought out a pair of sunglasses. Concerned, Jake touched her arm. She nodded. "I need to cover my eyes because they're daylight bulbs."

"Wait here please." Rita snapped, relocking the front door. "You can't be too careful. They're everywhere and out to get everyone who knows, you know."

"Sorry, I'm not sure what you mean," Jake said.

Rita rolled her eyes. "Please. No more stupid questions. Thank you. This way please." She scurried off down the narrow corridor.

"Touchy, isn't she?" Jake whispered. He looked over his shoulder and saw a faint redness appearing on Amanita's cheeks and the back of her hands. "Are you okay?"

"Not really. But I hope she isn't using these bulbs in the rest of the house."

Finally Rita pushed open a door and pointed a long finger at them. "You," she said to Jake. "Sit there. And you sit over there." She gestured Amanita to an old chair in the corner of the shabby living room. She smiled smugly and left her guests alone.

"What's going on here?" Jake asked.

"She's very frightened." Amanita rose and wandered about the room.

"She'll tell you off."

Amanita smiled at Jake, and then went back to studying the collection of leather-bound religious books in a large glass fronted cupboard, an odd mixture of Christian based religions, Paganism, Eastern philosophy, and the Occult.

"What's so interesting?" Jake surveyed the untidy room with mild interest.

"For a lady who isn't in tune with reality, she has an interesting collection of books."

Jake studied the back of Amanita's head as she squatted before the cabinet. Her white hair covered most of her narrow back. Less than twenty-four hours ago he would have thought she was dying after coughing up so much blood.

"I cannot believe they have a copy of The Sermons of the Master by Samuel Hieron. My father purchased a copy when it was first published in 1624…" Amanita reached into the cabinet just as the door opened. Rita entered, carrying a tray. On finding Amanita with the cabinet door open, she screamed. "Lady, you've no right to touch things. Now, please, sit down!"

Jake took the tea tray from Rita and placed it on the table. "Oh, you've only brought three cups in?"

"I'm sorry, but it looks as though you've come a long way for nothing," Rita said, all smiles.

"Isn't Lisa here then?" Jake bit back in a harsh tone, his voice rising.

Rita poured the tea into a fine, bone china cup, placed it on a matching saucer, before passing it to Amanita. "Is the tea to your satisfaction, lady?"

Amanita smiled and then sipped her tea. "This is very good, thank you. How is your cousin, Rita? Well I hope?"

"You'll have to forgive my cousin. You're aware she was the only survivor of a dreadful situation? She has good days, but mostly bad days. And today is a bad day, so your journey is a wasted one. Enjoy your tea." Rita grinned at them, her mouth a red slit.

Jake smiled broadly. Rita, clown-like, returned Jake's smile, but it didn't reach her overly painted eyes. Jake guessed her to be between her late forties and middle fifties. She wore her dyed auburn hair piled up with light, wispy strands that hung in soft ringlets around her oval face. Her large eyes stared out through thick layers of green and blue make up.

"I was eighteen when my cousins died." Rita spoke more to herself than her two guests. "I don't remember much about what went on. The adults were more worried about Lisa than me. No one knew what had happened to them." She continued in the same monotone pitch. "When the search party finally got there, they found everyone dead. Well, they weren't, were they, because Lisa was alive. Only they didn't know it at the time, did they?"

Jake wanted to ask a question, but her glare stopped him.

"Don't interrupt me," she snapped. "For once, someone will hear me out! I've spent years looking after her." She pointed to the ceiling. "For years, everyone wanted to listen to *her*, not me. I'm not *her* bloody servant?"

"Rita, we just want to ask Lisa some important questions and then we'll be gone."

"It's my turn to speak!"

"I'm sorry but we don't have much time…"

Rita leaned back, folded her arms across her narrow chest, and said, "Then you better go now."

Jake and Amanita sat on the edge of their seats and waited.

Chapter Thirty-Five

Seekers Of The Dark

"When Lisa arrived home from the hospital she locked herself away, wouldn't talk to anyone but herself. We thought she'd gone mad. She talked a lot of mumbo-jumbo about the Dark and the Destroyers. No one believed her, but you will." Rita turned her narrowing eyes onto Amanita. "You're not like us, are you? You're a sin seeker."

"How did you know?" Amanita asked.

"You've come seeking the Dark, haven't you?" Without waiting for an answer, Rita's attention was on Jake. "She isn't mad, you know. They're here, and she's seen them."

A door slammed somewhere upstairs, and Jake and Amanita looked up. The sound of footsteps on bare floorboards could be heard. Rita moved quickly, but not quick enough as the door burst open. A tall, thin woman entered, dressed in a faded white t-shirt and brown creased trousers. She mumbled incoherently while twisting the ends of her greying, blond hair. Her watery blue eyes glanced anxiously about until they came to rest on the two strangers. She timidly took a step backward.

Jake thought for a brief second that she might flee in terror. He stood and held out his hand. "Hello Lisa. I'm Jake Eldritch. My father was Robert, and my mother was..."

"You're here. At last!" Lisa's eyes brightened. "I've waited so long..." She turned to Rita, her voice raised an octave. "Why didn't you tell me?" Her face hardened as her eyes narrowed. "There is so much to tell him and so little time."

"Yeah, yeah," Rita snapped, child-like. "So you keep telling me. Year in, year out until I was sick of it. When Jacob comes! When Jacob comes, it's all over!"

Lisa flicked a dismissing hand at her cousin. "Please make some drinks. Thank you."

Rita shrugged and glared pure hatred at her guests. She gathered up the dirty cups and stomped through to the kitchen. A thin unnerving smile crossed Lisa's sunken face as she clasped Jake's hand and led him to the sofa. "How's Kate?"

"Kate is fine. She sends her best wishes." Jake caught a slight whiff of something lingering on Lisa's breath, but put it down to her just getting out of bed along with her unkempt appearance.

"I begged her to bring you to me so long ago. She kept telling me you were too young."

"Kate did what she thought was best." Jake tried to free his hand from hers as a slight stinging sensation travelled along his fingertips.

"I knew you would come seeking the truth. Have you seen the film yet?"

"Yes. How did you know?" Jake creased his nostrils as he caught another whiff of her breath. An image of decay and stagnant water filled his mind. He turned towards Amanita who nodded and smiled encouragingly. "Lisa, we've come to ask you about a Doctor Cula who worked with my father."

Lisa's face twisted. Her eyes widened unnaturally and rolled back in their sockets. The tingling in his fingers increased to a stabbing pain. Lisa's long talon-like nails clawing at the backs of his hands as she arched her back. Jake felt a surge of a dark physical energy course up his arms. Panic rose in his gut as she increased her painful grip on his hands. As blood oozed between her fingertips, an uncontrollable shiver racked his body, and the darkness swamped his mind, taking control.

Suddenly, in the confusion, his mind cleared as his panic subsided. The darkness seemed to lose its grip, and he became aware of another physical energy coursing through his body. Then he heard a soft, gentle voice summoning him to the light. "Jacob, I'm here." Instantly his hands were free.

Lisa sprung forward, snarled in his face, her breath putrid. "No one escapes the Dark. They'll find you in the end."

"Lisa," Amanita said, her voice, soft and as light as a butterfly's wings. "They found you too?"

She blinked, seemingly aware of Amanita. "No, they didn't," she said, haughtily. "I'm too clever. They killed my twin brother."

"We know. We're sorry for your loss. Can you tell us what happened to the gold boxes?" Amanita asked.

She giggled, her eyes flat and unblinking. "The soul boxes? I hid them. Doctor Cula says... No loose ends."

"Where did Cula come from, Lisa?" Jake rubbed at the backs of his hands.

"He didn't travel with us. About the second day, he appeared. Darkness for souls. Two more with him. They never spoke just stared into our souls."

"Were they carrying guns?"

"Guns?" A dark shadow crossed Lisa's face. She stood transfixed, something dark stirred within her memory. Then she collapsed in a heap holding her head. Mumbling, she rocked side to side.

Jake bent to help her, but Amanita stopped him.

"Guns! Stay Lisa! Ban... Gary finds you. Playing hide and seek. Mustn't let the bad people take the secret, mustn't find the angels." Torment flicked across her skeletal face as she stared blankly. Her long grey hair hung around her face like a faded veil as heavy lines appeared around her sunken eyes and mouth. She rocked slowly, hugging herself tightly. "Please, God, I want to die too!" She banged her fist on the floor. In a sudden sweeping movement, she cradled an unseen object in her arms, whispering, "Gary, talk to me!" With a sudden jerk of her body, she stood trembling. A low moan escaped from her followed by an ear-piercing scream as she stared down at her shaking hands. "Blood! Oh sweet Jesus. Too much blood."

Amanita placed a hand on Lisa's arm. Lisa's face softened

as though all her torment had left her. "Where are the gold boxes, can you tell me?"

"They're in my special room. I've been looking after them until Jacob comes."

"Can you show me?"

"Show you?" Lisa arched her brow. "I've something important I must tell my son first." She took Jake's hand again. "You must understand, my son."

"I'm not your…"

"Wait and listen," Amanita shushed Jake.

"Our time is short," Lisa said in a low, fevered voice. "The Dead Sea Scrolls told us what the Bible didn't. Eve never betrayed Adam. His betrayal opened her eyes. He fathered children with an angel, betraying his creator and her. The Father punished the disloyal angel and forgave Adam. The children of the union worshipped the Father with love. After many years, a war broke out in heaven. The Father's elite angels, a symbol of the purest of light and love, betrayed him by fornicating with the children of Adam and Eve. This time, The Father did not forgive.

Angered by his punishment, the Fallen Ones bestowed the knowledge of plants and herbal medicines, incantations, weapons and warfare along with arts and sciences to humanity. Within the knowledge was the key to not only our destruction, but to the destruction of the once peaceful world the Father had created. We cried out in pain for his help, and he sent forth the Archangel Uriel to warn Noah of the flood to cleanse the world of its sins."

Her breathing deepened and with trembling lips, she went on. "By now, evil had spread its wings too far across the world. The seed of man's self-destruction had become part of his own making. Cast out of heaven, the angels walked among us in the shadows of darkness while bearing the mark of the first betrayers the serpent. To free themselves from their punishment, they must first free us from our sins by feeding off them to regain their birthright. To do this, they bring to us the eternal sleep of the damned."

She released Jake's hands and fell back. "I must go now,

my son. Beware of the Dark for he walks in the light and carries the darkness." She gasped as her eyes rolled back. "Seek out the soulless ones Jacob and find the gold boxes." Lisa shook violently, arching her back.

"No!" Amanita shouted. "The boxes, Lisa, where are they?

"She's fitting! Quick phone for a doctor!" Jake leapt forwards, pulling Lisa to the floor, and laying her flat on her back. He leant over her and listened for her heartbeat. He pushed down in an effort to resuscitate her, and watched in horror as thick red, congealing goo oozed out of her mouth and fell in large droplets to the floor, scenting the air with blood and decay. "Oh my God. She's bleeding!" Jake continued to compress her chest.

"Jacob, stop! There's nothing we can do. She's been dead too long."

"Make the call, Amanita! There's a chance she can be saved."

Jake counted and then pushed. Suddenly a cracking sound echoed around him and his hands disappeared into Lisa's chest cavity. Shocked, he moved back and stared down at his red dusty hands. Before him, Lisa's body twitched and pulsated as though alive. Fine lines scurried around her eyes and mouth forcing them open.

For a brief second, Lisa's grinning death head smiled knowingly at Jake as decay etched away her features. Jake, unable to move, watched as death consumed her body. "What's happening?"

"Time's catching up with her, Jacob. I knew when she entered the room that she possessed someone else's soul."

"She called me son?"

"Your mother's love was strong, Jacob."

"My mother's soul has been here, waiting for me all these years, why?"

Before Amanita could answer, the door banged open.

"Here you are, cousin." Rita held out the tray. She stood transfixed, taking in the brightly lit room as Jake knelt beside her cousin's rapidly disintegrating body. The tray crashed to the floor, sending shards of milky, brown teapot and delicate china in all directions. Rita fled from the room, with Amanita close behind her. Jake followed. "Rita, wait!" The dark corridor seemed to shimmer ahead of them as Rita turned a corner, and slammed a door shut.

Amanita touched the door lightly, calling out, "Do not be afraid, Rita. Please open the door. We need your help."

"You're the dark ones! What have you done to my cousin?" she whined.

"No! I am a seeker, remember." Amanita pleaded. "I need one of the gold boxes. Please help me, Rita, to return to the Kingdom of my father."

"Are you really a lost angel?" Rita said, catching her breath.

"Yes. The Dark killed my parents. Please help me."

The door swung open revealing a myriad of portraits inside. In the flickering candlelight, Amanita saw hundreds of snapshots of Jacob's mother plastered across all the walls. They depicted Charlotte kneeling, walking, talking, and working. In the centre, black satin drapery surrounded a large photo of her holding up one of the fanged skulls. Below it, a makeshift altar covered in a black satin cloth that reached to the floor. On the altar, two large ornate candlesticks stood either side of an empty glass dome. The room had a feeling of reverence, but Amanita felt the dark forces skulking in the shadows. It crept along the floor engulfing everything it touched. Part of her screamed to leave now but Rita's mutterings brought her to her senses.

"Angel or no angel... you can't come in here," Rita wailed. "Lisa's special room!"

"What the fuck's going on here?" Jake appeared in the doorway.

"What have you done to Lisa? Not angels, you're the bad people!

"Listen. Look into my eyes, Rita. Tell me what you see," Amanita said.

"Please don't hurt me." Rita lowered her tear-stained eyes.

"Where are the gold boxes?"

"How did you know about them?" Rita whispered.

"Lisa said you would help me if I asked you."

She shook her head. "She told me I'm not to show anyone. They're special. I need to ask her first."

"Please help me."

"No!" From nowhere, Rita produced a large ornate knife and pointed it at them. Jake pulled Amanita aside, but she blocked him.

"Put it down. You've nothing to fear from us," Amanita said.

"I want to see her now." Rita lowered the knife, but her voice, soft and questioning, betrayed an underlying current of guilt that hung in the room.

"In a little while. First the box. Where is it?"

"As soon as I've asked Lisa. She'll be very cross with me if I don't."

Amanita placed a hand lightly on Rita's shoulder. Rita looked at it, studying the slender, pale fingers, before making eye contact. Amanita smiled softly, and Rita saw Lisa looking at her.

"You've done a good job. No one else could have done better. But you need to tell them where the box has gone."

"Oh no… Lisa, I'm so sorry. I had to…It wasn't my fault. We'd run out of money. I thought we'd get lots for it, but…"

"You fucking sold it?" Jake exploded.

The room filled with a demonic scream as Rita lunged at Jake with the knife.

Amanita bared her fangs, knocked Rita to the floor and swooped down sinking her teeth into her neck. Rita let out a yelp, writhing under Amanita's weight, kicking her legs out, and knocking Jake backwards as he tried to hold her down.

"It's gone—gone for good!" she shrieked.

Jake felt a surge of energy move through Rita's flailing body as the light in the room dipped. Her wild laughter soon died away and she became still. Amanita sat back, her ragged breathing steadying.

Jake studied her.

Amanita sensed his shock and blinked slowly as she ran her tongue around her lips, wiping a thin trickle of blood away. "Sorry. I could not allow such evil to possess her."

A sudden flare of brilliant light enlightened them to the presence of something else in the room. Jake pulled himself off the floor and inhaled deeply. "Something's burning."

On the altar, one of the candles lay on its side. Flames licked the wall in all directions as they engulfed the satin cloth and photographs. Jake tried to douse them, but the growing heat held him back.

"Get out of here now!" He pulled Rita's body towards the door.

"Jacob, she's dead. Leave her. You must come now."

Thick black acrid smoke spread into the corridor. Coughing, Jake stared at Amanita who seemed unaffected by the smoke though black ash already stained her face and hair. As if she read his mind, she said, "Bring her, if you feel the need to explain her death to the police." Then she disappeared around the corner.

Jake dropped the body. His attention drawn to his mother's twisted, distorted, and fading features as the heat reclaimed her. He tore at the photos closest to him, stuffing them into his pocket.

Amanita ran along the smoke-filled hallway, and ducked into the kitchen, just as the lights began to flicker. She turned back to see where Jake was and saw flames escaping from another room. "Come on! We must leave now!" she shouted.

"I'm coming. You get out!" he shouted back.

Amanita grabbed a tea cloth, soaked it, and held it to her face. As she passed the sitting room doorway, amid the flickering orange glow, shafts of silver light caught her attention. They were coming from Lisa's brain cavity. Amanita rubbed at her stinging eyes with the damp cloth and dropped to her knees. She pushed her fingers through the translucent skull and plucked out the bullet that had lodged in Lisa's brain twenty-six years ago. As she withdrew her fingers, the husk of Lisa crumbled to dust. Amanita popped the bullet into her pocket and hurried to the front door.

The acrid smoke seeping through the house was starting to make her cough. She wrapped the wet cloth around her head to cover her mouth and nose while trying to unlock one of the many chains and bolts fastening the door. As another lock clicked open, she tried to pull the chain free.

"Jacob, where are you?" she called. The burning in her throat stifled her shout. She listened and could hear him coughing and gasping for air. Dropping to her knees, she crawled towards him as overhead a light bulb blinked out leaving her in darkness.

Chapter Thirty-Six

Filmmaker

The garage door slowly lifted to reveal Elizabeth standing in the shadows. As the car came to a halt beside her, the passenger door swung open revealing Jake slumped in the seat. Amanita killed the engine and emerged, her hair and face blackened by smoke and ash.

"Oh, Elizabeth, so good to see you." She coughed and brushed her hair back from her face. "Please help me get Jacob out."

"What's happened to him? I've been so worried. Hope came here to warn you."

"We got into some difficulties when Jacob and I followed up on a lead on some gold boxes."

Between them, they half carried and dragged him through to the sofa in the parlour. "You go and get cleaned up. I'll make him comfortable and give him something to drink," Elizabeth said, unlacing his shoes.

"He's an amazing man. Do you not think so, Elizabeth?"

Elizabeth smiled and winked.

"No, Elizabeth, I know what you are thinking but I'm far too old for him," Amanita said laughing as she left the room

Tired but somewhat refreshed after a shower and a change of clothes, Amanita found Elizabeth in the kitchen. "How is he?"

"Much better now. He's had some tea, but is desperate to go home and get out of his smoky clothes. You're both very lucky."

The heavily-curtained windows showed no signs that the

day outside was in full swing now. Most early risers were enjoying the promise of a beautiful day ahead as the clouds broke over the ruined abbey on East Cliff. Inside the dark room, Jake sat studying the large painting of Amanita and her parents. On hearing the sound of Amanita's voice he stood as she and Elizabeth entered the room. "Oh, I thought you would be asleep."

"How are you, Jacob?"

"I've had better days."

"We've a problem." Elizabeth said. "I think you need to sit down, Amanita."

"Then we have two problems," Jake said.

"What's happened?" Amanita asked.

"Walker's been to my house looking for Hope, but he also questioned me about John. He knows about the website and that's what led him to me."

Amanita lowered herself stiffly on to the soft white leather sofa. In slow, agonising movements, she rubbed her face. "I think I will need to face my demon."

"You can't do that!" Elizabeth gasped. "It's too dangerous. You'll have to move, go to your other house."

"No, I shall not be driven from my home by him. My parents would not have wanted me to."

"Amanita." Elizabeth's voice softened. "Your father was always aware that the time would come when you would have to. That's why he put things into position for your safety."

"I do not want to be alone, nor running away. There must be something I can do to finish this once and for all."

"Maybe there is something I can do to help. I have a contact within the police force. An ex-copper, I'm sure he'll know a few contacts. I'll find out all I can about Walker. It might give us an insight into the best way to deal with him. You rest now, and I'll be back later after I've had a rest and shower, too."

"Thank you, my friend."

Jake leaned over and kissed her gently on the forehead. With a nod to Elizabeth he said, "I'll show myself out."

***

Well-rested but hungry, Amanita checked out her website. Paging through the latest golden rats, she paused and ran her tongue across her lips as one name leapt out at her. She and the filmmaker had some unfinished business.

The night club heaved and pulsed to the beat of the music, though no one was dancing.

Amanita sat at the bar, sipping a glass of bittersweet wine. Its taste made no difference to her whether the grapes were ripened on the hillside in Tuscany or not. All she needed it for was to keep up the appearance that she was drinking alone.

She watched her target. Marco Le Bianco greeted the men with firm handshakes and kissed the giggling scantily dressed young women on their fresh cheeks. Bianco was an elegant dresser in his dark suit and open-necked shirt. His hair showed no signs of greying, though he was much older than he appeared.

Finally, he looked her way and greeted her with a nod and a smile. Cocky and so self-assured, Amanita thought, as she set her glass down. For the first time in her long life, she felt nervous and wondered why the giggling young women didn't sense the danger too. Bianco wasn't the only one lying about his age she realised as she studied the girls.

"Good evening my amore," Bianco said with his false accent, brushing his thick hair back with a sweep of his hand. "You are very bel-lo... how do you say, err beautiful my amore."

His smile told Amanita far more than he realised. He wasn't Italian. His mother's side maybe, but he had never been to the land of his ancestors.

She giggled and lowered her eyes. Men like Bianco loved being in control, which was why they hunted out girls. They didn't see themselves as paedophiles and nor did the law, but still they destroyed girls' lives with their promises of stardom and excitement. Amanita made eye contact. By staring into her victim's eyes she could be sure that the dark wasn't lurking there ready to destroy her. The fact was the Dark had no soul. It didn't matter how much evil resided within the souls of men; they could always be saved.

Bianco's eyes sparkled with excitement as he picked up her glass. The game of seduction had begun. "Let me refill your glass, my amore, then we can talk business."

"Business?"

"With your looks, my sweet, you could go far. Come, work with me."

"Doing what?"

"Let me get that drink first and then we can go somewhere a little quieter." He winked at her before disappearing around the side of the bar.

Amanita perused the crowd. On her website, the girl's words echoed within her psyche. "*I'm finding life difficult that no one believes me. I can't find the words or anything tangible to show them what has happened to me. It's just vague shapes, feelings, lost time, and ultimate horror of not knowing who he was, and at any time or place he could be standing next to me in the street, in a crowd, in a shop or when I'm at a party with friends. I'm too frightened to go out now.*"

Amanita watched Bianco at the bar, sensing him hesitating as he passed his hand over her drink. Turning from the bar, he moved towards her, beaming.

"I don't think I've ever seen such a beautiful woman in my nightclub before," he said, setting her glass before her. "Come upstairs to my office. We can get to know each other a little more, my amore."

As she took a sip of the wine, she nodded. "Show me the way."

"It is good, is it not?" He gestured with a nod to the glass she held. "I like my ladies to drink the best Italy has to offer." He took her hand lightly in his and led them through a door marked private. He smiled reassuringly at her as he led her up a narrow staircase at the back of the building.

Amanita paused for a moment, held on to the banister, and fiddled with the thin strap on her shoe, giving herself time to look around for another exit. At the top of the stairs, Bianco waited for her. "Bella donna, don't look so nervous. I will not hurt such a beautiful lady. Come through here, my amore." He held a door open and ushered her in. "I find it so relaxing up here after the hustle and bustle. It's my own little quiet place."

The room was simply decorated, with white walls and large unframed Japanese landscapes. A pair of white leather sofas faced each other and between them was a dark wooden coffee table. One wall was dominated by a huge picture window with a view of Scarborough's harbour outlined in a ring of brightly-coloured lights that sparkled off the water in the bay.

A little unsteady on her feet, Amanita dropped onto one of the sofas. "Wow, it must be beautiful in here during daytime, if the night view is anything to go by." She stifled a yawn.

Bianco grinned. "Please relax. Then I shall be back to give you my full attention. I'm waiting on an important email." He switched on his computer.

Amanita nodded and rocked gently as she cradled her drink.

"Are you okay?" His fingers clicked rapidly across the keys.

"I feel a little odd." She creased her brow and rubbed her forehead.

"It's probably just the change in temperature after the hot dance floor."

"Hmm, it could be." She set her glass down and undid her jacket.

"Here, let me join you in a drink. Silly me, I forgot to bring one with me. Never mind, I've plenty here." He winked and opened a cupboard behind his desk, set a tumbler down and poured a drink. He laughed and gestured to a small cupboard. "I even have a few nibbles for when we're hungry."

"Do you bring many others here?"

"No. I'm shocked you could think such a thing!" He sat next to her and placed an arm around her shoulder. "You fill my heart with beauty. I've never seen such hypnotic green eyes before. You've stopped my heart, my amore. I've fallen in love with you and want to own you." He stood and turned his back to her. "You don't understand the passion you're creating in me with your beauty. If you were a glass, I would gladly drink from you." He turned around and dropped to one knee, his eyes blazed with his passion, he hoped. "With your dark Latin looks, we're made for each other. Drink up, my amore. We must put this beautiful night to shame with our excellent lovemaking. For I wish more than anything, my amore, is to find the passionate fire that burns within you." He handed her glass to her. "Let us drink to a night of love."

Amanita swallowed the rest of the wine as Bianco gathered the empty glasses and took them back to his cupboard.

"I need to go. Sorry, but I don't feel very well, Marco."

"Oh, my amore, let me call you a taxi."

Chapter Thirty-Seven

The Hunter Becomes The Hunted

Amanita squinted at Bianco. He stood holding his phone to the side of his face. The more she tried to focus on his voice, the more he seemed to be everywhere. She felt the drink trickle from the corner of her mouth, and slumped sideward, burying her head into a pile of cushions.

"My amore, my amore?" Bianco called softly. There was no longer any concern in his voice as he pushed her hair from her face. Amanita's eyes moved rapidly under pale eyelids. Bianco ran his fingertips over her cheek; her skin seemed to glow where he touched it. He pulled Amanita up into a sitting position and slipped her jacket off. The tightness of her white silk blouse pulled taut against the shape of her firm breasts, outlining her dark erect nipples. Unable to resist, Bianco ran his hand over them and pinched her nipples. Satisfied, she was under the influence of the drug; he gathered her up and carried her to the cupboard. With a slight kick of his foot, the back of the cupboard swung out.

The secret room would have put even a high-class brothel to shame. At its centre, a heart shaped king-size bed with heavy drapes of black and mauve cascaded from the ceiling down either side, while covering the bed white satin sheets flowed to the floor.

Bianco lay Amanita onto the bed, and then went back to collect her jacket and handbag. He closed the cupboard doors and pushed the back of the cupboard into place. He sat on the edge of the bed and emptied out her bag. To his relief he found that it contained nothing more than a lipstick, car keys, and a mobile phone, no recording device. Though, he was puzzled by no credit cards or purse. He tried to check the phone, hoping to find some form of identification, even pictures of friends and family. Most of the girls he'd picked up had pictures on their phone, some had taken unknown photos of him, but this one was locked. He shrugged, deciding she was worth taking the risk. He gathered up her belongings and dropped them back into the bag. Behind a wooden screen, Bianco typed a few words into a computer. After a second, he typed another sequence of numbers then went to check on Amanita. She lay on her side, her hair covering her face. One arm lay close to her body while the other was stretched across the fat satin pillows. She moaned softly as he rolled her onto her back. Her jet-black hair against the pillows excited him as he straddled her and peeled off her clothes. Bianco manoeuvred her body towards the centre of the bed and directly under the overhead camera before clearing away her discarded clothes.

Back at his computer, he checked all the cameras were working. Then a ping sounded letting him know what he was waiting for had arrived. He opened another small screen on his main computer and typed in the numbers given on the email before deleting it. In less than a second a messaging box opened.

'*Hello my dear friend,*' Bianco typed in

'*Marco, what have you got for me?*' the reply came.

'*A real beauty. Check your view.*'

'*Yes, yes lovely to look at, but that's not what we want. Your last one didn't really get me the excitement. Are you giving them a little too much of my magic? There's no fight left in them. We want to see their fear as they fight for their life. Now that's entertainment,*' the man replied.

'*This one will excite you, I promise. Why not feel the thrill for yourself?*'

'*You're asking too many questions, Marco. I'm not the sort of man you should be questioning.*'

'*I'm sorry, Mr Drysalter…*'

'*Don't use my name or take liberties with me. Remember your club was just a shit-hole until we met.*'

214

'Please accept my apologies.' Bianco opened the camera for live screening. Amanita lay as he had left her. *'Tonight you'll witness something special, I promise. Is she not a real stunner, maybe too good for you to share? Why not watch the action now?'*

'No, just send the film over once you've finished. Don't let me down, Marco. I'm becoming a little bored with your performance. Maybe it's time for us to part company, old friend. All good things must come to an end.'

'What do you mean?'

'I think you know. My customers enjoy seeing the fire in the young girls' eyes and the passion in their hearts when you take them, but your magic spoils our fun. Enough said.' Drysalter cut the link.

Bianco stared at the blinking cursor. "Old friend indeed. What did he know?" Though, he had never met the man, he knew enough about his sort. Like all of his other customers, they were hideously rich, fat old men with too much to lose if caught in the act with young, vulnerable girls. They enjoyed watching his firm, taut body entering the girls on their behalf while they fantasised.

Maybe it was time to get out, Bianco reasoned as he enlarged the screen. Take the money he'd stashed away and go abroad. What they expected no longer excited him, but turned his stomach. Once upon a time he was a seducer, making the girls believe they shared something special that they came back for more. Unbeknown to them, he controlled the cameras that filmed everything they did for an audience, but now a darker side had crept in.

One thing to give them drugs, to subdue them, allowing them to enjoy him as much as he enjoyed them, but to see the fear in their faces, and the madness in their eyes as they tried to escape the insanity in their minds, no, he hated that. It was one thing to rape their body, but their minds too, that was too much for him.

Back in the soundproof room, Bianco dimmed the lights and put on the soft music. If the girl wanted to scream with pleasure she could. Now dressed in black leather jeans, he pulled her into a seated position and forced her legs open. She swayed a little as he placed his hand between her legs, pushing his probing fingers hard into her.

"Now, my little pussycat, we're going to have some fun, so I want you to make some noise." He tilted her head back. "My fans will love you, my darling. Let's show them how good you really are."

Bianco wasn't sure who was more shocked, him or his camera. The girl's eyes snapped open, and he stared into the abyss of some unearthly creature. His erection melted away as her small hands gripped the top of his arms. In a sweeping movement, she pinned him onto his back. Fear caused a stream of urine to flow down his leg as he watched her jaw expand. Two bright drops of blood appeared in her gum line. Transfixed, Bianco saw two white tips come into view. He struggled against her as she leant into him and sunk her fangs into his throat. A blinding light filled his mind followed by a feeling of utter peace.

Amanita pumped in her drug of pleasure. With delight, she fed hungrily on his evil silencing the voices of the young girls who begged for their lives. She drew back and wiped the blood from her lips.

In the mirror above them, Bianco stared in wonderment while Amanita robbed him of his life. What a way to go at the hands of such a small, perfectly formed creature, he thought, while admiring the narrowness of her waist, the curve of her white buttocks, and the defined muscles in her back.

Amanita slid off the bed, stretched her arms, and arched her back before moving across the room. Bianco realised he wasn't dead. As the initial shock left his body numbness overtook. He tried to make sense of what was happening, retribution fluttered around his head.

In the small room off the main stage, Amanita sat before the screen. "So this is your little game, Marco." The live link flickered as Amanita's fingers danced across the keyboard. Three other small screens appeared. The faces of the customers in their darkened rooms had a look of puzzlement as they sat holding their flaccid cocks. The show they had expected hadn't materialised, what they witnessed held their fascination.

Their stud walked towards a dishevelled bed his muscles shone taut in the soft light. The camera loved him and seemed to know when to zoom in and pan round for the best shots. Close up, Bianco caressed his oiled body, sliding his hands easily over rippling chest muscles down over his abdomen and zoomed in for a close up as he slowly unzipped his leather jeans, pulling out his engorged cock. The ceiling camera swept in as Bianco pulled at the bed and held nothing up.

It recorded him saying aloud. "Now my little pussycat..."

On the video, Amanita saw utter confusion on his face when he found himself sprawled rag doll-like on his back looking up at himself in the ceiling mirror. After clicking a few keys, she hit the delete button. It didn't matter that she was invisible, but it was all the other unsuspecting girls whose pictures and films appeared on the computer hard-drive she worried about. She was, she knew, too late to stop them being watched by thousands of men.

She picked up her bag and checked her phone. A text from Jacob, letting her know he was heading over to Walker's and would catch her later. She dressed quickly, ready to finish her business and went through to where Bianco lay paralysed.

"Be prepared to meet thy maker, my amore. Do not forget to say hello to your old friend, Charles Keys." She laughed. Recognition was clearly visible in the man's eyes on hearing his friend's name. Overhead, the mirror reflected her final glistening kiss as she opened her mouth. Bianco saw the light glint off her extended teeth as she leaned in and sunk them into his neck. The unexpected peace left him as the darkness closed in.

In her car, Amanita slid off her shoes and stretched her toes. She laughed at her silly thought about being too old for creeping around back alleyways. In her special mirror, she was able to check her make-up and refreshed her lipstick. On starting her car she wondered how long it would be until someone found the hidden room.

On pulling out of the side street, she caught sight of a car in her rear-view mirror. There was still plenty of traffic about, but her senses buzzed. She pulled over and held her phone to her ear while watching in her mirror. The car sailed by. After counting to ten, Amanita drove on at a steady speed not wanting to be stopped for speeding. Her energy levels were beginning to drop. The new blood mixing with the old took time to balance out until the hunger began again. Amanita glanced in her mirror. The car was back. This time her senses told her who was following behind. If she could keep the car behind once they hit the moors, there wasn't many places where he could force her off the road. The only thing in her favour was her car was faster than his BMW.

She headed out of Scarborough, putting the distance between them. Did he know the route she would be taking to home? How safe would she be there? She checked the mirror. He was gaining.

The dark moor loomed as the flow of traffic like the night faded. Amanita couldn't afford to get stuck on the moor and put her foot down. Allowed its freedom, the car roared and gave her distance. Then to her surprise and relief the car suddenly spun in the middle of the road and shot back the way it had come. Relief washed over her as she slowed down coming into Whitby.

Chapter Thirty-Eight

Battling The Dark

On entering his flat, Jake paused. He was desperate to strip off his smoky clothes, have a shower before climbing into bed for some much needed sleep. The door to the sitting room stood open, he had definitely closed it, a habit left over from his childhood, instilled by his aunt Kate. *'In case of a fire, closing doors behind you slows its progress'* was her mantra.

From the hallway he peered in. To the untrained eye the room looked to be messy, but someone had been in moving things about. Jake went to his television room. Here, the door stood ajar. Again, he pushed it open with his fingertips.

The box Caroline had brought over stood on the coffee table where he had left it, but the piles of notebooks had been disturbed. Jake took out his phone.

"Caro, have you been back to my flat?"

"No. Why?"

"Someone's been here."

"You've been burgled?"

"No, but they've had a good nose about."

"Are the things I brought over okay?"

"Yes. You don't think your friend Miles would've come looking for the photographs to show his collector friend, Samuel whatsit, do you?"

"No, Jacob. Miles wouldn't break in."

"Just a thought. Do you still have a key to my flat?"

"Yes, of course. Is everything okay?"

"Everything is fine. Could you come over about 10ish?"

"If you want me to."

"I won't be here when you arrive, so make yourself at

home. Come anytime. I'll call you when I'm on my way. If I don't call, and just turn up, don't let me in."

"What's going on?" She laughed. "It all sounds pretty ominous."

"It's important, Caro, otherwise I wouldn't ask. Just remember, if you don't receive a call from me first under no circumstance let me in. No matter how much I plead and beg."

"If you say so, Jacob, but I wish you would explain."

"I will, I promise. Now write this number down. If anything happens. You must phone and ask to speak to Elizabeth Blackstone; she'll know what to do. Then just sit tight and wait for me, Caroline, please."

"I will, but what's going on?"

"I've got something to sort out first, and then I'll explain all. I want to keep you and Aunt Kate safe, and this is the only way I can do it."

"Okay, give me the number, but don't keep me waiting, Jacob." She laughed, but he heard the fear in it.

Jake showered and grabbed a bite to eat, while checking his emails. Someone had interfered with two of his files both related to his on-going research. There was only one person he could think of who was interested enough to break in. His phone buzzed. He didn't recognise the number. "Hello?"

"Jacob."

"Hello, Walker."

"I hope you don't mind me calling you. Another body has been found."

"How did you get my number?"

"From lovely Mariana. You know how much she likes to help you with your obsession. This is off the record. Just thought you might be interested. A drug dealer known as Dog has been found dead.

"What do you want, Walker?"

"We need to talk. No more going around in circles."

"I've helped you all I can."

"I can have you up in court for being a reluctant witness.

220

You were there at the time of the two deaths, so lovely Mariana tells me."

"You're threatening me because I withheld evidence?"

"Now we're speaking the same language. Where would you like us to meet? Name the most convenient place for you. But do it soon."

"That's thoughtful of you, Walker."

"We're here to serve the people, it's our job. Would it be easier if I was to come to your flat?"

"What again...? No, can I get back to you later. I have to be somewhere now; I'll ring you later on, as I have your number too now." Jake rang off. "Bastard!"

***

The row of late Victorian gothic houses stood large and imposing on the narrow street. Most of them were now apartments, apart from one. It stood set back from the rest on its own corner plot. It kept many of its original features, with its sash windows and fancy stained-glass in the front door. The front garden, divided into two, had a gravel area for parking a car, but was now covered in coarse grass and weeds. The rest of the garden lay hidden behind a high, untidy privet hedge. Jake's gloved hand rested on the metal gate. The house seemed to hold its breath as it waited for something to happen.

"You're just letting your imagination run away," Jake muttered and closed the gate quietly. He checked around to see if any of the other houses had a clear view of him. Satisfied, the hedge shielded him, Jake pushed against the side gate. At first it wasn't very forgiving until Jake put his shoulder to it. Around the corner of the house, on green-stained decking, was a collection of black plastic bags. Most showed signs that the local cats had enjoyed examining their contents as rubbish was spread over the garden. The neglected garden with its over-grown shrubbery hid Jake from nosy neighbours as he checked out the back of the house.

Through a small window, Jake could see the contents of a walk-in pantry. Stacked on the shelves were tinned food, a selection of cereal boxes, and cartons of long-life milk, all signs that the occupier was a single man. Jake checked the window. It was secure. Next he tried the patio doors. From his pocket he took a screwdriver and lifted the door out of its runner. Once inside, he closed the door and drew across a large dusty grey curtain.

The room was musty and uncomfortably warm. Jake turned on a penlight and knew straightaway Walker's wife had left him. The source of the smell was now visible - half-eaten takeaways, and cold, congealing cups of coffee littering the room. One end of the sofa, nearest the television, was clear of rubbish. If George was right then he would find the evidence he needed to prove what Amanita had told him. Jake, without thinking, picked up a discarded picture frame. Within it was a photograph of Walker, his face much softer, with clear, laughing blue eyes, as he cradled a new-born baby to his cheek. Jake photographed it with his phone before replacing the frame where he had found it, on the floor. From the coffee table he bagged a dog-end before going through to the hall. The hall showed the same neglect. A mountain of free papers and charity bags were heaped up against the wall, pushed there by the opening of the front door. Jake picked his way over unopened letters, bills, and junk mail.

At the top of the stairs, the only brightness in the unloved house came through the large, ornate stained-glass window at the far end of the landing. The fading sun burst into life, showering the dirty cream carpet in blues, greens and reds before the sun slipped below the horizon.

An unpleasant smell grew stronger as Jake pushed open the first door and quickly closed it again. The bath was full of green slimy water, and someone hadn't flushed the loo. After two rubbish-filled bedrooms, Jake found what he had been looking for.

The small office was situated off one of the bedrooms. In the semi darkness, Jake shone his penlight around. On shelving, rows of files stood colour coded and numbered. On the opposite side was a sofa bed, a blanket tossed casually over it along with a couple of scatter-cushions. Someone spent a lot of time here, other than just working. Here too were plates of penicillin and stale coffee cups that added to the unpleasant aroma.

Jake stopped himself from opening a window and instead reached for the mouse beside the computer. The screen cleared to reveal a picture of Amanita as a child. In her small hands she clasped a gold soul box.

"So she could've returned to heaven at any time, but had decided to remain here to help us," Jake muttered. "The bastard knew who she was all the time! Walker may be innocent of killing my parents, but the entity isn't. Now I need to know how it came to England, if it had been in Albania when my parents were killed."

Most of the files were Walker's reports on petty crimes and stored emails to and from work. George's information showed Walker was a happy family man and a dedicated hard-working copper before his breakdown, so what had changed him?

Jake read on. Still nothing accounted for Doctor Cula's presence within Walker. He clicked back to the desktop and pondered what to look at next, when one of the icons jumped out at him, *picture*. Who kept their picture icon on their desktop? He clicked on it. As the screen opened, Walker stood next to the ruined temple at Amantia, Albania the same one where Lisa had hidden the day his parents were murdered.

"Was that it?"

As Jake moved the cursor across the screen it highlighted a word among the ruins behind Walker's smiling face. He moved the cursor back again. The word *Angels* flashed up. A hidden file opened when he clicked on the word. There were dates and times at the top of each entry. He tried to read the journal of sorts, but wasn't taking it in enough to make sense, so took a series of pictures with his phone to read later. He was about to page on when the atmosphere in the house changed. Jake moved to the door, listened and heard nothing.

He stepped out onto the landing. Again heard nothing, but the flow of the traffic in the distance

The journal started before Walker left on the trip. He had been a little unsure about going, but Lucy wanted him to enjoy himself, to come back as her fun-loving Bard. The entries mostly seemed to be about his thoughts on the trip with his old school mates. Things started to change after they hired a car for the weekend and took a trip into the mountains. Walker wrote about how amazing the views were across the unspoiled countryside. On following a narrow mountain track, they arrived at a ruined city known as *The City of Angels.*

Jake read on. Bard wrote about how excited they were on finding the hidden chamber and began to explore it. "That's when the problems had begun," he wrote.

"What problems?" Jake paged down and then paused, his finger hovering over the down key. He listened, and then clicked to close the file, certain that he could hear something. After making sure nothing was out of place, Jake closed the door behind him and went downstairs. On entering the living room, a blow to the side of his head sent him crashing to the floor. Jake wasn't sure how long he had been out. On coming to, he reached up and touched the side of his head and flinched. His fingers came away wet and sticky as the pain increased.

"So this was your choice. You should've told me. I would've tidied up. Got some drinks in." Walker laughed. "If I wanted to kill you, I would've. After all, the rogue copper would get the blame. I'm just a shadow."

Jake focused on the direction the voice came from and pulled himself up into a sitting position. The pain in his head made it hard for him to concentrate. "So who... are... you then?" Jake asked though his words came out slurred. When his eyes finally focused, he saw the dagger in Walker's hand.

Walker sat cross-legged on a table. The only source of light came from a desk lamp, which was pointed at Jake's face. It left the rest of the room in darkness. Walker rested the bronze dagger on his lap. Its hilt was pure gold, with a jewel-encrusted pommel, and shone an array of colours around the room as though it had a life of its own. In the blinding light, Jake could just make out that it was ancient, maybe ceremonial.

Walker held it before him, playing with it in the same way some people sit clicking a retractable pen, slipping the blade into its scabbard, and then withdrawing it only to sheathe it again. Decorating the leather scabbard were gold medallions and thick bands of gold depicting scenes with wild-haired warriors of some sort. Jake could see from where he sat that their mouths opened as though shrieking, bloodcurdling cries as they drove two wheeled war chariots. They held a sword above their heads as they rode in to battle.

"It started before I was born." Walker slipped from the table and held the knife to Jake's throat. "Then again, it's as old as time itself. You weak humans will never understand because you've got it so wrong. You see it as a struggle between good versus evil. If only it was that clear cut. Now try to see it from my perspective, Jacob."

Walker exhaled in short breaths as though trying to calm himself and focus his mind. "You can't begin to understand what it is like waking up in a strange bed, in a different place, in a different time and in a different life. The face you see in the mirror is not your own." He stepped back from Jake and sheathed the knife. "I don't even remember what I look like anymore." Walker leaned forward so close Jake felt his breath on his face.

"What do you want?"

"*Her*! That's what this is all about, and why your parents died."

Jake flew at Walker. Years of pent-up rage burst from him. The dagger shot across the floor and disappeared in among the rubbish. Jake raised his fist and hit Walker. A snapping sound brought him to his senses. His heart pounded as he tried to breathe.

Walker pleaded with Jake, his eyes shone bright blue. He lifted his hand to his face and wiped the blood from his lips. "Help me! Please, God, help me!" the voice came like a whisper in the chaos.

"Walker...?" Jake asked stepping back and lowering his fist.

As Walker's eyes began to change back to green again a cracking sound like a bone snapping, echoed around the room.

"I like your spirit, Eldritch." The harsh Eastern European accent returned to Walker as his eyes darkened. Walker pulled himself upright and turned his neck back into position. "Let's take a little word like *evil*," he said, as though nothing had happened. "In the Middle Ages, your image of evil was clashing swords, fighting demons and the image of Satan bearing down on humanity with his pointed tail and pitchfork. You got it wrong?" Walker kicked the rubbish aside as he hunted for the dagger. "The trouble is you've been too busy blaming beautiful Eve, the mother of humanity, instead of God. How does that make you feel, you who have no faith?" Walker picked up the dagger. "My father was right about one thing; you've wandered too far off the path to care anymore. That makes it so much easier for me."

"You're one hell of a bastard, Walker!" Jake sprung at him again and Walker went down, narrowly missing the coffee table. Jake's hands tightened on his throat.

"Jacob, I can't die." Walker laughed and pushed Jake aside as though he was sweeping dust from his shoulder and picked up the knife. "But you, my friend, can!" Walker pointed the dagger at him. "I'll just find some other poor sucker to inhabit. I was created to hunt out evil, but instead I enjoyed destroying my own kind. Don't look so shocked, Jacob. Humans have been doing it for thousands of years. You have a saying— if it's good enough for you, then..."

A fury rose in Jake's gut. Amanita's words haunted him. But somehow, now, Walker's crazy talk had penetrated his mind. Was the entity wriggling its way into his thoughts? An unknown voice filled Jake's mind and he grabbed for the dagger knocking Walker backward with such force he shocked himself. Everything slowed as a fountain of blood, warm and sticky, sprayed him.

Chapter Thirty-Nine

Salvation

Caroline stood before Jake's research display board and shook her head slowly. To her, there was no real proof of the existence of vampires, only folklore, and Bram Stoker's Dracula.

The call from Jake came mid-afternoon. Though he'd sounded his jovial self, she had detected something in his voice, something she hadn't liked. But he had dismissed her concerns. A job to do first, but he wanted her at his flat before ten o'clock.

She had arrived early, wanting to get the place warm and to cook him a meal too. After preparing the dinner in a slow cooker, she busied herself around the flat. On finding a pile of clothes that smelled of smoke, she stripped the bed and added the sheets to the clothes in the washing machine. As the machine started up, she wondered whether he was putting himself in danger for the sake of another story. Caroline closed the bedroom door, pleased that it smelled fresher, and turned her attention to the rest of the flat.

She gathered up the piles of books and papers that lay scattered around what Jake laughingly called his TV lounge. She began to dust and hoover the neglected corners of the room. On picking up a large green folder, she misjudged its weight and it slipped from her hand, scattering newspaper cuttings across the floor. She sat down and hoped that she was picking them up in the right order. With the folder on her lap, she began to see what Jake had tried to explain. Reading all his underlining and scribbling in the margins, she saw the pattern to *Dead Men Sleeping* too. As she slipped the pages back into the folder, the phone beside her rang. "Jacob... is that you?"

"Caroline, I've killed him. Dear God, I've killed him."

His voice sounded far away as though he was fading from her. "Who? What's going on?"

"Oh Caroline, he was going to kill me. I had to."

"Where are you?" Panic rose in her.

"No, you can't come here. Not safe for you. You must do as I ask. Phone her now. Just do as I ask—"

"Please Jacob, I love you. Where are you?" Caroline cried, but he hadn't heard her as the buzzing of the phone told her he'd gone. She dashed into the kitchen and emptied her bag out, hunting for her notebook. She picked up her phone and hit the number she had entered earlier. The phone seemed to ring forever.

"Hello." The voice was soft and patient

"Am I talking to Elizabeth Blackstone?"

"Yes...Who's calling?"

"You don't know me. I'm Caroline Cooper. Jacob told me to call you. He needs help. What do I do? None of what he said made sense to me."

"Caroline, listen, do exactly what he said."

"I will, but he said he's killed someone."

"Do you know where he is? It's important."

"He didn't tell me where...but..." Caroline heard Elizabeth saying something. "Hello— who's there with you?"

"Caroline, listen, we can help Jacob, but you must stay calm."

"I don't know who you are, but Jacob told me it was important that I told you. Maybe I should phone the police and let them deal with it."

"Please listen to me. Don't call anyone or don't let anyone into your house."

"I'm at Jacob's. He told me to meet him here."

"Then don't let anyone in, especially not Jacob."

"I've no idea what's going on, but if he needs me, then I will."

"Listen, Caroline." Elizabeth's voice became harsh and authoritative. "It's very important. I know you're confused at the moment, but you will be helping Jacob more if you do what I tell you. The person may look like Jacob, sound like him, but it's not him…"

"You sound like a crazy lady," Caroline interrupted. "Maybe I should phone the police."

"If you're serious about helping Jacob, then please pay attention. Its sounds crazy, I know. The bible tells us there are more things in heaven and on earth than we fully understand. Such things as malevolent spirits that possess a living body…"

"Are you talking about dybbuk?" Caroline interrupted again.

"Yes. If you let him in, then he'll destroy you too. Jacob is only trying to keep you and his Aunt safe."

"That's what he said."

"Right. In an hour's time there'll be a knock at the door. If Jacob arrives with a woman, let him in. If he is alone, tell him, he's not welcome. No matter what he tells you, or how much he begs, don't trust him. Do you understand?"

"If it's true what you are saying, then how can you help him?"

"Have faith. We have the good guys on our side. One hour and everything will be all right.

"Okay. I'll do as you say. Please phone me if there are any changes.

"We will, I promise you."

***

The wind-driven rain whipped Amanita's hair across her face as she stood on the main street. She sensed the occupants within the houses tossing and turning in their disturbed sleep while fighting with demons in their dreams. Tomorrow in the brightness of a new day their nightmares will be forgotten.

Amanita reached the side gate of Walker's house and slipped through it. The patio door stood ajar. Amanita closed her eyes and sensed the scene within. A pain shot through her head as bile rose in her stomach. Evil ebbed from within, smothering everything it met. With her ear still ringing, she entered the house. The airless room stunk of decay.

She pushed open the living room door and was met with the sight of Jake standing over Bard Walker's lifeless body, a dagger in his hand.

Jake turned, on seeing Amanita, he dropped the dagger. Around him, images began to pulsate, as he tried to focus on them. In desperation he clutched at his head trying to free his mind from the terrible images.

A clear azure sky appeared, and he could feel the sun warm on his face and smell the sweet-scented air. Jake knew the place, but he hadn't been there before. A weight in his hand made him look down. A gun.

The sweetness of the air was gone in its place a heavy metallic stale smell. Jake screamed, but not in terror… excitement, but not his. Something stronger than him was moving him. He lifted the gun, feeling its weight. Eagerness washed over him, driving him on. Then he saw her. A look of betrayal and fear in his mother's eyes as his finger tightened on the trigger.

A pain shot through his head scattering the image of his dying mother to be replaced by Walker's eyes opening. Had he shot the blood-soaked man? Where was the gun he had used to kill his mother?

Another flash of pain and he was trying to focus on the man again. The deepest of blue eyes were now at peace. His mouth moved slowly. "Thank you…for freeing me." The eyes flickered and closed as his life's blood soaked the carpet. The pressure in the room altered and Jake turned. A shining light filled his vision. A name came to mind, but he couldn't acknowledge it.

"Jacob."

He turned towards her, but she knew he was following the sound. There was no recognition in his eyes. The entity was taking control. Once it had entered his subconscious mind Jacob was lost forever.

"Jacob, it is Amanita."

"I've killed because of you."

Evil seeped out of the walls and rose through the floorboards swamping Amanita with an overwhelming desire to flee, but instead she stepped forward.

"I didn't think it would be this simple, Amanita. Not after all these years."

The centuries disappeared as the pain and loss tore through her. The man before her no longer had soft blue-grey eyes now they were cold and mocking.

"Do you see your destiny?" Jake pulled her hard against him. His stale breath filled her nostrils as the dagger dug into her throat. Lines of centuries rippled across Jacob's face and etched into the corners of his mouth and around his eyes. Amanita knew Jacob was fighting back. She prayed he had the strength to survive what she had to do.

Chapter Forty

Into The Light

On the floor, Jake lay panting, unable to open his eyes. He inhaled a metallic smell and a trickle of blood slipped down his throat. He retched. Panic rose in his chest as he gulped in air and tried to steady his breathing. For a moment he wondered if he had become a dead man sleeping. He tried to move an arm, but a sweeping numbness made every part of him too heavy to lift. He turned his head and forced his eyes to open and found he was looking into Walker's dead eyes.

He pulled back, his head pounding. It was true. No longer was it Walker, the entity and killer. It was now the body of a police officer. Jake turned away.

Now he faced another horror.

Amanita lay in a pool of congealing blood. Her clothes slashed revealing deep scratches on her legs and across her face. Jake's heart rate slowed as his breathing became shallower. He wanted to join them both in death, rather than face what he had done. No longer could he smell blood, but more of a sweeter aroma. He inhaled deeply, filling his nostrils with the scent of wildflowers. A soft distant voice silenced his troubled mind.

"Jacob, are you all right?"

He turned his head in the direction of the sound and saw Amanita kneeling beside him. Her white hair hung limply around her battered face. "Oh, thank you my dear Father. I was scared you would not make it. Can you stand?"

Jake raised his hand to his face and touched his lips. He tried to run his tongue around his mouth. "Water."

"Of course. I'm sorry."

Amanita moved into the darkness of the house. Fear gripped Jake. When she returned, she held his jacket around her bruised shoulders and squatted before him, pressing a glass of water to his lips.

"We must leave now. The police will soon be here. Can you walk? My car is parked close by."

***

When the doorbell rang, Caroline hesitated in the hallway, unable to speak. It rang again closely followed by urgent knocking.

"Who is it?"

"Caroline. I cannot hold him much longer."

On opening the door, Caroline was confronted with a petite, dishevelled woman desperately clinging to Jake. "Please help me..."

With great difficulty, they managed to get him into the sitting room. While Caroline supported Jake, she watched as the woman swept the piles of folders and notebooks onto the floor, kicking them aside. After they laid Jake down, the woman asked, "Where is the bathroom?"

"The door on your right." Caroline led the woman into the hall and pointed to a door. Back in the living room, Caroline knelt beside Jake and wondered if he would ever be the same again.

***

Amanita watched Caroline stroke Jake's forehead. The touch so intimate a pang of longing raced through her body. She stepped back into the hallway, dropped to the floor, buried her head in her arms, and wept. The shower had refreshed her, and the use of Jacob's shirt had helped to cover the bruising on her arms and body, but it hadn't taken away the loneliness of her existence. Her dreams of returning to her real home, with her parents lay in tatters. For a moment the possibility had seemed real, knowing that some of the gold

soul boxes had survived. Now that the Dark knew where she was, she would have to leave everything behind and move south.

"Are you all right?"

Amanita lifted her head as Caroline knelt beside her.

So this is what captivated Jacob's heart, a beautiful smile that lit up sparkling jade-green eyes. The entity hadn't reckoned on Jacob's loyalty to this beautiful soul, when it had invaded his body.

"Are you all right, Elizabeth?" Caroline asked.

"I am not Elizabeth. How is Jacob?"

"Oh. He's still out of it. Who are you? Where's Elizabeth? What's been happening?"

"So many questions." Amanita pulled herself off the floor and gathered Jacob's shirt around her. "I'm Amanita Virosa. Elizabeth is my housekeeper. Jacob was helping me to track down the missing gold boxes..."

"You know about them?"

"Yes. They belonged to my people. Jacob's parents uncovered them in a graveyard in Albania, but the boxes went missing. I need to find them."

"Your people?"

"We'll talk when I know Jacob is okay."

Jacob lay on his side, eyes still closed. His face bore the marks of the struggle between them. A small cut on his chin, a slash across his left cheek and under his right. His clothes were torn and sliced where the dagger had made contact. Amanita placed her hand on his arm. "Jacob, wake up. Please."

The large man stirred. His chest heaved as though he gulped in air for the first time. He let out a low moan as he rolled on to his back. Caroline saw blood oozing from a gash across his thigh.

"My God. He needs the hospital." Caroline snatched a tea towel from the kitchen and held it on the wound.

"That won't be necessary. Remove the towel."

"We need to stop the bleeding."

"I will, but I need a moment. Jacob, we need you to wake

up, please."

Jake's eyes opened slowly. On seeing Caroline, he smiled. "Caro, are you all right? He's not here, is he?"

"Who?" Caroline glanced up at Amanita.

"He's gone, but I do not know where the boxes are."

Jake moved to sit up and let out a moan. Blood trickled down his leg, soaking through the tea towel.

"For goodness sake." Caroline put pressure on the wound. "That needs stitches."

Amanita pulled the towel away and put her hand in its place. She stared into Jake's eyes and he lifted his hand to her cheek. For a moment they melted into one.

"It's healed, but how?" Caroline said.

The wound on Jake's leg was gone, not even a scar. Amanita placed her hand on the rest of his cuts. All that remained was a small amount of bruising. "You need some sort of trophy to show you lived to fight another day."

"Are you going to tell me what's been going on, Jacob?"

Jake and Amanita stared at each other.

Caroline gave a shrug. "Don't see why I should be left in the dark, when Elizabeth seems to know too."

Jake sat up and pulled Caroline into his lap. "I'll explain, but you won't believe it. Oh, before I forget, I've something for you, Amanita." Jake kept one arm around Caroline as he pulled a small oval gold frame from his pocket. "Hope it didn't get damaged in the scuffle."

"This belonged to my mother." Amanita's voice caught in her throat. "She carried it with her wherever she went." Holding the frame in one hand, she twisted it slightly to reveal two other paintings within. On one side, a picture of her father, a slight smile played across his lips. His eyes the same as his daughter's stared out full of love and peace. On the other side, her mother, the artist had captured within a few fine brushstrokes, all the peace and beauty of the angels. "Thank you, Jacob, for returning my parents to me."

"I'm glad it's over. Sorry I didn't find any boxes."

"Jacob, it is not over. The police officer, Bard Walker, is dead, but the entity still has the box somewhere."

235

"I looked for it when I first arrived at Walker's."

"No, it would not have been in the house. It's too precious, along with the dagger. It has to be hidden somewhere ancient that will not change. The entity comes and goes freely. Space and time does not matter to it. The gold boxes are what hold me here. Once they are all destroyed, it will have destroyed me too."

"Where did the dagger go after I tried—?" Jake's voice faltered. "I mean to say it isn't something you could lose so easily, especially when you've just stuck it into someone's chest."

"I am not too sure. It follows him wherever he goes, and the box too, I guess."

"Won't the police want to question you about his death? You were spending time with him. He's bound to have your name on his files," Caroline said.

"Don't worry. The police already have me down as a crazy person. There's nothing to link me to his death. Even my fingerprints at his house would be down to me helping him with the murder cases."

"But you'll tell them, Jacob. It wasn't your fault."

"What do I tell them then, Caro? The man has no wounds. He's just another Dead Man Sleeping."

Amanita took hold of Caroline's hands. "All you need to know is that Jacob made the right choice for everyone, and I mean everyone. The police don't have anything to link Jacob to any of the crimes. If they dig enough, they will find DI Walker was already dead."

"Already dead," Jake and Caroline said in unison.

"Yes, he died along with his friends in a car crash in Albania. That's when the entity invaded him," Amanita explained.

"So that's how the Dark could've taken over the body of historian Dr Cula. By being there at his moment of death."

"Yes, or caused it somehow, and then made him an offer to live, and he accepted."

"But why didn't he use Cula's body? The man was in his eighties."

"Someone else must have been there at the time. The younger man who took the historian's name and killed your parents."

"So once they had all the information needed from Cula about the site, they discarded his body and took on the younger one. He was the one we saw killing everyone at the site once the gold boxes were uncovered. So we'll never know who killed my parents."

"No, Jacob. Just that it was the Dark."

Jake pulled Caroline tighter to him and kissed the side of her head, breathing her in.

"Only they didn't know about the gold box Lisa had. Now if I was going to hide a gold box, there's only one place it would survive untouched for centuries," Caroline said, "Whitby Abbey."

Jacob kissed her forehead. "That's my girl. Now you're coming with me, and I shall explain all that happened when I took on the Dark, on our way over to Amanita's."

Chapter Forty-One

Beyond The Darkness

The sea fret rolled in smothering the ruined abbey and swirled around the small houses clinging to the cliff face. The spotlights, used to highlight the ruins, added to the eeriness of the night. The moon, like a silent witness, watched over the scene as the mist dampened and chilled everything it touched.

The moon wasn't the only one watching and waiting. Three crouching figures moved off the narrow footpath that ran along the abbey's boundaries. They dodged between the beams of light that strobe across the abbey field. For a split second, it highlighted everything in its path, and was gone, giving a brief moment of darkness. The three figures disappeared into the gloom and resurfaced on the other side of the abbey wall.

"The buzz from the Goth festival below hides everything so well," Jake said as they moved between the shadows. "Hopefully Martin and his team will be kept busy for hours, hunting among the costumed figures."

Caroline pulled her hood down at the front. Together, with Amanita also dressed in Goth costumes they moved between the ruins trying to hunt for any signs of disturbance to either the ground or stonework.

"Martin is bound to come up here sooner or later," Caroline said.

"It's a chance we'll have to take." Jake cast his torch beam over the wall and along its base.

Caroline leaned against the wall and pulled her wet hood up over her damp hair as she shone her penlight up part of the north transept. "It's too showy up here to hide anything. Someone is bound to notice if anyone started digging."

"You're right. It's too obvious."

"Of course. How stupid of us." Amanita wrapped her heavy black velvet cloak tightly around her. "Jacob, where's one place you would not think of looking, if you were going to hide a box?"

"Right under your nose," Caroline said, turning to Amanita. "The most obvious place would be your parents' grave. It's old and safe."

Jacob helped first Amanita and then Caroline over the boundary wall. From behind and because they were similarly dressed, he couldn't tell one from the other. They crossed the abbey car park and disappeared into the misty graveyard of St Mary's, making their way between the stones, towards the large flat grave marker of the Virosas,

In the spa car park, Elizabeth checked her phone to see whether her daughter had any news. Hope was in her gothic finery - heavy black and white makeup, black-laced dress, and cloak with heavy motorbike boots. She enjoyed the chance to prove to her mother what a responsible adult she had become. She tailed Brookbanks and Martin along with their police officers as they moved among the living dead. Hope pleased that Martin and his team hadn't shown any signs of looking for them anywhere other than the noisy head-banging music venues. Surrounded by all sorts of Goth costumes, Hope saw the frustration growing on Brookbanks' face as they moved from one venue to another through the crowds.

From his vantage point, Jake could let Caroline know if anyone came up the hundred and ninety-nine steps, or around the side of the abbey, by phone.

Suddenly the two figures in the church graveyard stopped, crouched and disappeared from his view. Jake knew off by heart what had been inscribed on the stone, now washed and faded by wind and rain. A large corner of the tomb's lid was missing, leaving only the last two lines.

And I saw a new Heaven and a new Earth.
Behold, I make all things new.

Jake checked his phone again. Nothing. He jumped down from the abbey wall and made his way to the top of the steps. He stopped and listened. Someone was calling his name, and by the sound of it, whoever it was, was pissed off.

Another unearthly sound filled the air above him. The mist seemed to sense the change and began to thin. Jake pocketed his phone, just as Detective Chief Inspector Martin appeared at the top of the hundred and ninety-nine steps, with five other police officers in tow. Overhead, the mechanical whooshing noise of a helicopter illuminated Jake in its spotlight.

"Eldritch, where is she?" Martin snapped.

"Who?"

"Don't be a fool. You know who. Amanita Virosa. One of my men is dead. You're hiding the woman responsible. Now where the bloody hell is she?"

"If you're looking for the Virosa I would say you're about two hundred and twenty-four years too late. As for Amanita, I wouldn't know. Try a deciduous wood rather than a graveyard. You're not 'gothed' up enough for the festival, though the mechanical bird is a nice touch in the mist, if not a bit dangerous." Jake gestured to the helicopter hovering over the cliff like some prehistoric bird.

"What the hell are you talking about, Eldritch? Two hundred and twenty-four years? DI Walker left evidence. It pointed to you and a woman called Virosa as being responsible. So where is she?"

"I've told you. Look, if you don't believe me." Jake pulled out his phone and entered Amanita's name in a search engine then passed his phone to Martin.

Martin stared at it. "What the fuck! A picture of a pure white toadstool appeared on the screen."

"Commonly known as the destroying angel. So you better check your evidence again."

"No one makes a fool of me!"

"No one is, apart from you," Jake called back over his

shoulder as he continued down the steps. *We're all fools to think we have freedom of choice for ourselves when all we are doing is allowing the dark to win,* Jake thought.

In a gloomy alley, a cloaked figure grabbed Jake's arm and yanked him in, covering his mouth with theirs.

"There you are," Jake whispered softly in her ear as he slipped his arm around her waist. "I wondered where you went." He pushed the hood back, ran his hand over the soft, bobbed black hair, and kissed Caroline passionately. As they broke free, he took her hand in his. "Don't ever do that to me again, leaving me wondering where you are." He kissed the back of her hand. "Did Amanita find what she was looking for?"

"Yes, but it's not over yet until she's finds two more gold soul boxes to help her parents." Caroline rested her head on his shoulder. "Will we ever see her again?"

"I've no idea. All I do know is how much I love you."

"Oh, Jacob. I thought you hadn't heard me."

"Well, I was a little busy at the time."

***

Three months on: in the South of England

Woodrow Merrill stood in the noisy auction room watching the numbers on the board. Why the auctioneer saw fit to place the two objects together when all he wanted was one. It was maddening.

Earlier in the day he had studied the book. It was the genuine article, he was sure. Yes, it had been recovered. Well, you didn't expect something like that not to have suffered. After all, it was three hundred years old. His hand shook as he held it. His long, slender fingers slid over the open page tracing every word on the thin onionskin paper. He could almost taste the power of the small, insignificant book on his tongue. The impulse to slip it into his pocket was so unbelievably strong that beads of perspiration gathered on his forehead.

Well, what difference would it make; it did belong to his family after all.

A voice at his shoulder made him turn. "Have you seen enough, sir?"

Woodrow nodded and handed the book back.

"Good luck in the auction this afternoon, sir." The young man locked the glass cabinet and walked away.

After the auctioneer's assistant had left, Woodrow pressed his hand against the glass door, willing the book to pass through it and back into his hands.

"I know exactly how you are feeling. You just want to own it right away."

Woodrow found himself staring into the deepest green eyes he'd ever seen. The sunken face of an almost skeleton-like man stared back at him, while offering Woodrow his bony hand. "Samuel Hieron. I'm pleased to meet you."

On taking the hand, Woodrow was surprised to find it was a firm handshake. "I'm Woodrow Merrill."

"I'm mighty pleased to meet you, Woodrow."

Woodrow, unnerved by the unexpected attention, focused on the glass cabinet, but sensed the man hadn't left. He turned back. "Is there something else?"

"Well, Woodrow... May I call you, Woodrow?

He nodded.

"The book, I sense, is your desire." He gestured to the cabinet. "I have my eye on the box." He pointed to the small-engraved gold box. "I'm the collector."

"The collector?" Woodrow smiled weakly.

"Do you not think it is silly for us to bid against each other, when we both only want one of the things?"

Woodrow shrugged.

Samuel looked about nervously, and then leaned into Woodrow. "Let's go outside and talk business."

Outside, the grey sky pressed down heavily. The pot-holed car park showed just as much enthusiasm for the day as the mud, splattered cars that stood in uneven rows. Sheltering under a large, bare oak tree a group of smokers danced to the music of the icy wind. Samuel looked warily about before taking hold of Woodrow's elbow and guiding him through a small open door.

They stepped into an unused auction room. Another odd-looking couple stared back at them as they stepped in. The shorter of the two looked familiar to Woodrow. A thin, mousy man dressed in a thick-hooded, beige duffel coat and faded blue jeans. Woodrow smiled nervously at his reflection in the mirror that stood leaning up against a gothic sideboard. Samuel threw himself down onto a worn out 1950s sofa and gestured to him to take a seat.

"Bloody crazy standing out there in this weather, do you not think so, my good man?" Samuel smiled up at him. "I have never partaken of the evil weed myself. And you?"

"No. Couldn't see the point myself." Woodrow sat on the sofa's matching worn-out armchair.

"Now you are comfortable, my good man. Let's talk business."

"Business, sir?" Woodrow tried to judge the character of the wizened man.

"Please, do call me Samuel. Yes, business. Are we not after the same thing?"

"Mr Hieron. Sorry, Samuel. I'm at a loss here."

"Now, now. You're after the book."

Woodrow nodded.

"I'm only after the little gold coloured box."

"What's so interesting about it?"

"The box! Oh, it's a bit of folly on my behalf. I like the look of the thing. We could land up paying silly money for our madness. Do you not think so?"

"Aha, now I understand. Outbid each other when all we both want is one thing."

"Exactly, my good man. Exactly that!"

"Who will bid then, and with whose money?"

"Aha, a businessman after my own heart. I knew it." Samuel's wild eyes glinted.

"I'm not a rich man. I do have my limits."

"Don't we all?" Samuel leaned forward. "So, you're not

desperate for the book then?" A thin smile widened his eyes.

"I didn't say that!"

"Maybe not in so many words, but you're willing to walk away from it?"

"No, I'm not! What's your game?"

"I can assure you, Mr Merrill, I do not play games!"

"So why are you being so cagey about the box?"

Samuel's eyes darkened as he stood. "It's just a box." He peered out of the door. The smokers were heading back to the main auction room. Samuel turned back to Woodrow. "My good man. Are you willing to let me do the bidding, on the understanding you'll have the book at the individual price given by the auctioneer?"

"He has the final say?"

"Yes, after we've won them. We'll split them and pay half. Is that not fair, my dear fellow?"

Woodrow studied his nails. On sensing the other man's impatience, he said, "Yes, I agree, but before we go back, will you sign this for me?" Woodrow scribbled something down on the catalogue, and then passed it along with his pen to the man.

Samuel nodded slowly as he studied what was written in the catalogue. "Book of Angels?" He met Woodrow's stare with a broad smile, revealing a row of broken and rotting teeth. The pen hovering over the page as he asked casually, "What is the book about then?"

A cold shiver engulfed Woodrow. "Shouldn't we be going back to the salesroom now?"

Samuel took out an old pocket watch and peered at it. "There's plenty of time. Now, about the book." He leaned forward and fixed his narrowing eyes on Woodrow.

Woodrow swallowed hard and looked to the door. *Something told him he should've kept his mouth shut and taken his chance.* "Have you thought we might not be the only ones who are interested in this lot?"

"Mr Merrill, please do not panic. Now about the book."

Woodrow sat, defeated again, the small child with his brut of a father standing over him. *"I can't trust you to do anything, Woodrow, can I?"*

"But dad, I..."

"Don't give me your lame excuse, boy! Come here!" The
stinging belt of his childhood and his weakness at not being
able to fight back returned. "The book once belonged to my
family. My father's dying wish was that I should get it back."

"Oh, I see. So you know nothing about it?"

"Only that it once belonged to my second great
grandfather, James Murrell."

Samuel's thin, wry smile lit his face up. "How very
interesting. I take it you mean *the* James Murrell?"

"Yes, you've heard of him then?"

"Hasn't everyone? But weren't all of his books
destroyed?"

Woodrow stood. "I'm not sure whether this is one of his
books. I just thought it looked interesting. It's just a family
story, a myth. My family, that is, thought great grandfather
James was just a crazy old man. No one in the family
believed all that stuff about him talking with the angels. Why
are you after the box? I don't believe for one minute it's
nothing."

Samuel scribbled on the catalogue and passed it to
Woodrow. "We better get our seats."

Fantastic Books
Great Authors

darkstroke is
an imprint of
Crooked Cat Books

- Gripping Thrillers
- Cosy Mysteries
- Amazing Horrors
- Fascinating Historicals
- Exciting Fantasy
- Young Adult Adventures
- Non-Fiction

Discover us online
www.darkstroke.com

Find us on instagram:
www.instagram.com/darkstrokebooks

Printed in Great Britain
by Amazon

61716073R00149